THE FIREMAN AND THE FLIRT

A SINGLE DADS CLUB NOVEL

A.J. TRUMAN

Copyright © 2024 by A.J. Truman

All rights reserved.

No part of this book may be reproduced in any form or by any electronic or mechanical means, including information storage and retrieval systems, without written permission from the author, except for the use of brief quotations in a book review.

Cover Illustratation: Sierra Summit Designs

Title Design (illustrated cover): Robin at Wicked by Design

Editing: Heather Caryn Edits

Chapter heading design: Eli Calkins @greygaymer

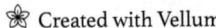 Created with Vellum

1
CARY

I thought I'd been in shock before, but those other times were total fakers. This here, right now, was the real deal. I could feel every cell in my body freeze as I processed the three-word sentence my friend Cal had nonchalantly tossed off.

Derek is back.

Derek, as in Derek Hogan. As in the guy I was obsessed with in high school, the guy that made going to high school bearable at all, the guy that confirmed every time I laid eyes on him that yes, I was one-hundred-percent, balls-to-the-wall gay.

When I was in high school, I believed that Derek Hogan was the most attractive guy I'd ever seen in my life. Now, twenty years later, with the benefit of hindsight and an adulthood exposed to copious amounts of porn and all four famous Chrises, I could confirm that my teenage self was correct. Derek Hogan remained the most attractive guy I'd ever laid eyes on.

Broad shoulders and big chest.

Shaggy, dirty blond hair that I would've given my soul to comb my fingers through.

Jason Priestley-esque sideburns, which—believe me—were *it* back in the day.

I hadn't laid eyes on him in twenty years though, but that didn't stop my mind from rebooting my crush at the mention of his name, like some perverse Pavlovian experiment.

"Cary, did you hear me?" Cal snapped his fingers in my face, loud enough for everyone in the diner to hear over the Christmas music.

"What? Yes. Town's back in Derek."

Good Lord. Just the mention of Derek was making me stroke out. I was convinced that the crushes you had as a teenager did something to your brain. It permanently and irrevocably wired your neural pathways. Anytime I went out with a guy, it was inevitable that I'd measure them against Derek subconsciously. Here I was, a forty-year-old man instantly reduced to a horny puddle of a fifteen-year-old at the mere mention of a guy that I'd said no more than a few words to in my life.

You had to be there. Derek Hogan was a moment in time. He and his fellow hockey players had barreled through the halls like it was their own personal kingdom. The twinkle in his eye every time he smiled, as if life was one ongoing inside joke, made me fall harder for him.

Meanwhile, I was short, skinny, invisible, and deep in the closet. The only thing in my eye was astigmatism. Fortunately, that was corrected with contact lens, while puberty gave me height. I was trim now, instead of skinny. But I'd always be that invisible twink stuck in the late '90s.

"Cary." Cal snapped his fingers in my face again, this time with growing impatience. "Stay with me."

The Fireman and the Flirt 3

"Sorry. I'm here. Derek is..."

"Back."

"Right." I nodded, picturing the V of his corded back muscles through his T-shirts.

Cal held up his fingers, about to snap for a third time. I gently pushed them down.

"What's going on with you? Have you had your iced coffee yet?" Cal asked, which was a fair question.

"I've had two. I thought Derek lived in Alaska or something." From what I remembered, he moved out there shortly after graduating high school. The Inuits were so lucky.

"He was living out there with his daughter..."

"Working on an oil rig, right?" I asked, mostly to confirm that my fantasy of his jacked body slicked up with oil was accurate.

"He had transitioned to working as a foreman once his daughter was born."

Oooh, that meant he liked to give orders. Hot.

"And he worked as a volunteer firefighter," Cal said.

A fireman? Double hot.

"Hot," I said, my brain and mouth not thinking that one through. "I mean, are fires hot in Alaska since it's so cold there?"

"Yes. Fire is hot. Do you want me to order you another iced coffee?" Cal was about to flag down our waiter, but I shook my head no and managed a weak smile as an apology.

I played with the silver tinsel strung along the top of our booth. I was a total sucker for Christmas decorations.

"I'm just distracted with year-end stuff and getting a client's house ready for the market." Being a real estate agent meant that I had a never-ending list of stuff to do. I was either trying to help people buy or sell houses.

"Yeah. You seem very distracted."

"Usually, end of year isn't so busy for me because people wait to buy or sell in the spring. But the market isn't calming down." Talking about my work helped keep dirty thoughts of Derek at bay for the moment. Because my thoughts about him *always* went there eventually. "Go on."

"Anyway, since his wife passed away, he's had some trouble on his own, so he moved back here to be closer to family. It's hard raising a child by yourself." Cal had ample experience with that, since he was a single dad for the first decade of his son's life. I could barely care for a succulent, let alone another human being. "He's been back for a little over a week."

"That's great. The Hogan brothers will be reunited."

"Something like that." Cal shrugged.

In high school, Cal and Derek didn't seem that close, and I supposed things hadn't changed much. They were so different. Derek, as I'd already established, was a jock with overflowing sex appeal. Cal was a big theater nerd. Derek being Cal's big brother protected us from getting harassed by the popular kids for a while. It also meant I got to see Derek whenever I hung out at Cal's house afterschool, even though I could never build up the nerve to talk to him.

"How's he doing with the..." I waved my hand, trying to think of a nice way to say *the dead wife thing*. "How is he coping?"

"He doesn't say much, and he says even less about that. He becomes a brick wall. He and Paula were such a great couple; they were so in love. It's tough...but I think he and Jolene are doing well considering the circumstances. It's been six months, so a lot of the initial shock has worn off."

Cal shook his head and stared out the window. "I didn't know healthy people could get aneurysms."

"It's awful. I'm so sorry." I sent Cal a bouquet of flowers when Paula died. It was terrifying knowing we could lose somebody close so quickly. I didn't have Derek's address in Alaska to send him one, too, and I felt awkward asking for it. He barely knew that I was a person who existed in high school, one of his little brother's uncool friends.

"Coming back to Sourwood, to a community he knows, will be a good transition."

"He can really start to move on," I said.

I'd seen pictures of Derek online. He didn't have social media, but last year, Cal and his family had gone out there to visit him. Derek still looked good. He had middle-aged heft, less hair on his head, more hair on his face, and the start of distinguished wrinkles at the corner of his squinty smile.

Wasn't it weird how as we got older, we found older people attractive? When I was a teenager, I never would've found a gut and wrinkles sexy. And yet here we were.

I rubbed Cal's arm in support and to let him know I wasn't zoning out. "You're a good brother. He's lucky to have you and Russ and the boys."

"And you."

"What?"

"That's what I wanted to talk to you about," Cal said. He scratched at his own beard. "He's going to need a place to live. I gave him your information."

"You gave him...he has..." All blood drained from my face. All the air drained from my lungs. "What? Why would you do that?"

"Because you're a real estate agent?" Cal cocked an eye at me. He pulled one of my business cards from his pocket.

Damn me for giving them out so freely. I should've known it would come back to bite me in the ass.

"Right. I am." My business thrived on personal referrals. It was just that nobody had ever referred a former crush to me. "What did he say when you brought it up? Does he even remember me?"

I wished Cal had ordered me that third iced coffee.

"He took your card and shoved it in his wallet. I'm sure he remembers you. He just has a lot on his plate."

"Right, right."

"Rather than rent an apartment and wait until spring, it's best if he starts looking now."

"Absolutely. Because prices will only go up if he waits." Speaking of things going up, I crossed my legs when another flash of Derek hit my mind.

"So you'll take him on?" Cal asked, hopeful. "You remember Derek, right?"

"Vaguely."

"I hate to say it, but he hasn't changed much since high school." Apparently, neither had I. "He's not the most talkative person. It'll be hard to get any opinions out of him, but I know you're up for the challenge."

"That's me. Up for the challenge." The real challenge would be speaking in complete sentences around him without my throat going dry. "But maybe there's someone else he could work with."

"Are you serious, Cary?"

"I don't want it to be uncomfortable, since he's your brother and all."

"Why would it be uncomfortable? We're friends, and I trusted you to sell my house when Josh and I moved in with Russ and Quentin."

Heat prickled at the base of my neck.

"You're the best in the game," Cal said. Not even the compliment could help me shake the discomfort seeping through my pores.

Cal leaned back in the booth, an amused smirk on his face. "You know, this is going to sound crazy, but I always thought you had a little crush on my brother back in high school."

I sputtered out a laugh. "Really? What made you think that?"

"I don't know. You loved hanging out at our house even though we never did anything."

"My house was never fun to hang out in. You guys had PlayStation."

"Are you sure?" Cal seemed to derive a weird pleasure thinking about me crushing on his brother.

"Yes. I said maybe five words in my entire life to your brother. It was high school. None of our brains were fully developed anyway." I waved off his line of thought. "I will help your brother and your niece find the house of their dreams if he wants to work with me."

The summer had not gone like I planned. Deals fell through. Buyers got cold feet. I wouldn't let my resurfacing crush mess up the chance to clinch a commission.

It was early November, but it might as well have been the Christmas season. I glanced out the window at the decorations going up around downtown. I was due for a Christmas miracle.

"Do you want to work with him?" Cal's tone changed. It was a real question. I couldn't blame him for being confused at my reaction, but I couldn't tell him the real reason why I was terrified of seeing Derek. I couldn't tell him that all those years ago, I'd shot my shot with his older brother, and it was a huge disaster.

I handed Cal my card. Maybe this one would actually get used by Derek. "Have him give me a call."

I was a professional. I was an adult. Derek was merely a potential client. No crush or huge disaster would get in the way of that.

2

DEREK

I sat on the pullout couch of my makeshift bedroom and stared out the window at the quiet cul-de-sac. I remembered when this development was being built back in my high school days. My friends and I would come to the empty houses and drink. It was perfect. The fuzz never found us. We called these places douche castles because only boring-ass adults would choose to live in Sourwood, or so we thought. Now I was one of them.

Twenty-some-odd years later, I was temporarily living inside one of these douche castles, which I had to say was very nice. Those boring-ass adults made very savvy investments.

I turned around when Cal's husband Russ knocked at the door. They'd met because their boys were in school and a scouting troop together, and their blended family was quite adorable. Russ always had a concerned look on his face, unless he was with my brother, then it changed to lovingly annoyed.

"How are you holding up?"

"I'm almost recovered from the jet lag. It only took a week. How many time zones did I cross to get here?"

"Four."

"Fuck me." I hadn't been back in Sourwood in years, not since my parents passed away. I sometimes forgot how far I'd traveled. Four time zones wasn't fucking around, though.

Russ opened his mouth to say something, but I knew what was going to come out. I saved him the trouble. "I meant fork me. Sorry."

Bless his heart for trying to keep his household profanity-free. My nephews were ten. He could keep all the cursing out of the house he wanted to, but fuck and shit would eventually become a major part of their vocabularies.

"You just rest. Moving is exhausting, and a cross-country move by yourself would wipe anyone out. Jolene is hanging with the boys in the living room."

"How does her jet lag seem?"

"Non-existent."

I used to worry about Jolene being so cut off from family. She was a quiet toddler, didn't speak until she was almost three. But she eventually came into her own, and now she was a thirteen-year-old with boundless energy. I had trouble keeping up. Curiosity fueled her, sending questions out of her mouth so fast the thick glasses perched on her nose would shake. I loved watching her develop into an interesting young woman.

"You and Jolene can stay here as long as you need, you know that. Don't let Cal rush you out."

Cal wanted me to meet with his friend about getting a house. The last thing I wanted to do was overstay my welcome. And as much as I loved Russ as a brother-in-law, the guy was a neat freak, which would get tiresome soon. I didn't know how he and Cal, the sloppiest man on the planet, made it work. Love was truly a mystery.

Russ sat on the pullout beside me, the mattress squeaking under his weight. "And listen, if you ever need to talk about Paula...I know it's been a few months, and it seems like life has gone back to normal, but that's never the case."

He patted my knee. Russ had lost his first husband in a car accident. He loved Cal dearly, but he would carry the memory of Malcolm forever. Cal, to his credit, tried to make Malcolm a member of their new family, giving Russ a card on his birthday and waving at Malcolm's picture in the living room whenever he passed.

The initial shock over her death still weighed on me. One moment, she was informing me that I bought her the wrong kind of milk (oat milk, not almond); the next, her spirit had left her body, wine overflowing from her glass as she was mid-pour.

"She was a wonderful woman. She was an angel on earth, and now she's an angel watching over us," said Russ.

Six months later, there were still wounds that wouldn't heal over Paula. She left us with so much unfinished business. I was devastated that Paula had died. My heart broke for Jolene. But it was hard to hear people talk about what an angel she was, and how we were such a great couple, knowing that she was on the verge of leaving me for another man. In those final weeks, things had been said that couldn't be taken back. I was blindsided and hurt, but there was no chance to clear the air or talk through things. I didn't want to tell people the truth and sully their memories of her. That didn't seem fair to Paula.

And so I was left with a weird jumble of emotions. I

loved her, I missed her, I was angry with her, I couldn't understand how any of this had happened.

I couldn't get into that with Russ, or anybody. People preferred the pitiful widower, not the confused, angry one.

I patted his leg back. "Thanks Russ."

He waited on the pullout for an extra few seconds, likely waiting for me to open up. That wouldn't be happening. Not yet, anyway. Maybe not ever.

"I'm making some of my homemade pizza for dinner." He stood up.

I detected hints of basil and garlic wafting in the air. "Smells good. I'll be down in a little bit."

A LITTLE WHILE LATER, I joined what had blossomed into a little party in the living room. Cal and Russ watched Jolene and their two sons Josh and Quentin play Mario Kart. According to Cal, Russ had been strictly anti-video games until Cal and the boys launched a "multi-pronged campaign" (Cal's words, not mine) to change his mind. He did not elaborate on the prongs.

Jolene sat on the couch, long legs folded under her. Her face immediately brightened when she saw me. She had soulful blue eyes and an avalanche of red hair that could either be flowing waves or a frazzled mess depending on the day. I loved this girl more than words could ever describe. Thankfully, Paula and I had managed to keep our fighting contained between us, so Jolene hadn't suspected anything was wrong. At least she got to believe that her parents had been in love until their final day together.

"There you are! You're missing all the fun," she said,

thoughts of jet lag and living on a new side of the world not seeming to affect her. "Did you want to play?"

"I'll pass," I grumbled.

"Dinner's almost ready. Ten more minutes," Russ said.

"I'm starving!" Quentin protested.

"It will be ready when it's ready." Russ didn't take any guff from his sons.

"It would've been ready now if you'd gotten the salad mix like I insisted," Cal said. "I don't see why you need to make your own croutons. People who make their own croutons are just showing off."

"Uh oh. Cal's hangry." I knew that tone well from dinners as kids. Cal ate every meal like he'd been locked up starving for a month.

"I'm trying to be respectful of our guests." Cal arched an eyebrow at me.

"You're being a butthead," I said, proud of myself for not cursing. "Don't make me give you a noogie."

"Wait." Cal covered his head. "My hair is too beautiful to be messed up."

"I've never had homemade croutons," Jolene said. "Dad's only dipped his toe into cooking."

"I make a mean mac and cheese."

Paula handled meals since most of my time was spent at work. One bright spot of all this was that I became a more hands-on dad. I did all the things I had been too busy to do, like cooking meals with her and going with her on stargazing adventures. I was relieved to leave the oil rig behind. It was an all-encompassing grind. I couldn't even attend Russ and Cal's wedding.

Ten minutes later, we finally sat down at the dining table. Just as I noticed two empty chairs, the doorbell rang and in walked a blast from the past.

"Holy moly." I popped out of my chair and gave one of my best buds Mitch a bear hug. We were tight in high school and had played hockey together. He was one of the guys who had gotten drunk with me in the unfinished douche castles.

"Look who's back," he said. He and Cal had grown close over the years, bonding over being single dads.

It was weird to see Mitch as a middle-aged man, like myself. We both had beards and heftier mid-sections, and yet him being here made me feel seventeen again. Funny how that happened.

A shorter guy with a big, golden retriever smile stepped out from behind Mitch. This had to be Charlie, his husband.

"Awesome to meet you!" Charlie said.

"Likewise." I gave his hand a hard shake.

Maybe moving back to Sourwood wasn't the worst idea I'd had. I had friends and family here. Jolene and I wouldn't be alone.

Cal had been hyping up Russ's homemade pizza for a while, and it did not disappoint. It was ultra-thin with a tart taste to the homemade sauce, apparently from special tomatoes that came from Italy. I kept looking over at Jolene, and it warmed my heart to see her bonding with her cousins, whom she barely saw. The boys were telling Jolene all about the Falcons, their scouting troop, different badges they'd earned and brave tales from camping trips. Jolene regaled them with facts from her nights stargazing in Alaska, which had a perfect sky for it. She wanted to work for NASA one day, and she had the grit and smarts to get there.

Mitch asked me about life in Alaska. I gave him the basic strokes.

"I was sorry to hear about Paula. She was quite a woman. Sounds like she loved you like crazy," he said solemnly, quiet enough not to draw the attention of Jolene. Charlie nodded along.

My stomach tensed again, as it did earlier when I was with Russ. "Cal tells me there's a movie shooting at Stone's Throw."

Mitch grunted out confirmation then epically rolled his eyes.

"Don't get him started," Charlie said. He turned to his husband. "It's called A Mountain Man Christmas. It sounds awesome!"

"It's one of those cheesy Christmas TV movies. Big city guy gets stuck in a small town, falls for a grumpy lumberjack. Ridiculous premise." Mitch shook his head.

"That's how we met, though," Charlie said.

"Ours was more complicated than that." Mitch turned back to me. "Because it's set at Christmas, there's fake snow clogging my gutters and strings of Christmas lights draining our power. And I had to close down for three weeks so they could film. I don't know why I said yes."

"Because it's a great opportunity! People will want to visit the bar where Colt and Jaxon fell in love. Think of the business," Charlie said.

"I'm thinking about the crew guys tracking in mud day in and day out and the director chain smoking on the balcony in between takes."

"They're going to clean everything up when they leave. Maybe Brad Pitt will make a cameo." Charlie bit off a piece of his crust.

"Brad Pitt isn't making a cameo," said Mitch.

Charlie shrugged his shoulders, his face full of boundless optimism. "You never know."

"And then there's dealing with questions from these Hollywood actors about what life is like in a small town and being a bartender. One of them wanted to shadow me." Mitch rubbed his face with his hands.

"Why don't you get off the ba humbug bandwagon, you sexy Scrooge?" Charlie tossed his last piece of crust in the air and landed it in his mouth. He made a touchdown sign with his arms. "What do you think, Derek?"

"Don't they usually film Christmas movies in the spring? We're already in November," I said.

"If they shoot it now, apparently it'll be ready to go by late-December. The Christmas movie industrial complex is a well-oiled machine," Charlie informed me.

"We'll have to host a party when it premieres," Cal said.

Mitch cocked a skeptical eyebrow that suggested he'd rather jump into the Hudson River naked. Russ passed around another homemade pizza fresh from the oven. We all grabbed at slices like hungry wolves. Even though I was getting full, it was too good to pass up. I hoped Jolene didn't expect this level of cooking from me.

"So how long are you planning to stay?" Mitch asked me.

"Indefinitely," I said. My eyes flicked to Jolene to see her reaction. Her cheeks bunched up into a pizza-filled smile. She'd had an incident with some girls bullying her on social media last year. Like me, I suspected she also wanted a fresh start away from Alaska. "Sourwood is a great town. Our family is here. We're not going anywhere."

"Derek's in the process of buying a house." Cal loved to be my spokesperson.

"I am?" I asked Cal. "That's yet to be determined."

"Yes. You're planning to stay. You need a house."

"But you're welcome to stay here as long as you need," Russ threw in.

"He knows that, but he and Jolene don't want to live out

of a suitcase forever." Cal tipped his head at his husband. "Have you called Cary yet?"

"It's on my to-do list, just under finding a job." I had a meeting with the fire department. They had openings from what I'd seen online, and my experience as a volunteer firefighter should make me qualified.

"You don't want to wait. Cary says the market is still busy this time of year. All the good houses will be gone by January," said my brother, ever the drama queen.

"It's okay. I packed a tent." I smirked at him, finding a small pleasure in getting under his skin. I was too far away to kick him under the table.

"Who's Cary?" Jolene asked.

"He's my friend, and a killer real estate agent," Cal said. "He helped me sell my old house. I promise you, nobody will work harder on your behalf."

"He takes his job very seriously, if I remember correctly," Russ said. "Talks a lot."

"What's wrong with talking? Humans were meant to communicate," Cal said in a serious British actor accent. He did voiceover work for commercials, and he loved to throw in a random voice to emphasize his point. I was not born with the same dramatic flair. We came from opposite ends of the womb.

Cal turned back to Jolene. "We went to high school together. We used to hang out while your dad and his friends got into trouble."

Mitch and I shared a busted look, memories of smoking up in my room and sneaking my dad's *Playboy* came to mind.

"We have no idea what you're talking about," I said.

"I'm sure you don't." Cal huffed out a laugh.

"Cary was that weird, skinny kid," Mitch said.

"Weird how?" I asked.

"I don't know. Kinda dorky. He'd say awkward things and laugh but they weren't funny, stuff like that. Didn't he pull a muscle when he tried out to be the school mascot?"

"Being a mascot is a very physically intensive undertaking," said Cal, forever defensive of his friends.

"And didn't he have a nickname?" Mitch scratched at his beard, and now that he mentioned it, an image of Cary came into view. Eager eyes, shy, skinny, awkward. The name had vaguely sounded familiar, but I couldn't think of who he actually was.

"There was no nickname," Cal said.

"Yeah, there was some story about him in high school. It was after we graduated. What was it? He was at a party and did something in a car…" Mitch punched my arm, his way of asking if I remembered. Again, things were vague with Cary. My mind was a million other places in high school. Hockey, girls, my car, life after graduation. "I think he was trying to flirt with a guy on the soccer team or something, so he put the whole gear shift knob in his mouth, and then he threw up."

"Lovely," Russ muttered.

"Gearhead. That's what people called him! Because it was like he was giving…" Mitch's eyes darted to the young children at the table, then at Russ who was two seconds away from full-blown panic.

"We all have different ways of expressing our interest in someone. Cary had a crush, and he took a chance, and it didn't pay off," Cal said.

"You could say his chances were stuck in neutral," Charlie said.

"He doesn't deserve to be mocked. That was over twenty

years ago, and we don't need to rehash it over dinner." Cal got up and took his dirty dish to the sink.

"What happened? What happened?" Quentin asked, dying to be included in adult conversation.

"Nothing," Russ said firmly. "It's nobody's business except Cary's, and I doubt he wants to bring up stupid things from high school."

Cal returned to the table and cleared the boys' plates. "Everyone does something stupid when they're sixteen."

"I jumped off my friend's roof when I was sixteen," Charlie said.

"Why?" Russ asked.

"What do you mean why?" Charlie laughed off the question.

Jolene was three years away from that age...and from guys that age. I gulped back a nervous lump in my throat.

"Dad, can Josh and I jump off the roof?" Quentin asked.

"No," said Russ and Cal in unison.

Cal turned his laser focus on me, his dark eyes burrowing into me, cutting past all my bullshit as only brothers could. "Cary is a great real estate agent. Call him. At least discuss your options. You might even be able to move into a place and be settled by the time winter break is over in January."

I knew what he was getting at. It'd be an easier transition for Jolene, one less interruption in her school year. Uprooting her two months into a new year wasn't my smartest move. But I couldn't stay in Alaska and be reminded of Paula.

"Fine. I will call Weird Cary."

"It's just Cary," Cal said.

3

DEREK

That night, I tucked Jolene into bed. Yeah, yeah she was a strong, nimble young woman, but there were still times when I wanted to baby my little girl. I wanted to cherish these moments together, since we hadn't had enough of them when I worked on the oil rig.

"How you doing, Jo?" I asked her as I pulled the covers up to her neck. She pushed them down to her chest, a reminder that she wasn't a little kid anymore.

"Good. I like it here so far," she said. "Uncle Cal has a friend with twins around my age. We're going to meet up tomorrow for hot chocolate."

"Are you talking about Ari and Lucy, Leo's kids?"

She nodded yes. "Lucy likes to make movies, and Ari makes video games. They sound cool."

"Before he was Uncle Cal's friend, he was my friend. Leo, Mitch, and I hung out in high school." I was glad that Cal had become friends with Leo and Mitch. They were good guys. But a part of me had a twinge of jealousy at what I'd been missing out on. I had some friends in Alaska, but they weren't keepers like my Sourwood crew had been.

The Fireman and the Flirt

I adjusted Jolene's pillow behind her.

"I know things happened pretty fast, moving here, and this is a big transition. Thank you for going along with it."

"Did I have a choice?"

"You know what I mean." I wasn't yet used to having a sarcastic teenager in the house. "I did this for us. We'll have family here. You can spend more time with your uncles and cousins."

"The sky won't be as clear here, though." She glanced at her telescope, shoved in the corner of her guest room.

"We'll find a good place for stargazing. I'll drive us out to the country. And we can go into New York City to their planetarium."

"Deal," she said.

"I love you." I stroked a hand down her soft hair. There was no better feeling than spending time with my daughter.

She looked down at her comforter, her eyes getting cloudy. "I miss Mom."

"Me, too, Jo. Me, too."

"I was thinking about going to the storage locker, maybe get some stuff of hers I could keep in my room." Cal and I had already owned a storage locker where we put our parents' old stuff. Piles of memories from growing up were collecting dust, but neither of us had the heart to get rid of anything. There was enough space to store my and Jolene's items from Alaska for the time being.

"I'd like that," I said with a heavy heart. I kissed her atop the head. "Good night, ladybug."

"Dad, I'm too old for that nickname."

"No, you're not."

I smoothed out a wrinkle on her comforter and turned on the light on the bedside table. She pulled a thick fantasy novel from the shelf underneath. She was a voracious reader. We used to read together, but she was too old for that now. Another little signal that time stopped for no man.

She let me kiss her goodnight on the forehead, a brief moment where I could still be her big ole dad.

I clicked the door shut and made my way upstairs to Russ's office, where the pullout couch was set up.

I stripped down to my boxers and looked at myself in the window reflection. I was once muscley and smooth. Now my chest and arms were covered in hair. It seemed that each year I got older, I got more hair on my body and less atop my head.

The exhaustion of the past few days hit me like a snowball that had finally avalanched down the mountain.

I plopped onto the pullout. Just before my head hit the pillow, I spotted the business card Cal had given me perched on Russ's desk. I grabbed my phone from the floor. Knowing Cal wouldn't leave me alone about finding a house anytime soon, I dialed Weird Cary's number.

"Hello! Cary Perkowski here." Cary chirped into his end of the phone like a squirrel that had guzzled a pack of pixie sticks.

"Uh. Hey." I wasn't quite ready for this level of perkiness. I was still jet-lagged from crossing an entire continent. The tiredness seeped into my bones. "I got your number from my brother Cal Hogan," I grumbled out.

"Derek. Of course. Welcome back to Sourwood."

"Thanks."

"You're looking for a house for you and your daughter."

"Yeah."

"That's wonderful. Fantastic. People think that this is a sleepy time to buy, but the market's been surprisingly robust. Now that means there will be more competition, but it also means that more sellers are choosing to put their houses up for sale. Ergo more inventory available. I choose to look on the bright side." The words tumbled out of his mouth at lightning speed. He reminded me of those uber-chatty morning talk show hosts that my late wife would constantly watch. How could people just talk and talk for three hours straight on live television?

"Uh...good."

"Excellent! Very, very excellent. Or as they say south of the border, excellente! In Alaska, when people say south of the border, do they mean the regular United States? Or Canada? Or maybe they don't use that expression. Don't you say 'the Lower Forty-Eight?'"

"Yes?" I was trying to keep up, but I regretted not having a cup of coffee after dinner.

"I know Sourwood isn't Alaska, but it's still a beautiful place. Different from when you were living here, more built up, but still a great town. Great schools, perfect for families."

"You don't have to sell me on Sourwood. I'm already here." I cracked a smile at his boundless, borderline-chaotic energy. I was glad to see he hadn't let his freak flag fizzle out in adulthood.

"Right. Well, we're happy to have you back here. And by we, I mean the collective we. Sourwood never forgets one of its own, right? That makes us sound like a cult, doesn't it? Anyway, we should schedule a meeting to talk through what you're looking for, and then I can start putting together a list of houses for us to tour."

"Sounds good. I'm around tomorrow. I'm still adjusting to being back."

"Get yourself a sub from Deli Street Main and you'll feel right at home."

"Shoot. They're still open? They haven't been swallowed up by Subway?"

"Big Sandwich hasn't gotten to them yet."

Originally, they were Main Street Deli, until another place in Massachusetts sued them for copying their name. So they flipped it. They had the perfect crusty bread, toasted just enough. Nice and crispy. Alaskan cuisine couldn't hold a candle to the places of Sourwood.

"They were my favorite. Especially their homemade chips," I said.

"I remember."

"You do?"

"Uh, yeah. Yes. I mean, you and your friends used to bring it in. Cal and I would sneak a few chips when you weren't looking."

"We figured." A hit of nostalgia flickered in me. Life used to be as easy as ordering subs with friends after school. "It was a thank you for not tattling to my folks that we were getting high in my bedroom."

"You guys were smoking up? For real?"

"You didn't know?"

"No!"

I full on guffawed out a laugh, probably my first one since I was back in town. My friends and I thought we were geniuses for exhaling into a toilet paper roll covered with a dryer sheet…and it turned out we were.

"Thanks for inviting us to join!" Cary teased.

"Hugs not drugs." I wasn't going to let my little brother or his weird friends get high. "It's not as fun now that it's legal."

"Next time, you'll have to invite me up to your bedroom. Shit. No, I mean. That was a joke." Cary sputtered as he tried to put back on his professional voice. "I meant if you were still doing drugs, I would gladly partake. Shit, no that's not it either."

Keep being weird, Cary.

"I know what you mean. I'll see you tomorrow."

"I'll text you details."

"Cool. Good night, Cary."

"Clockwise. I mean, likewise. Likewise. I should probably go before I shove my foot deeper in my mouth."

I shut the light and plugged my phone in. I found myself smiling as I drifted off to sleep.

4

CARY

Today was the day. The moment of truth.

I woke up thinking of Derek and his growly, sleepy voice. Were sex operators still a thing because he would make a killing.

Oh, this would not be good.

In all my years as a real estate agent, I never fell for a client or crushed on a client or had any sexual spark for a client. They were clients, i.e. potential income. I wanted to be the best in my field and show my bullies that their names and teasing didn't keep me down. That didn't happen by fawning over clients and messing up potential sales.

The Prescott Realty Group's office was located smack in downtown Sourwood. It was a prime location in the center of town, pretty much equidistant to any houses for sale. The office's front windows overlooked the bucolic perfection of our town square all decked out for Christmas. Strands of garland curled around lamp posts and lined the perimeters of store windows. Strings of lights criss-crossed above the main intersection, giving the streets an ethereal glow. People were in a better mood during the holidays. We were getting gifts, buying chocolate, and receiving year-end bonuses.

And as an added bonus, the office was next door to Caroline's, a greasy spoon diner with French toast so yummy it made regular toast embarrassed to be seen in public.

As I walked to the PRG office, I gave my morning middle finger to the bench ad with the two stupid, punchable faces of the Morris brothers. We were all associates for PRG but rival franchises. Real estate was funny that way. We were on the same team yet wanted to crush our teammates to be the number one franchise. Tad and Chad Morris loved to play up their clean cut, good ole boy image. They were on boards for different charities, where from what I heard, they didn't do anything but take pictures with disadvantaged people for social media clout. And they played dirty. Hiding listings from agents. Poaching clients. They claimed it was all in the name of delivering a premium experience for their clients. I called it being fucking assholes.

I swept into the office and waved to my co-workers. Fortunately, the Morris brothers weren't in yet, so I didn't have to be fake nice to them. I headed into my office cubicle, which I shared with my partner Hannah.

"I have to get my shit together," I said as I clicked my cup against hers. It didn't matter how cold it was outside. A day could not start until we had our frigid cold, iced coffee. Hannah still drank Starbucks, despite my interventions to get her to break the habit. Friends didn't let friends drink Starbucks.

We had partnered together ten years ago, and it was a professional match made in heaven. We could divide and conquer, going after different demographics. Hannah was great with young families, as she had three kids under seven. She could give the whole lowdown on Sourwood's school system and overall family-friendliness. My strengths were with older people in life transitions: the newly divorced, empty nesters downsizing. I had to be part life coach.

"You have your shit together, Cary." She swirled her iced coffee around, letting the cream flood the entire cup. Hannah had what I called a Gone Girl aesthetic. She was a pretty blond woman with a sweet smile and extensive J. Crew wardrobe. But underneath her basic white girl veneer was a killer saleswoman who knew how to nudge buyers into making an offer. I loved her, I was terrified of her, and I wanted to be her.

"You say that, Hannah, but do I have my shit together? Do I really?" I checked my hair in the mirror. I'd chosen a slim fit shirt to accentuate what little muscles I had. The shirt's color was a shade of red called oxblood, which made me feel more imposing. I preferred bold colors in my wardrobe. They projected confidence. "Maybe I'm just pretending."

"Honey, we're all pretending."

I sat in my desk chair and wheeled over to her in one big whoosh. I spun myself around, too. I was on a little bit of a high, still buzzing from my conversation with Derek last night.

"I have a meeting today with a potential client. He's a widower with a daughter. They just moved back to Sourwood, and they need a house."

"Okay. Sounds great. Why are you freaking out?"

"Because this isn't just anyone. This is Derek Hogan."

"Who's that?"

Oh, right. Hannah wasn't a mindreader.

"I had the biggest crush on him in high school. Bigger

than James Van Der Beek. Bigger than Heath Ledger. RIP. And now he's back, and he needs a house, and he called me last night, and I tried my best to sound like a functional human, but I don't know how well I managed."

Hannah chuckled. She understood. There was no judgment in her eyes. Before she met her husband, she would come to me with dating horror stories all the time.

"I'm sure you sounded fine. And hey, he's single." She shrugged a shoulder.

"He's straight. And a widower. He's in mourning. He probably sleeps under a blanket made of his dead wife's hair."

"Ew."

"Sorry. That was kind of graphic." I took a gulp of iced coffee until the caffeine willed itself into my bloodstream. "But the point is, I need to get my shit together."

"We all get a little flustered around old crushes when we first reconnect with them. But once you see him, you'll remember that he's just a regular guy, probably with a beer gut, and high school was forever ago."

"Right, right." Somehow, in the recesses of my soul, I doubted I would ever see Derek as a regular guy. And per the photos circulating on Cal's social media, he had a slight beer gut, but it was drowned out by the wall of muscle in his chest and shoulders.

"It won't be awkward unless you make it awkward."

"Also right." I twisted the straw around in my drink, letting it make squeaky noises. "Um, so it might be awkward. Definitely awkward."

I didn't have a bachelor's degree, but I did have a PhD in awkward.

She quirked an eyebrow, her face flashing with curiosity. "Did something happen between you two?"

"Sorta."

"What do you mean sorta?" She wheeled closer to me, cornering me against my desk.

Here it came. The Big Awkward Thing. The Huge Disaster. I had to purge this from my system. I hadn't told a soul about the note. I locked it away in the part of my brain where I stored all embarrassing moments, which I then thought about for no reason at three in the morning.

I gripped my iced coffee until the frigid plastic seared my hand.

"I had the biggest crush on Derek," I started.

"This has already been established."

"But he never noticed me. Even though I was friends with his little brother, and I would hang out at his house afterschool, I was invisible to him. We never had a conversation or any kind of inside jokes. That wasn't all his fault, though. I was too nervous to talk to him."

"You? Too nervous to talk?"

I tipped my head, just as surprised as her. "One time, we were in his kitchen together, and he asked me to pass him a paper towel, and I handed him the pepper shaker like an idiot. Then I promptly left the kitchen without saying a word."

I needed a pillow to bury my head in. The embarrassment was as fresh as ever. I'd forgotten just how awkward I was as a teenager. It was a miracle I had any social skills at all. (Though in my slight defense, "paper" in Derek's sexy mumble sounded like "pepper.")

"That's the something that happened between you two?" Hannah deflated slightly, unaware that we were only getting started.

I shook my head no. "I'd had a sneaking suspicion that

he might've been gay, or at least bi. Sometimes, I'd catch him checking out a guy in the hall."

"You were watching him that closely?"

I nodded in the most unfortunate manner.

"There were never any rumors about him, and I've never heard of him hooking up with a guy, so it was in my head. It was my subconscious willing him to bat for my team. I told myself that all he needed was a little nudge, a secret signifier to know that he wasn't alone." The nerves raged up my spine as acutely as they'd done all those years ago.

"He was getting ready to graduate. It was the end of my sophomore year," I continued. "The night before the last day of school, I could not fall asleep. My brain was wired. It was one of those nights where in the height of exhaustion, your mind gets clear and comes up with a brilliant idea. And so my brilliant idea was to slip a note into his locker giving him that nudge."

Instinctively, I clutched my legs into my chest, hugging myself tight, braving the choppy waters of mortification.

"What did the note say? 'I'm gay, you're gay, let's talk?'"

Oh, Hannah. Despite having gay friends, she had no idea how the mind of a gay man worked.

"It was slightly more explicit."

She full on gasped, eyes bugged out like she was in a cartoon.

"I wrote him a letter telling him about how hot I thought he was, how every time I saw him in school or at Cal's house, I stopped breathing. I said that if he were curious about being with a guy, he could use me to experiment. And then I detailed all the things I wanted him to do to me during said experimentation." I pinched my ankle, hoping that maybe this was a dream, and I would wake up screaming.

That did not happen, except for the screaming part, which came from Hannah.

Hannah was usually cool as a cucumber, but my story had reduced her to a hyper teenage girl high on gossip. She slapped a hand over her mouth as soon as the scream left her body, followed by a tear-filled laugh that she was trying to hold in to no avail.

"Cary," she said through her hand. The hope that I was fucking with her was very much implied.

"I shot my shot. And I was sleep deprived. Don't forget that part. Teenagers need like nine hours of sleep to properly function. Go big or go home, right?" I dipped my head into the crevice between my chest and my knees. Could I physically burrow into myself?

Hannah began cackling again. There was something sweet about it. I had a friend I could finally laugh about this with.

"Teenage Cary was a horndog," she said.

Being a horny virgin compounded on itself. The more action one wasn't getting, the more obsessed one was with getting it. And being a closeted horny virgin compounded that even further because one couldn't even talk about the action one wasn't getting. There was a whole life that my teenage peers got to lead that I couldn't. At the time, the only person I had been out to was Cal, but I couldn't talk to him about wanting to offer every hole in my body to his brother as if I were a mini-golf course.

It was repression cubed.

Hannah slapped my knee. "Don't stop now. What did he say?"

"Nothing! He had no reaction. He never mentioned it. He didn't look at me any different." That was the worst part. I was still invisible to him.

"Maybe he never got the letter."

"But I put it in his locker."

"Are you sure it was his?"

I shot her a look that equated to *Girl, are you serious with that shit?* "You think I didn't know my crush's locker?" I leapt out of my chair, hit with a sudden urge to pace around. "Did he read the letter and just not care? Did he laugh it off as Cal's friend being weird? Or did he not even open it? What if he saw it was from me, shrugged, and tossed it into the trash?"

"He wouldn't do that. He'd be curious enough to read it. Nobody is chill enough to ignore a personal letter written to them."

She had a point, which only added more confusion.

"The next year is when the whole gearhead shit started up, so maybe he was going to say something, but he was scared off." In my junior year, I decided to shoot my shot with another closeted athlete, one who I thought liked me back. It backfired horribly. He cast me aside, outed me, and turned me into a big joke. Fortunately, Derek was already in Alaska before I got unfairly pegged as a car-fucking weirdo and had my social status ruined. Even though the nickname followed me for the rest of high school and then some, I chose to believe that the story never made it to him. Cal said Derek worked on an oil rig in the ocean. Gossip couldn't travel over water, right?

"Maybe he didn't want to embarrass you. He's most likely straight, and rather than make a big deal out of it, which would put his brother in an uncomfortable spot, he might've thought it was easiest to just let it go."

"So he was kind of being chivalrous?"

"In a way," Hannah said. "Or maybe he never got it."

I sat on her desk, which was cleaned off except for her laptop and pictures of her kids. "Which is it?"

"I don't know."

"How can I go into this meeting not knowing? Either he never read the letter, or he did. And if he did, does he even remember it? I can't bring it up to him, but I need to know." Our phone call last night gave me no hints. He was normal, casual. It was actually a nice conversation with an easy flow, despite my awkwardness.

"Wait for him to bring it up. And if he doesn't, make like Elsa and let it go."

Easier said than done.

Hannah leaned back in her chair and propped her legs on my lap. "You know, he might feel the same way about you. Maybe he's loved you back all these years."

"Doubtful. And for the record, I never loved Derek. It was never about love. It was about lust. I didn't doodle *CP plus DH 4ever* in my notebook. I had very vivid fantasies about him, but none of them involved a fairy tale ending."

I'd learned the hard way that it was safer to bend over for a guy than to bare your soul. Bad sex was bad sex, but betrayal cut to the bone.

"I'm not letting a little crush and a little letter get in the way of a potential commission. We are so close to beating the Morris brothers for the year."

Hannah grunted out a sound of disgust from the back of her throat, a common response to the thought of Tad and Chad. Despite all their underhandedness, we were neck and neck for top team of the year. The winner received an all-expenses paid trip to Bali with the other top performing agents across the country.

"If I'm able to find Derek the house of his dreams before the end of the year, then we can stop Tweedle Dee and

Tweedle Dickhead from getting our trip." So that meant I had to keep my awkwardness to myself and ignore all pestering thoughts about the letter.

Our office line rang with a call from Brenda, the admin up front. I put the call on speaker.

"Hey Brenda! What's up?" I asked.

"There's a gentleman here to see you. Derek Hogan."

Hearing his name made my stomach plummet twenty-seven floors. Hannah and I shared a look; she was equally nervous for me.

It was go time.

5

DEREK

The Prescott Realty Group lobby was the type of place I usually avoided. It had sleek black leather chairs around a glass coffee table dotted with copies of *Vanity Fair* and *Architectural Digest*. I clocked a sparkling water dispenser in the corner. Way too fancy for me. But I was doing this to get Cal off my back.

I hadn't seen Cary in over twenty years, and I barely remembered what he looked like, but when a man swept into the waiting room in a whoosh of barely contained manic energy, I knew instantly it was him.

My little brother's quirky, nerdy friend, all grown up.

He was well put-together, not a surprise at a place like this. His dress shirt was a vibrant shade of red, fitted to show off his trim figure. His gray slacks funneled down to shiny black loafers that were likely some high-falutin designer. A stark contrast to my ratty boots with frayed laces.

"Derek. Nice to see you." Cary studied me for a moment, perhaps looking for recognition in my face. My memories of him were fuzzy.

The Fireman and the Flirt

We shook hands, his grip surprisingly strong and confident.

"It's been a minute." He let out what I perceived as a nervous laugh, though I couldn't understand why he was nervous. He seemed like someone who sold lots of houses and worked with all sorts of people.

"Yep. I'm back in town."

"I heard, I heard. You look different. All grown up. I guess you were grown up back then, but you know what I mean. I don't think you had a beard."

"You look grown up, too," I said. "Nice shirt."

"Thanks. Tis the season."

Something told me he was the kind of guy who wore bold shirts like that all year.

Cary stood on his tiptoes and bit his lip for a second, another slip of nerves. I had to admit it was endearing to have someone be nervous around me. Or maybe that was how he naturally was, a guy perpetually on edge.

"How does it feel to be back in town?" he asked.

"Uh, good." I never did well with these small-talky questions. I hope he didn't think I was still some monosyllabic jock who spoke in grunts. "I'm happy to be back, happy to be around family."

"I'll bet. Well, since you are back, you need a place to live, which is why I'm assuming you're here this morning. Let's go and talk through what you're looking for." Cary waved for me to follow him back into his office. "Did you want anything to drink?"

"Coffee, if you have it."

He walked us through a maze of cubicles to a glass-walled, brightly-lit conference room.

"Shoot. I should've picked you up a coffee on my way

here. I'll get you a coffee from our break room. It's good coffee, but not as good as a cup of Caroline's coffee."

"Caroline's. Blast from the past."

"And still the best. Take a seat and take off your coat. Get comfortable. I'll be right back." He darted out of the conference room, then quickly swooped back in. "I should ask how you like your coffee."

"Black."

"That tracks."

"How so?" I asked.

His cheeks began to redden. "You just seem like a black coffee kind of guy. Like *me mountain man on oil rig. Me no time for cream or half and half.*"

"Is that how I sound?"

I knew what Cary was getting at, but there was a fun pleasure in watching him turn a deeper shade of red to match his shirt.

"No. I don't know where that came from." Another nervous laugh. He had a great smile, even when it was full of discomfort. "I'm going to get you that coffee. Be right back!"

I shucked off my coat. I wore a black T-shirt and felt very underdressed. I never settled in well at corporate settings. I was a man who worked with his hands and preferred to be comfortable.

Cary swooped into the conference room with a coffee for me and a water for him. Good call. I didn't think he needed anymore caffeine. Under his arm was a thick folder and tablet.

"You're not cold?" he asked, pointing at my T-shirt.

"Nope. I wear heavy coats when I'm outside, but inside, every place is heated, so there's no need for bundling up in sweaters and shit."

"That's actually pretty smart." He slid the folder across

The Fireman and the Flirt 39

to me. "This is our welcome packet. It has information about PRG, how we've been in business since 1952, so we know what we're doing. Plus there's a packet that describes the process of buying a house, as well as gives some information on Sourwood. You can read all that on your own. Since you've bought a house before and grew up here, you probably know a lot of what's in there."

"Do I have to read it?" I eyed the thick stack of glossy paper.

He shook his head and laughed. "No. But I'm required to give it to you and strongly suggest that you read it cover to cover."

I quickly flipped through the folder's contents. Shiny graphics and big charts and stock images of satisfied homebuyers standing in front of the houses of their dreams. At the end was a one-page bio of Cary with his picture. He and a blonde woman were sitting on a desk, like powerbrokers, but for houses.

I held up the picture.

"Hannah is my partner. She's on a call with a client, but she's also here to assist you or answer any questions you have. We're a team."

"I was going to say you look like a badass."

"I was going for professional and competent. But I like badass."

"How'd you get into real estate?" From what little I remembered about Cary, he didn't strike me as the salesy type of guy. He was shy and awkward. Cal seemed like the leader in their friendship. Although, after hearing that gearhead story, there was a whole other side to Cary I didn't know about.

"I wasn't the best student. Things fell off my junior year...anyway, I went to community college, thinking I'd figure out what I wanted to do for my bachelor's. I got a part-time job working at the PRG office, doing filing and data entry. And I got swept up in the excitement of real estate. I liked that anyone could do it. There are people here with all kinds of backgrounds. Stay-at-home parents who wanted a side hustle, former addicts who turned their lives around, veterans looking for something after their tours of duty."

"What about them?" I pointed to a poster behind him of two guys who had to be brothers, their faces shellacked of all human character, creepy smiles plastered on their lips like they were recruiting for their cult.

"Real estate bros. We have those, too." Cary rolled his eyes. "Even though I'm an agent with PRG, I like that I have my own book of business. I can set my days how I want them. There's never a dull moment."

"That's what I like about manual labor. People think it's boring and repetitive, but every day is a new challenge. On the rig, mother nature would throw something new at us. You had to think on your feet. No two days were the same. My brother-in-law works at a tech company in operations. He stares at spreadsheets all day. I could never."

"I do look at spreadsheets, but not all the time."

"Same." I acknowledged. "I didn't love being a foreman. It was steadier hours, but I hated all the administrative work."

Since when was I this chatty? Maybe I could smalltalk. Cary must've been bringing it out of me.

"I couldn't have a job where I was in front of a computer all day. Some days are admin days, while others, I'm showing houses or doing walk-throughs of new builds or working on a staging shoot with a photographer."

I couldn't imagine Cary sitting behind a desk all day. He was too energetic, too curious.

He put his hands on the table, signaling us to move on, or else we'd be here all day. "Let's talk about your dream house, Derek."

"I'm not looking for a dream house. I just need a house that works."

"Okay, but you're going to be in this house for a good, long while, so hopefully we can find one that's slightly better than 'a house that works.' And what does that even mean?"

I chuckled. "I don't know."

"I promise I won't show you any houses that don't have running water or are filled with broken appliances."

Buying a home was more of an ordeal when it wasn't your first house, the thrill of newness replaced with the stark realities of homeownership. But I found myself relaxed with Cary, the tiniest bit eager to start the homebuying process.

Cary began typing on his tablet. "What are your must haves?"

"Um..." I was stumped, and I couldn't say a house that works again. "A garage would be nice. One attached to the house."

"We can definitely do that." He bit the corner of his lip to fight back a sarcastic smile, and damn if it wasn't the cutest thing. "Anything else you would love to have or not have? There's no wrong answer."

"I guess it would be nice not to deal with too many stairs. Carrying laundry up and down can be annoying." I shrugged, unsure if there actually *was* a wrong answer. My house in Alaska had a steep staircase, and I hated forgetting something upstairs. Fortunately, Cary didn't flinch at my suggestion and entered it into his tablet.

"I totally get that. Our knees aren't getting any younger.

There are some really nice ranch houses in town. What else?"

"Nothing I can think of. I have basic needs." This was why I stuck to wearing T-shirts and jeans everyday: one less decision to make.

"Two-car garage for when Jolene starts to drive?"

"Sure." A flash of panic tore through me that my daughter was only a few years out from that reality.

He typed the note into his document. "Do you want a basement or attic?"

"A basement would be nice for storage."

"Unfinished okay?"

I nodded yes. "How did you know her name?"

"Cal told me. She's beautiful. I hear she's whip smart, loves astronomy. She'll have to go to Renegade Park. I've been told there's great stargazing there."

A surge of warmth flooded me. It was an uncontrollable response to hearing someone talk so highly about Jolene.

"We'll have to check it out. She was worried that Sourwood wouldn't have the same skies as Alaska."

"I doubt we can compete, but we're not too shabby. Although, I can't remember the last time I took a moment to look up at the stars."

"I never used to until she got me started. The night sky is stunning." I was grateful to have someone in my life who made me stop and look up once in a while.

"It's kind of funny that we never take the time to admire it. We're all too busy." Cary pondered this statement for a moment, his lips pouting for a second, before he got back to business. "How about number of bedrooms?"

"Two."

"You don't see a need for more bedrooms in your future?"

"I'm past the age of wanting more kids. My back still hurts from picking up and putting down a toddler all day long."

A sly smile hung on Cary's lips that was hard to look away from. "Noted. I recommend two full baths. You and Jolene don't want to be sharing if you can help it."

"Good point. Sharing a bathroom with Cal in high school was a nightmare."

"The man has always loved his beauty regimen."

"The hell that would rain down on me for using his shampoo..."

Cary bit the corner of his lip to hold back a bigger smile, transfixing me once again.

"Now, in your bathroom, would you need dual sinks, or is one sufficient?" Cary glanced at me before looking away.

"Why would I need two sinks?"

"Well, you know...it makes it easier...for two people to get ready in the morning."

"Like I was sharing my bedroom with someone?"

"Yes, technically. That's your prerogative. It's your bathroom and you can share it with whoever you want. If you do see fit to do that." Cary turned red again. "What I mean is, dual sinks are popular and more in demand."

"I only need one," I said definitively, and he didn't follow up.

We continued to talk about features I might want in a house. The more questions Cary asked me, the more I realized that I did have opinions beyond a house that works. There were things I hadn't thought about like backyard space or neighborhood preferences. He made it easy to make this a free flowing discussion, and I was surprised at how much I discussed. He knew his shit, and with each question, I saw a spark glow behind his eyes. I was in the presence of someone who loved what he did, and his excitement was starting to be contagious.

Before we knew it, we'd hit an hour and those two annoying brothers were knocking on the conference room door and pointing at their watches.

We'd gone through his entire checklist, but a part of me didn't want the meeting to end.

"Where are you off to now?" Cary asked as he walked me to the lobby.

"I don't know. I might grab some lunch. After our call last night, I've been thinking about Deli Street Main."

"That does sound good. I can get you set up on our listings site so you can start poking around and liking properties you might want to see."

I forgot house hunting was a job in itself. I didn't like to spend much time on a computer. It made my head hurt. "Is that site accessible on your tablet?"

"Yep."

"Then what if you joined me for lunch and we went through the listings together? Or else I probably won't get around to it. I'll even let you steal chips from my plate for old time's sake."

"Uh, sure." Did I detect hesitation in his voice? Maybe I was overstepping client/agent boundaries.

"Unless you have another appointment."

"Not until the afternoon. I'm always down for Deli Street Main. Let me grab my coat." Cary pointed at his cubicle.

Outside, dark gray clouds on the verge of snow hovered over downtown Sourwood, making the strands of lights over the main intersection sparkle in cozy warmth. It was good to be back.

6

CARY

A good real estate agent knew how to read people. Were my clients feeling a house? Were they happy with an offer they'd received? These were some of the questions that never got straight answers. A good agent was able to cut through the niceties and indirectness to know the truth of how a client felt.

I considered myself a good agent in that regard. Say a seven-point-five out of ten. But Derek was proving difficult when it came to one question in particular.

Do you remember my letter?!

I spent the start of our meeting trying to assess his reaction to me. Did he seem uncomfortable to be around me? Did he seem nonchalant? The answer was...a mix of both. He appeared clueless about the letter, but every now and then during our conversation, there would be a tiny shift in energy, a second or two where there was an added weight between us, kind of like seeing a bolt of lightning blip in the sky before it disappeared into the blackness.

Or maybe I could be overanalyzing.

Whatever he thought about the letter, he wanted to work

with me as his agent, and that was paramount. We walked through downtown Sourwood to get to Deli Street Main. It seemed that the town got more into the holiday spirit with each passing hour: a new decoration added to a store window, another piece of garland spotted in a door frame.

"You ready to order?" Derek asked. His eyes crinkled into a gleefully nostalgic grin, his dimple making a deep crease in his bearded cheek. Alaska had made him broader, wider, stronger. I could not get over how rugged and attractive he was—and how much restraint I needed not to flirt with him, my half-assed attempt to ask about his current relationship via sinks notwithstanding.

"I'm ready. Are you? It's been a while."

The owner of Deli Street Main was notoriously impatient. You had to give your order right away and step down the counter. Best practice was to look at the menu above the cash register before stepping in line. He hated when people got to the front and hemmed and hawed, holding everything up. If a person couldn't say their order in ten seconds, he would boot them to the back of the line.

We got to the sandwich shop, which had a lunch line starting to form. Derek hung back to scan the menu, a smile curling onto his lips.

"They still have it," he said. "The BBLT."

The BBLT was a BLT with extra bacon. The owner wasn't one for coming up with cute names for his grub.

"What are you having?" he asked me.

"My mainstay. The heart-healthy turkey."

"Heart healthy?" Derek cocked his eyebrow in this way that could get the most hardened criminal to confess on the stand. "Your heart is fine."

"For now. Because I'm eating heart healthy. How much bacon does one man need?"

The Fireman and the Flirt

"Unlimited. C'mon, Cary. Live a little." He tipped his head to the side, another move that sent an unwelcome pulse of heat down my back.

"How is eating bacon living?"

"Because it tastes so good. Unlike turkey, which tastes like cardboard."

"Thanksgiving begs to disagree with you."

Derek stepped up to the counter and delivered his BBLT order as if he hadn't missed a beat. "And extra chips."

He shot me a wink, which was basically a lit match dropped onto a path of gasoline.

He is your client, Cary. Commission. Not coming.

Was this what it would've been like to go out to lunch with Derek in high school? Bantering about food choices and standing shoulder to shoulder in line, close enough to smell his cologne mixed with the lingering scent of oil on his jacket.

"You're up." Derek put his hand on my lower back, in the exact border spot that could either be friendly or erotic.

His touch made me lose all sense of verbal communication for a second. His hand spread across my lower back, igniting every nerve in its path.

"Your order?" The owner asked, already at the highest level of impatience.

"My order? Yes, I...well, I'll..." I looked up at the board, panicking, my brain not functioning as long as Derek's hand was on me. Could gravity please kick in and let that hand slip onto my ass?

Back to reality. Time was ticking. I couldn't be booted to the back of the long lunch line in Derek's presence.

The owner raised his arm, about to shoo me to the back of the line.

"BBLT," I blurted out.

I breathed an epic sigh of relief as I shuffled down the counter to pay.

Derek gave me a thumbs up. This man was going to be the death of me.

Luck was on our side. A gaggle of co-workers with their company's ID badges hanging from neck lanyards and belt loops cleared off their high top table. It was nestled in the crook of the front bay window, perfect for people watching. Downtown was alive with the bustle of the day. People walked past us carrying full shopping bags. I loved the buildup to the holidays. There was an indescribable excitement in the air.

"How's your bacon? Bacony?" Derek asked. The man was only capable of taking big bites, his hardy, bearded jaw devouring his helpless food. No nibbling for him.

"Yummmm. Pig." Though I couldn't protest as I'd already made my way through a quarter of the sandwich. My arteries would have to deal. This was damn good bacon.

"Next time, you should get extra mayo."

"Mayo is just liquid fat."

"Sounds tasty," he said with an extra-squinty smile that hid his eyes. Derek had a good sense of humor, a new fact I filed away in my head. He'd always come off as serious and reserved. Maybe the bacon brought it out of him.

He pushed his basket of chips in my direction. I spent way too long deciding on the proper amount to take. I didn't want to be greedy, but taking a single chip would be abnormal human behavior.

I settled on three.

"Thank you." The chips were a perfect burst of salty

crunch. A theory: food taken from someone else's plate always tasted better than your own.

"Bacon *and* chips. Don't tell your cardiologist." Derek's massive jaw easily took down a chip.

"I'm not a health nut," I said, part of a compulsion to perpetually explain myself. "I don't like to eat heavy while I'm working because it can drag down my energy and put me into a food coma. Nobody wants to buy a house from a guy falling asleep."

"Okay. It's cool if you are."

"Not all of us are as naturally buff as you, Derek."

Crap. Was that a flirtatious comment? For as long as I'd known Derek, he had a natural jackedness to him thanks to his size. I was merely commenting on his genetics.

"And don't get me wrong. I really like meat."

Crap. Was *that* a flirtatious comment?

Derek chuckled while taking another huge bite, a wheel turning in his head. What did that smile betray? *Do you know about the letter or don't you?*

"I like meat, too," he said, but he was likely talking about bacon. Before I could dig into that statement and simultaneously dig myself further into this one-way flirtatious hole, he changed the subject. "Thank you for asking about the sinks."

"Uh, yeah. I mean, that's what I do. I want to get a full sense of what my clients are looking for."

"You don't have to call me your client."

"But you are." Calling him my client was a reminder to myself to curb my desire to climb him like he was El Capitan and I was the *Free Solo* guy. Besides, what else would I call him? We weren't friends technically. "Why are you thanking me for bringing up a dual vanity?"

"Because nobody in my life ever will." Derek put down

his sandwich, a pained look creasing his brow. "It feels like people want me to stay the sad, lonely widower forever. You are the first person who hinted at the possibility that I could date in the future."

I blushed slightly, happy that I could unintentionally provide this glimmer of light for him. I couldn't imagine what it was like to continue on with daily life without your one true love or boo or whatever straight people were calling their spouses nowadays.

"I do miss my wife. It's been a very tough year. But I hate how it's this dark cloud hanging over every interaction in my life. Except with you. I like how we can just talk, and talk about my future, without you bringing up the sad, lonely widower thing."

I had a twinge of guilt hit the back of my throat. Selfishly, I didn't want to bring up his late wife because I clung to a one-percent chance that I actually *had* a chance with someone like him. Knowing how badly he wanted to move on from mourning, I was more determined to find him and Jolene a house they could fall in love with. I would help them make a fresh start.

"Cal and Russ and my friends...I can tell they're always thinking about it, constantly worried about me."

"They care about you. You went through a very traumatic thing. You lost your soulmate."

Derek cut his eyes to the window for a moment, a tense reaction on his face. I was doing exactly what he didn't want me to do. I was bringing the dark cloud over.

"You should get back out there," I said.

"I will. But I don't want anything serious."

"That's fine. Get back on the saddle and ride somebody." Shit. Why did I always go there with him? "I mean, you need to take your time to find someone special."

"Honestly, I don't know if I ever will." He chased the admission with a few chips.

"I feel that," I said. "Friends and family ask me when I'm going to settle down, but I like my life how it is."

I wished I could tell everyone the truth: that I would rather get a Prince Albert piercing than a husband. I didn't want to risk opening myself up to someone again and giving them that power over me. I wouldn't be a victim of love anymore. But that wasn't something one was allowed to say in polite conversation or else one was branded a cynic or curmudgeon or some other depressing euphemism. Here was the simple truth: maybe I was built to live life alone. I channeled those feelings of incompleteness into building up my business.

Derek and I made nerve-wracking eye contact, a tentative understanding between us. We both refused to wear the label of sad, lonely guy.

I took out my tablet, and we went through a few properties on the listing site. It turned into a fun game of Derek giving a thumbs up or thumbs down. We were laughing like two teenagers trying to study but getting no work done. By the last property, Derek held his thumb out sideways and built up the suspense before sending it down.

I balled up my sandwich wrapper. "I hope you're ready, Derek. Because we are going to go on an epic house hunting sprint. Stay hydrated. It's going to be busy, but a lot of fun, too!"

"Got it."

"Come on. I'm going to need more excitement from you. How about we put our hands in and yell 'dream house' on three."

He shot me a look that told me that would not be happening. Fair enough.

I offered my tray for Derek to dump his plate on. I took them to the trash. It was quickly becoming a pesky habit of pre-missing Derek as our time came to a close.

"Listen," he said when I returned.

"Yeah?" I took a sip of my water.

"I just need to get it out there, that I know about your note."

Rather than spit out my water in shock, it went straight up my nose, making me cough and my eyes water. Derek bolted out of his chair and offered me a leftover napkin. I held it to my face to catch the leaking water. Well, there went any chance of being the suave professional.

"Sorry. Wrong pipe," I said. "So you know about the note?"

He nodded. "Cal gave me the note you passed along to him, about the market being unusually tight this time of year, and so I can't lollygag on making a decision on a house."

"Oh. That note." I gave my sinuses a bath for nothing.

But what about the other note, I couldn't stop wondering. *The note about me wanting to gag on your lolly.*

"Cal warned me not to drag my feet. I will do my best."

"And I will do my best to find you the most ideal property." I tossed my snotty tissue into the trash and applied a generous amount of hand sanitizer to my palms.

We put on our coats and shimmied from the tight squeeze of our table, as another party waited for us to vamoose. The cold air hit my face, a harsh wake up call.

"Thanks for lunch, and for everything, Cary. Looking forward to working together." Derek held out his hand to shake.

I shook it back, but there was something overly clinical about the gesture that dug at me. Not to mention, Derek looked super cute with his knit winter hat plopped on his head, a softening of his hardened image.

"Derek, I need to ask you something," I said before he could launch into a formal goodbye. "And I know it's going to be awkward, but I just have to ask it because we can't keep dancing around it. Do you remember the letter? Are you pretending that it doesn't exist because if you are, we should probably get it out in the open."

I caught my breath. That was so much word vomit my BBLT almost came up with it, and as soon as I finished, I realized what a big mistake I'd made. I should've let it lie. If there was ever a time in my life to play it cool, now was it.

"What letter?" he asked simply.

"*The* letter," I said with emphasis. "From high school."

He raised his shoulders to his ears. The only letter Derek seemed to know about was the letter C, as in the crazy real estate agent directly in front of him. "I don't know what you're talking about."

If Derek were lying, then he should've been on Broadway acting his heart out because he was that good. But no, he was not lying. And I was making an ass out of myself in real time with no ability to stop.

"Oh."

"What was in this letter?"

"Nothing. I can't remember."

"You seem like you remember." He stepped closer, blocking us off from passers by. A lamp post hit my back. "You seem like you remember vividly."

As it did at the Deli Street Main counter, time was ticking. I searched my memory for a believable lie. Fortunately, spending half my life in the closet had given me the ability to come up with fake stories on the spot. "I wrote you a letter sticking up for Cal. He was mad at you about something, and so I wrote a letter and slipped it into your locker trying to play peacemaker. I shouldn't have gotten involved, and I don't know why I brought it up now. But in case you were still mad at me for getting involved in a brotherly dispute..."

Did that word vomit make sense? God, I hoped so. The one upside was Derek staring at me with his dark, swirly eyes to determine what level of bullshit I was spewing.

"Yeah, I never got that letter."

"Good. Great. Let's forget I said any of that." I tossed the thought behind my shoulder like it was salt and banged my knuckles against the lamp post. "I don't know what made me think of it. Maybe what you were saying about Cal only seeing you as a widower."

"Sure." He continued to stare at me like I was crazy, which I probably deserved.

"Sorry. I just made things weird. You weren't supposed to see that until *after* we closed on a house."

To my enormous relief, a smile slunk onto Derek's lips. "Keep being weird, Cary."

He meant it genuinely, which gave me mixed feelings. We liked being different but didn't like others pointing out we were different. I studied his face, checking for any fleeting signs of letter recognition. I slowly backed away and waved goodbye. "We'll be in touch about looking at houses."

I pivoted on my heel and walked three blocks in the wrong direction until I was sure he wasn't anywhere near me.

7

DEREK

While I didn't see Cary over the next few days, we were still in regular communication. He emailed me over listings he thought I would like. When I didn't respond to those, he began texting them. A house should've been at the top of my to-do list, but I'd gotten the job at the Sourwood firehouse and was immediately pulled into training. Because I'd been a volunteer firefighter for years, the training was a formality and more about getting to know the guys in my squad.

I got out of training one early afternoon and walked around downtown before Jolene got out of school. So far, her teachers raved about her. I breathed the sigh of relief that every parent breathed after their kid's first week of school.

I forgot how much I loved it in Sourwood. Bare trees lined the mountains in the distance. The water of the Hudson River shimmered under the sunlight. Alaska was beautiful, but Sourwood had its own charms.

My stroll was interrupted with yet another text message from Cary.

Cary: You haven't been looking at any of the houses I've sent you...

Derek: I will.

Cary: One of the houses I sent you already has an offer.

Derek: Then it wasn't meant to be.

For the record, I didn't believe in the meant-to-be bullshit of houses. There was no such thing as a dream house. No house was perfect. All we could do was find a suitable home that checked a majority of our boxes and learn to live with its imperfections. The same thing could be said for relationships.

Cary: Check out this one!

He sent over a link to a ranch house at the end of a cul-de-sac that badly needed a paint job.

Derek: I went to a party at that one. I think Mitch threw up in the front bushes.

Cary: And they're still standing. Great landscaping!

I legitimately LOL'd, getting weird looks in the process from strangers.

Cary: Doesn't vomit count as fertilizer?

Derek: I'm going to pass. I don't want to think about what shenanigans went on in that house.

Cary: We can get it deep cleaned. I work with a cleaning service that are miracle workers.

Cary: Fine.

Derek: Sorry that I'm making this difficult.

Cary: You're not difficult. You're a challenge 😀

Cary: I'm making a running list of things you say you like and don't like. No to open concept. Yes to wood-burning fireplaces. No to puke-fertilized bushes.

There I went laughing to myself again like a crazy person.

The Fireman and the Flirt

Derek: Only when I know the person who puked in the bush.

Cary: Fair. Would you be up for seeing a house tomorrow? I can get us in early before the official open house. I have a good feeling about it.

I smiled at the phone, admiring Cary's persistence and work effort. It was a 180 from my last experience working with a real estate agent.

Derek: Let's do it.

I tucked my phone into my pocket and headed into Stone's Throw Tavern, Mitch and Charlie's bar, off the downtown strip. It had a hole-in-the-wall vibe but was nice enough for the suburbs. The spacious floor of the bar had floor-to-ceiling windows overlooking the river, and upstairs was a small loft space with Mitch's office.

But this afternoon, I found Mitch at the bar talking with someone. His flannel shirt stretched across his back. I tapped his shoulder.

"Hey, I got a blast from the past for you."

The man who turned around was not Mitch, although he looked disturbingly similar. His features were softer, his beard more of a stubble, and was he wearing makeup?

"Oh, sorry. I thought you were someone else."

"Did you think I was Mitch?" The man's eyes lit up. They were not dark menacing coals like my friend's, but rather filled with sweetness and a desire for validation.

"Yeah. Is he around?"

"Allison!" He called out to a woman in a huddle by the high top tables. "Allison!"

She emerged from the group of people frazzled, mind elsewhere. "Yes?"

"This man thought I was Mitch!"

"Great," she said with a fraction of his enthusiasm.

"Allison's our director. Did I read appropriately small-town and surly to you? Did I look believable as someone who owned a bar?" The man studied my face for a response. His gregarious voice did not jive at all with his Mitch-esque appearance.

I didn't know what rabbit hole he was taking me down, and I didn't want to find out. "Is Mitch around?"

"I'm right here." Mitch came up to our circle and let out a sigh that reminded me of when I'd get annoyed with toddler Jolene's incessant questions.

Seeing Mitch and his doppelganger side by side was an odd sight. The man took note of Mitch's gestures and tried imitating them. Around the bar, I noticed crew members and lighting equipment set up. It all began to make sense.

"Are you the actor from the movie?" I asked him.

"Lucien McDaniel. Did you want a selfie?"

"That's all right," I said, deflating him like a balloon.

"What is this blast from the past story you wanted to tell Mitch? I could use it for my backstory."

"Lucien, for the last time, you're not playing me in your Christmas movie," Mitch said.

"It's called *A Mountain Man Christmas*, and you are very mountain man-esque. I'm drawing *inspiration* from you. What do you think of the outfit?" Lucien gave us a modeling pose of his flannel and jeans. "Doesn't it absolutely scream mountain man?"

"Is that my shirt?" Mitch asked.

"Heavens no. I had our costume designer find comps. The jeans are designer from a boutique in Beverly Hills. What do you think?"

"I love it!" Charlie said, joining our circle. He was followed by a man with a pretty face also doused in makeup who was wearing the exact same green henley as him. I assumed it was the other actor, or else this was one hell of a practical joke. "Guys, this is Skip Houston. He's studying me."

Charlie beamed with excitement. Skip imitated his nodding head and gave us a wave.

"Mitch, how cool is this?" Charlie said.

"Not cool at all," Mitch replied with a deep-throated grumble.

Which Lucien then tried to imitate, although he sounded like he was hacking up a lung.

"Question: When you do that grumble, does it start in the throat or is it more in the nose?" Lucien tried it a few more times. I was tempted to hand him a tissue.

"Do you still think this Christmas movie was a good idea?" Mitch asked his husband.

"Do you still think this Christmas movie was a good idea?" Lucien repeated in a below-average Mitch impression.

He shot Lucien a cold-blooded grimace that shut him up for good. Then he nodded for me to follow him.

Mitch and I ascended the spiral staircase. He collapsed onto a messy couch across from his desk and rubbed his temples. "I am never watching another Christmas movie for as long as I live. At this point, I don't even know if I can watch *Die Hard* again."

"You will survive." I plopped down next to him and patted his knee in support.

"I wanted to talk to you about something," Mitch said. "Remember Bill Crandell?"

"Billy?"

"Well, he doesn't go by that anymore, but yeah."

"Of course I do. The king of the penalty box." Mitch, Bill, and I all played hockey at South Rock High years ago. Bill was someone who used the ice to take out life's frustrations, and that made him all the better as a player. I liked Bill and regretted that I'd let myself lose touch with my teammates. "What's he up to?"

"He works in insurance. He lives a few towns over. He's starting up a team. There's a regional extracurricular league for adults. What do you think?"

Hockey had been a major part of my life. It gave me grit, discipline, camaraderie, and a healthy way to let go of my anger.

"I think I'm too old to get knocked around the ice."

"We all are."

"Are you joining?" I asked.

"I think I'm crazy enough. Could be fun."

"Getting back into all that gear? Can our bodies take those blows?" Once I hit forty, my back and legs ached for no reason, as if it were a delayed reaction to years of hockey and manual labor.

"Bill's looking at recruiting guys our age, so we can commiserate together. What do you say?"

"I'll think about it." The chance to get back on the ice was tempting. "When does it start up?"

"January."

I wondered where I would be by then. Hopefully in a house and enjoying my job as fireman.

Mitch grabbed us waters from his mini fridge. "So what was this blast from the past story?" he asked.

"Remember when you tossed your cookies outside that party in high school? And then Leo pointed and said matter-of-factly, 'You puked in a bush.'" A laugh ripped through me as the memory came back to life. When I said it aloud, it didn't sound that funny, but you had to be there. I'd forgotten how stupid we could be as teenagers and how freeing that feeling was.

"Not my finest hour."

"The house is for sale." I kicked my legs up on the coffee table. "Cary is being very diligent."

"He seems good," Mitch said.

"Have you been hanging out with him?"

"He and Cal are friends, so we see each other from time to time."

"What's he like?"

"What do you mean?" Mitch shrugged. "He's nice. A little weird."

"But a good kind of weird. That gearhead story was kinda funny." There was something sexy about buttoned-up people who let their freak flag fly from time to time. Why was I thinking something sexy about Cary? "He seems like a fun guy. Odd, but fun."

Mitch gave me serious side eye. Why was I trying to get nuggets of info about Cary out of him?

He might've given me more information on present-day Cary had the sound of shattering glass not distracted us.

"My bad. I thought those were prop glasses." Lucien's voice floated up from the bar. "Allison, where's the film set medic? I cut my pinky."

Mitch clamped his eyes shut and grumbled.

———

BEFORE I DROVE to pick up Jolene from school, I stopped by the storage facility, an anonymous-looking building situated off the highway. My storage locker was at the end of a long, quiet hallway bathed in depressing fluorescent lights. Here was everything to my name, everything that had made it from Alaska.

When our parents passed away and Cal sold the house, he rented a huge locker to hold all of our old crap. I wasn't one for holding onto things. Cal was. He didn't like letting things go, just in case there was the tiniest bit of sentimental value to be found.

I wasn't sure what I was looking for. It was kind of nice being around my old belongings from Alaska, a reminder that my life was currently on pause until I found a new home. Boxes of pictures and clothes were stacked against the wall.

I opened boxes on Cal's side of the locker, burrowing further and further into my past until I found my high school yearbook. I looked like such a handsome schmuck in my senior picture, the gauzy blue background glittering behind me, thinking that I was god's gift to the world with my unearned cockiness. "You miss 100% of the shots you don't take" was my quote. How original.

I flipped to the sophomores section, then to the P's, and finally to Cary Perkowski. The underclassmen pictures were small squares in black-and-white. His angular face had a trio of pimples dotting his chin, and oppressive amounts of gel reflected in his hair.

He was practically begging to be shoved into a locker.

And yet...he was cute in his awkward way. His wide, eager smile hadn't changed. There was a sweetness to his picture, and I hoped that my high school self had stopped him from getting shoved into his locker. Were kids actually shoved into lockers or was that just a cliché from the movies? From what I remembered, the lockers at South Rock weren't full-length. They were stacked in two rows. It would've been impossible to contort someone into one of them.

There I went...I was sounding like Cary.

I winked at Cary's picture. He'd grown up into a successful, good looking guy. He hadn't let past setbacks keep him down. High School Cary would be happy to know where he ended up.

"You done good," I said to his picture.

―――

THE NEXT DAY, I met Cary to look at my first house, and I quickly learned that photographs in a real estate listing rarely matched reality.

"The front yard looks smaller," I said. Overgrown hedges and eroded mulch bunched up by the walkway, a stark contrast to the neatly trimmed yard in the pictures.

"The listing probably used a special lens. But it's still a great-sized yard. And less space means less you have to mow in the summer."

"It's...dumpier than I pictured."

"A little TLC will fix that." Cary clapped my shoulder and held it there for an extra second. "Let me get the door."

He punched a code into a large lock hanging on the doorknob. It flopped open, revealing a key to unlock the door.

"And here...we...are." Cary opened the door, and I suddenly felt like a giant who had stumbled into the Keebler Elf tree.

The living room was stuffed with furniture that spanned the entire rainbow. Two hot pink sofas were up against the orange-painted walls with an aqua blue coffee table between them. It was a full-bodied assault on the eyes, and not at all the empty room as shown in the listing photos.

"I'm guessing they used old photos for the listing," Cary admitted.

"It's small," I said.

"It's cozy. People in big houses are constantly running from one end to the other to grab something they forgot. How exhausting."

Bless his ability to find the silver lining to anything.

"For two people, this is a good amount of space." Cary banged his hip against the couch arm and muttered a curse. "Keep looking around. This house has a lot of hidden nooks and charms. I know it's hard, but try to ignore the paint and the furniture."

I placated him with a tour. At least he kept it fun with his need to spin every facet as a positive.

"Plenty of mature trees in the backyard," he said. "You could put up a hammock in the summer, host barbecues."

I had to hand it to him. He was managing to paint a picture, to make me forget about the flaws that I'd seen. I couldn't yet tell if he was naturally optimistic or a killer salesman.

I stopped in the hall when something green caught my eye in the bathroom. I blinked to make sure I was seeing it correctly. Hundreds of Shreks stared at me.

"Is that Shrek wallpaper?" I pointed into the bathroom.

Cary's face dropped when he saw. "That...is Shrek wallpaper."

"Was this a kid's bathroom?"

"Uh, no." Cary bit his lip.

"Have we checked the basement for any kidnapped girls?"

Cary scanned his tablet. "The basement is finished. Fresh carpeting installed a year ago."

I pushed open the door to the main bedroom, which had a twin-sized bed, a night stand, and lime green painted walls, which now that I thought about it, was the same color as Shrek.

"Walls can be painted," Cary said. "That's one of the easiest changes to make."

On the ceiling, above the bed, was a disco ball shooting off flecks of rainbow light.

"Cary, why is there a disco ball in this person's bedroom?" A slash of sunlight hit the ball, sending a ray directly into my eyes.

"Have you seen how much natural light these windows are pulling in?" Cary let out a nervous chuckle.

"Cary, if we're going to work together, I need you to drop the bullshit. Would you live in this house?"

"Yes, after a substantial remodel. A very, very substantial remodel. This house has good bones. Think of the bones, Derek."

"The bones of the murdered people buried in the backyard under the mature trees?"

"Walls can be painted. Disco ball lights can be uninstalled. But the things that matter in a house, like good structure, updated HVAC, and sturdy roofing, this house has. I wouldn't take you to see a real stinker. This place is a gem. Look at the main bathroom. Have you seen this shower?"

Cary led me into the en suite bathroom which had mirrors on the walls and ceiling, projecting unlimited versions of us. It was straight out of the '70s. The design of this house truly made no sense, and I feared for the sanity of its current inhabitants. He pointed to the shower stall, which had a bench installed.

"This is a nice shower. It's huge!" he said.

"That's the mirrors playing tricks on you."

"It's true! This is a great, big shower. Look at all this space." Cary stepped inside and spun in a circle. It might've been big for a slender guy like him, but for me, it was a place where a wrong elbow move could put a hole in the tile.

"It's a normal shower."

"It's not! It's bigger than your average one."

I quirked an eyebrow. Maybe the mirrors were throwing me off.

"Check it out for yourself." Cary waved for me to join him.

"You want me to go in there?"

"So you can see for yourself."

This guy was weird city, but to his credit, I was intrigued.

I stepped inside, momentarily impressed it could hold both of us. A small amount of space sat between our bodies, a space that made my heart pound in my ears.

"See?" he said, his voice echoing. "There's enough space for two people."

Electricity hung in the bits of air that separated us. I cleared my throat.

"So?"

"Well, that's a great thing." His eyes went wide. I was so close, I watched his pupils darken. "In case you don't want to shower alone."

"Why wouldn't I shower a...Oh."

An unsettling fog of silence coated the air. I became very aware of the quiver of his Adam's apple, the emerging stubble prickling his neck, the red of his lips.

"I mean, if that is your thing." He gulped back a lump.

Then I gulped back a lump, suddenly thinking about showering with another person, and that person being Cary. A flash of soaping down his smooth skin flitted in my mind, sending heat coursing up my neck.

"I think...I'm going to pass on the house."

"Understood. There are plenty to see." Cary wiggled out of the shower, his tight frame brushing against me and zooming back into the Shrek-inspired bedroom. "Onward."

8

CARY

I needed a cold shower after that session with Derek. How ironic.

"Hannah, have you ever accidentally flirted with a client?" I asked my partner when I returned to the office.

I found her in the breakroom hunched over her laptop. She was uploading pictures we had taken for an upcoming listing. We worked with a photographer and staging company to make every property look flawless. Too bad the house I took Derek to didn't follow our example.

"How does one accidentally flirt?" She took off her chic, oversized reading glasses.

"Funny story."

"Why do you always have funny stories when it comes to Derek?"

That was a question I needed to ask a professional. Somewhere on my long to-do list, right under starting a gratitude journal, was finding a therapist. Until then, there was Hannah.

"I basically told him the shower in the main bathroom was perfect for shower sex."

"I mean, was that something he described wanting?" We'd had clients who wanted hardcore bachelor pads, so the question wasn't out of line.

"No. It kinda came out of nowhere. Well, not nowhere. We *were* in the shower together..."

She slammed her laptop shut. "Cary."

"Hannah?"

"Did you hear the words that came out of your mouth?"

"I usually try not to." I didn't need to listen to my madness making its way into the world. "We weren't showering together. It's another funny story." I let out a nervous chuckle.

"Have you noticed that you're the only one laughing during these funny stories? And to answer your previous question, no I've never accidentally flirted with a client. And you're not supposed to either, especially with this one."

"I know." I slid into the seat next to her like I was a stream of molten lava. "I told myself to keep things professional. I couldn't help it. He does things to me. He triggers the flirty part of my brain."

"Your prefrontal whoretex?"

"Good one," I said. Hannah patted herself on the shoulder. "It's his fault for being so hot."

Derek put me on perpetual high alert, and yet he also put me at ease. Considering how nervous I could feel around him, we'd very quickly worked up a banter between us.

Hannah walked to the beverage station, poured herself a large cup of ice, and plunked it right in front of me. I tossed a pair of ice cubes in my mouth and munched away, as I'd done many times before.

"Did he say anything about the letter?" she asked.

"No. He has zero recollection of it."

"Well, that's good. You must feel relieved. The only awkwardness is in your head."

"Yeah," I said without her enthusiasm. I avoided a mountain of embarrassment. Yet it was hard to explain why I felt disheartened. I would never know what his reaction would've been, just like I'd never know what would've happened if we marinated in our uncomfortable silence in the shower for a few more seconds. The not knowing was its own punishment.

"Your secret is safe."

What good did a safe secret ever do anyone?

A loud ding of the sales bell cut through our conversation. Whenever a house closed, the agent on the sale rang a big bell in the center of the office. It was supposed to be about celebrating a teammate's success, but in reality, it was another way for an agent to show off.

The Morris brothers beamed by the bell, giving each other their stupid special handshake. Co-workers gathered around and applauded them.

"Bali here we come!" Tad shouted.

"We got ten grand above asking. We couldn't have done it without Jesus, of course, and all of you," said Chad, who only found Christ for the business connections in his church.

The brothers Morris caught me and Hannah looking at them. Tad gave us cutting winks.

Game on.

"Cary, we can't lose to these guys. I can't stand another year of the Morris brothers gloating and mansplaining my job to me." Hannah stood up and stuck her laptop under her arm. "Get your shit together, keep it in your pants, and make this sale."

"I will. I won't let this happen again."

Two days later, Derek texted me, and I had the unprofessional reaction of a full bodied swoon when I saw his name pop up on my screen. I would work on that.

Derek: I think I found a house I like.

Derek: Maybe a "dream house."

I could see his sarcastic smile through the screen. Nevertheless, I would make him believe in dream houses.

Cary: Send me the listing!

Derek: I hearted it on the website, per your requests. I don't want to break the rules. 😊

Was I imagining things, or was Derek flirting? Just because a straight man felt comfortable enough to joke around with me and use emoji in his texts didn't mean he was flirting.

I looked up the house on the website. No wacky interior design. Good location. It felt very Derek. Understated but sturdy and lots of character.

Cary: I love it! I'll set up a time for us to visit. Are you around today?

Derek: Yep.

Cary: I may also sneak in two other houses that just came on the market.

Derek: Haha. Cool.

Was that a genuine haha or a humoring haha? I could earn a PhD with all the time I spent trying to decipher the meaning in text messages.

I shot off an email to the listing agent and a few seconds later, she replied with the green light to give Derek a tour. Good real estate agents checked their emails obsessively.

Cary: We're in for this afternoon.

Derek: Can't wait.

Was that a genuine can't wait or a sarcastic one?

DEREK BEAT me to the house. He leaned against his truck in a coat just open enough to reveal his Foo Fighters T-shirt, giving the house a smoldering stare. This guy had no idea how hot he was, which only made him hotter.

Get it under control, Cary.

Commission, not coming.

No flirting.

Do not go anywhere near the showers in this house.

"Salutations!" I said like a dork. I'd never said salutations before in my life. My mind was apparently working overtime to keep myself in check.

"Uh, hey."

"You ready?"

"Let's do it." Derek put his hand on my back, once again in that exact spot that was on the border between "friendly" and "fuck me."

This house was in far better shape than the Shrek palace. It had been decluttered and the walls painted a neutral off-white color. It made the rooms feel bigger and allowed homebuyers to better visualize their own style.

"Look at all this natural light coming into the living room," I said as Derek made his way into the house. He took off his coat and hung it on a hook beside the front door. His beefy arms were on full display. I wanted to be suffocated by them.

Commission, not coming.

"They installed coat hooks. Great space saver!" I said.

He checked out the closets and studied the size of the hallways. I watched him go through a mental checklist.

The Fireman and the Flirt

People tried to be analytical when searching for a house, but one hundred percent of the time, emotions were the deciding factor. Derek would be no different, but he had to discover that on his own.

"What do you think?" I caught up with him in the kitchen, which looked out on a neatly kept backyard with a pergola.

"It's nice."

I wouldn't be getting much more from him, and that was okay.

"On a scale from No Way to Dream House, where are you?"

"Somewhere in the middle." He cracked a smile as he opened the fridge. Even the food inside had been organized. "Huh."

"What?"

"They drink a lot of Diet Coke." He pointed to the two boxes of Diet Coke cans stacked in the fridge. "Diet soda is terrible for you. You're better off drinking regular."

"That's a matter for their dentist, not you."

"If they don't care about their bodily health, do they care about their house's health?"

"Derek."

His face split with a smile that stretched up to his crinkly eyes. "I'm kidding."

The look of unabashed joy on his face sent a warm spark through me.

I cleared my throat. "The appliances are all stainless steel and less than five years old."

"Good to know." He leaned over the open fridge door, his biceps tightening against his shirt. "What was in your letter?"

"Huh?" I clutched my tablet to my chest.

"In your letter from high school."

"What made you think of that?"

He shrugged his shoulders, which belied a whole ocean of questions.

"I was flipping through the South Rock yearbook. You look mostly the same," he said.

"I doubt that, but thank you." Was that a good thing?

"I was rolling my eyes at my senior quote. I thought I was being profound."

"I'm sure it was great, whatever it was." The truth was I knew the exact quote. All of it. *You miss one hundred percent of the shots you don't take* was Derek's senior quote, and yes, teenage Cary found it deeply fucking profound.

"It's a bit cliché. But don't sidetrack us. What was in the letter?"

"I told you. I was sticking up for Cal."

"Okay." A glint in his eye warned me that my story was on shaky ground. Before he could grill me any further, and before I could let his steely gaze trigger more flirting from me, I shut the fridge.

"You don't want all their Diet Coke to go bad." I spun on my heel and headed to the bedrooms. Because we hadn't yet seen the bedrooms. Not because I was thinking about the *bedroom* bedroom.

"Let's go," I said over my shoulder. "Plenty more house to see!"

Derek followed behind. We walked to the first door on the right.

"This is the first of three bedrooms. And I know you don't need three, but one can be an office or a guest room."

A very large bed with a red, fluffy comforter took up nearly the entire square footage of the room. It had to be a California king at least. It reminded me of stories of sketchy nightclubs in the late 1970s that had rooms filled with only mattresses.

"That's quite a bed," Derek said. He squeezed past me to the window, which had a nice view of the street. But the only thing either of us could look at was this enormous bed swallowing up this tiny room.

One huge, welcoming mattress stood between us.

"Yep. It is a very large bed," I said. My heart rate chirped up. I struggled to keep cool. Why did my mind always have to find its way to sex around Derek? Why couldn't I think about grocery lists or the impending doom of climate change like normal people?

"It seems comically large for this room."

"It does." It was meant for a large, strong man...and a slender man that the large man could play with.

"It makes you wonder what the owners were thinking, why they needed such a big bed." Derek scratched the back of his neck. Did I detect the slightest hints of blush on the tops of his cheeks?

"Maybe they had big guests?"

"It's definitely big enough for two people." His lips curled up into a mischievous grin that got my blood pumping, a grin I hadn't seen since he was fucking around with his friends in the halls of South Rock High.

"For sleeping," I said, breath heavy in my chest.

"Or other things."

Other things.

"The room has a closet." I half-heartedly waved to it. Three dull hangers clanked in the center.

The bed was getting larger, expanding out, a black hole sucking everything into its vortex. I should not be thinking about holes and sucking...

"And you can put whatever you want in here. This room

doesn't have to have a bed, especially a bed this big. You can put a desk in here, or turn it into a TV room with a couch."

Derek rested a knee on the bed, and it squeaked back. This mattress was unapologetically loud, cutting through the thick silence between us. How loud would the mattress get if Derek was full-throttled fucking me?

Commission, not coming.

Derek isn't sexy. That's just the nostalgia talking.

Shut up, brain. You know that's not true.

"Have you ever..." He raised a curious eyebrow my way.

"Uh huh?"

There was that mischievous grin again making my dick stand at attention.

"Done it in a house you were showing?"

I felt red all over my body. Sometimes, talking about sex was hotter than having sex.

"No," I said simply, the word barely coming out.

"That would be wrong."

"Yes. We're not supposed to damage any properties we show."

"You would damage property?" He raised an eyebrow, his grin getting bigger. "Cary's got a wild side."

"Damage is a—is a broad word. Let's go look at the main bedroom. It has an upholstered window seat."

"You ever thought about it?" Derek's crystal blue eyes pinned me in place, clouding everything I thought I knew about him. I didn't know if he was flirting with me, blatantly hitting on me, asking genuine questions, or if I'd died and was actually in purgatory.

"N—no. That's a little too...I'm too much of a good girl to try something like that."

But good girls also needed to be spanked, right?

"Are you? I heard you like to get up to freaky things now and again, Gearhead."

There it was. The inescapable label, shattering this delightfully confusing moment. It was someone yanking open curtains, flooding a room with unwanted light. I thought I'd shaken it as an adult, but oh no, it would forever haunt me. Like a ghost. Or an STI.

"I actually have to get back to the office. I have a meeting I just remembered. I'll let you scope out the rest of the house on your own. Make sure to close the door when you leave."

I brushed past him, immune to the pull of the bed's vortex, immune to whatever spell Derek may or may not have been trying to cast. When I got back to the office, I would ask Hannah to be his point of contact moving forward. Why the hell did I ever think it was a good idea to work with a former crush?

9

DEREK

What the hell just happened?

I stood in the bedroom, me and one extra-large bed, going over the instant replay in my head. Cary and I were joking around, and then...did I start flirting with him? Was I seconds away from throwing him on the bed and tearing off his fancy shirt? He made it so damn easy with his cute smile and his big eyes. An electricity crackled between us, which made me keep going. But then just as fast, it was over, and I was standing in a stranger's house alone.

I had crossed a line with my flirting and made him uncomfortable. But was it something else, too? Because he seemed borderline upset.

I got into my car and let out a sigh. I was having a good time with him. And then my dick had to ruin it.

I'd had fleeting attraction to guys in the past. Nothing ever worth acting on, and something I had ignored while I was married. I supposed I was bisexual in today's parlance. Cary was the first man in a long time to make that side of me come out and play.

I checked my phone for a message from him. Nada. But another blast from the past popped up on my screen.

Leo: I hear you're back in town and hanging out with Mitch? I'm feeling left out.

Leo was my other good friend from high school. The three of us hung out religiously. Leo had more drive than either of us. He'd gone from being a successful lawyer to mayor of Sourwood.

Derek: You around now?

Leo: I got some time between meetings. Want to meet at my office?

Derek: Sure. Where is it?

Leo: City Hall, motherfucker!

———

FOR A SMALL TOWN, Sourwood's city hall was impressive. Inside, a big rotunda stretched up from the center, its round walls dotted with exhibits of Sourwood past. I vaguely recalled the mandatory field trip here in elementary school, although the highlight for me that afternoon was playing pogs on the back of the bus.

On the rotunda walls were photos of the city council members, with Leo's photo hung above them all. He was the head honcho. The BMOC of our hometown. I was proud of my friend.

I went down a long hallway of offices, which looked no different than a corporate setting, until I reached the last door. I gave my name to Leo's administrative assistant and sat in the waiting room.

"There he is." Leo strutted from his office, his dress shirt sleeves rolled up, black hair slicked back with touches of gray at the tips. He'd gotten older looking, but the sarcastic glimmer in his eye was the same as it'd been years ago. "Thanks for leaving the glacier to deign us with your presence."

"Alaska is a beautiful state." I smacked him in the stomach, a reminder that a fancy office didn't change a guy. "Are you going to invite me into your office, Mr. Mayor?"

"Right this way." Leo led us back.

I was expecting the Oval Office, but then I remembered this was a small town in New York. It was cozy, but had certain presidential touches: a large wooden desk that had to be a century old, a sofa by the door with a framed American flag hung on the wall.

"You're hot shit, man," I said as I looked around.

"I'm merely a civil servant to this great town."

Servants didn't have large, fancy desks. Nice try.

"I did some redecorating when I got re-elected." Leo was very into decor. Cal said he had renovated and remodeled his Colonial home where he lived with his boyfriend and kids. And he was easily the best dressed of our friend group.

"I heard you have a boyfriend now," I said. "A carpenter."

"Yep. I'm dating Jesus. No, his name is Dusty. We go way back, not as way back as you, me, and Mitch. You'll like him." He blushed for a second, a slip of his refined persona. He was in love. It was sweet to see. Leo threw a foam stress ball at my chest. "Let me know the next time you and Mitch hang out."

"Sorry. I thought you were busy with mayoral stuff. Why didn't you come over for dinner the other night?"

Leo rolled his eyes. "Cal's pissed at me because I wouldn't get his parking ticket cleared up. He claims he was only five minutes past the meter, but our records show it was closer to forty-five. I think Cal secretly wants to go to traffic court to fight it so he can give a dramatic courtroom monologue."

"That sounds about right." My brother was constantly seeking his *Erin Brockovich* moment, a movie he finally got me to watch the other night.

Leo got quiet all of a sudden, and I knew what was coming. I steeled myself for the kind words.

"Hey, I'm real sorry about–"

I held up my hand, as if I were pushing an invisible brake. "Thank you. I'm hanging in there."

"I'm here if you ever need..."

"I know, man. I know. I'm kind of all talked-out at this point."

"Cool." Leo nodded his head, a little unsure of how to proceed. Was proper friend protocol to keep prodding? I quickly switched topics.

"Jolene really likes Lucy and Ari. She's been playing Ari's video game nonstop at home." Unlike their dad, Leo's twins were very creative. Lucy made films, and Ari created video games on his computer. "They've helped Jolene get acclimated to a new school. You got good kids."

"As do you. Dads of the Year," he joked. "So I hear you're househunting. How's it going?"

I see-sawed my head. It had been going well, until it wasn't. What *was* that weird moment with Cary?

"It's going," I said.

Leo and I fell into reminiscing about high school, stories pouring out of us as if they'd just happened, laughing like we were sixteen again. He wasn't the mayor, and I wasn't a middle-aged sad widower. Before we knew it, Leo had a meeting he had to attend.

I checked my phone and did a double take at the email that had come though.

. . .

Derek,

I've realized that my workload is a little bit heavier than anticipated, and I fear I can't give you the attention you deserve for this important process. I've looped in my partner Hannah, who will be working with you moving forward. I'm still here as a resource should you have any questions, but anything you need, Hannah can help with. Good luck on your home buying journey!

Best,
  Cary

"What the fuck?" I said to my screen.

Leo stood up to escort us out. "What happened?"

"I think my real estate agent just dumped me."

———

I tried calling Cary twice, but each time rolled to voicemail, the cold, businesslike greeting sending a chill further down my spine. I preferred the warm, funny voice that was constantly forcing me to see the upside in every house.

I replayed the scene in my head, how the heat rose between us. The questions had tumbled out, fueled by a desire that overcame me, and it seemed like he was into it. Until he wasn't.

The Fireman and the Flirt

Derek: Hey, what's going on? You don't want to work with me anymore?

Cary: It's my fault. I took on more than I could handle. Hannah is great. You're in good hands, I promise.

The words came off as cold as his voicemail greeting.

Later that day, Hannah called me to introduce herself. She was nice and professional, and true to Cary's words, she made me believe I was in good hands. But they weren't Cary's hands.

Cary's hands...on my body.

Fuck. I had definitely made things inappropriate between us. I had to make this right, but I got the feeling that I would never be seeing Cary again.

Fortunately, the next day, I started my first shift on Sourwood's fire fighting squad. I used my required workout and time spent cleaning the firetruck to take my mind off Cary and houses and showers large enough for two people.

Hannah and I met to look at houses a few days later. She took us on a tour of four different properties, and by the end, the houses began to blend together. Which one had the breakfast nook? Which one had the two-car garage? Why had Cary cut me off cold?

She was professional and good at her job, but there were no Cary-like quips, no hints of nerves in her voice.

We stopped at a Starbucks to regroup and go over my opinions on each property. Hannah took out her laptop to take notes, but I only had one comment.

"I think Cary is mad at me," I said. I gulped down my black coffee and took a bite of the snowman cookie Hannah had gotten for me.

"He's bitten off more than he can chew. We share clients all the time. We're a team." There was something about her attitude that was trying too hard. "What's important is finding you the best house."

Yes, that was the most important thing...but then why was I letting this thing with Cary overshadow finding a place to live?

"Is he mad at me?" I repeated.

"No," she said, betraying a hint of doubt.

"Does he do this often? Handing clients off to you via email? It doesn't seem like his style."

"It is odd, I'll admit. I think he's just stressed."

"Hannah." I turned on my deep dad voice, the one used when I knew Jolene was hiding something from me, the voice that said *I'm not the enemy but I also won't allow secrets in my house.* "If you know something, please tell me." I leaned in. "I promise I won't drop you as my agent if you tell me the truth."

She sipped her coffee nervously. "Yes, this is unlike Cary."

"I knew it." I slammed the table.

"He asked me to start working with you, didn't say why. Maybe things...I don't know, maybe because you two knew each other from before, he felt it was a conflict of interest?"

She wasn't buying what she was saying. Neither was I.

"We were joking around at the last house we saw together, and I might've overstepped." I spun my coffee cup, letting the condensation form a perfect circle on the table.

She leaned forward, face lit up with curiosity. "What did you say?"

I could feel myself turn red. If I was going to get to the truth, then I had to be honest. "I asked if he'd ever had sex in a house he was showing."

Hannah snorted.

"I shouldn't have asked him something like that. We were joking around, and it got out of hand."

"That isn't something that would make him stop working with you. He has a good sense of humor."

"He does," I said wistfully. We hadn't spent much time together, but he was already one of the funniest people I'd known. He put me in a good mood, and I liked to think I did the same for him.

"What else did you say?"

"He said he wouldn't do something like that, like you said. And then I said something like, 'Are you sure about that, Gearhead?' Because of his nickname in high school."

Hannah's face dropped like it had plummeted down an elevator shaft.

"You called him Gearhead?"

"I heard that was his nickname. It was supposed to be a fun callback to high school."

"Do you know how he got it?"

"I just heard the story the other day. It was funny." The tale of how he got that name was also a little hot. Cary had a wild side. "It'd happened after I left for Ala–"

"Derek," she said firmly, shutting me up. "It's *not* funny. First of all, Cary was outed against his will by his secret boyfriend. Then he was teased relentlessly for the rest of high school because of it. It metastasized into this big story. People thought he had sex with a car or did other freaky shit. When he tried dating years later, there were some guys, guys who never went to South Rock, who would bring it up. It was awful."

Oh shit. I hunched over my coffee cup, furious with myself.

"No wonder he doesn't want to work with you."

"Fuck. I am such an asshole." I felt my whole body sink into itself, immediately overcome with an anvil of guilt.

"You really didn't know?"

I shook my head no. My eyes pleaded with her to believe me. It took a few seconds, but she eventually softened.

I wanted to kill Mitch. Did he know about the teasing? Probably not. Mitch would never be cruel to someone. Knowing Cary, he probably laughed it off, played the good sport because that was the kind of guy he was. And I was an asshole.

I clamped my eyes shut and silently cursed myself. "I really fucked up."

"Yeah. You did."

10

CARY

Despite working in real estate, my house wasn't anything to write home about. It was on the older side, on the fringes of town, and could use some upkeep. I'd spruced it up with a remodeled kitchen and a pair of cute flower pots outside the front door. My credit score wasn't great when I'd purchased, which limited what I could buy.

My family and I never really talked about money because we never had that much. My dad painted houses, and my mom did alterations out of our basement. There were never enough houses or pairs of pants most months. I learned how to shop for deals and look presentable on a budget, though I never had the effortless cool of a rich kid who lived a frictionless life. Being closeted and kinda weird meant that I already stood out without trying, so I didn't want to stick out with a bad wardrobe. When I turned eighteen, I was inundated with offers from credit card companies, and I discovered the magic of plastic—without being told that paying them off on time was actually, like, really important. Real estate had allowed me to get out of that hole. Now I could shop where the rich kids shopped.

There was a constant boulder of guilt sitting in my stomach around the gearhead debacle. My parents worked hard to provide for their son, and he turned around and became a laughingstock. I made sure to shield them from my petty high school drama, never letting them know what happened, never burdening them with my pain. They worked too hard to have to spend their free time wading through my teenage bullshit.

It filled my heart with the purest kind of joy when I helped them sell their house for a tidy profit years later, which enabled them to buy a unit in a very nice senior community.

I'd been tempted to buy myself a unit in one of the hot, new luxury condo developments popping up downtown, but a part of me preferred living away from town. I liked to be social, but I also liked my solitude. There was a fine line between loneliness and solitude. Solitude was something we chose; loneliness was something that happened to us. I was constantly riding that line.

Most mornings, I could step into my backyard, which faced quiet woods, and have a little kumbaya moment of zen.

This morning, though, I didn't find zen when I stared out into nature. I checked my email first thing when I woke up, which probably wasn't a good habit to keep up. I was technology-obsessed, a member of the hyperconnected twenty-first century, and that was that. Hannah kept me abreast of Derek's house hunting mission. Each new update chipped at my heart, the way creeping on an ex's social media page always made me feel lacking. I hated to say it, but I missed him.

I got dressed in an aquamarine button-down shirt and black slacks. Bright colors would cheer me up. I drove into downtown Sourwood, admiring the large candy canes hung on all the lamp posts. I didn't mind that it was mid-November. Let the holidays begin on November 1st!

As per my routine, I parked in the PRG lot and beelined to Caroline's for my daily iced coffee to go.

Caroline's was a greasy spoon diner which on the surface wouldn't be thought of as a great place for coffee. In fact, I was the only person who ordered iced coffee to-go from them. The brother of Caroline's current owner owned a coffee bean supplier in Manhattan and provided the restaurant with rich, delicious coffee from the heart of Costa Rica. Let the other mindless yuppies wait in line at Starbucks for average coffee. Caroline's was my little secret.

"The usual?" Kathy, the waitress at the counter who'd been there forever, asked.

"I'll take two today. I need the extra caffeine."

"Make it three," said a familiar deep voice behind me.

I wanted to be strong and not get turned on by the sound of Derek's voice and the sight of his lumbering body. But we couldn't get everything we wanted.

"Oh. Hi," I said, taking in Derek's black Dave Matthews Band t-shirt, which highlighted his strong chest as well as his protruding stomach.

Why did Derek's eyes have to sparkle? Sparkling eyes should be illegal.

"They have good coffee," he said.

"It's because they source it from a special coffee bean distributor, so it's better than the standard coffee that other places have." Fuck. Why was I giving all these details? I had to be better at being the strong, silent type. "But yeah, it's good."

"So three total?" Kathy asked, ready to update the order.

"No," I said. "We're separate."

"No, we're not. We'll take three iced coffees. I'm paying." Derek slapped down his credit card, letting me glimpse his strong, muscular forearm.

"He's not. I can buy myself my own iced coffees." I slapped my credit card over his. Watching our pieces of plastic touch sent an inappropriate vibe through me.

"It's my treat," he said, pushing his card forward to Kathy, who was confused by the whole situation.

"Will one of you pick a card, any card? I don't have time for this," she said, putting us in our place. She'd been on the clock since 1986, and her feet were tired.

"Let me," Derek said, unleashing the full power of those sparkly eyes. I pulled back my card.

"Why are you so adamant on feeding my caffeine habit?" I asked. "And also, thank you."

"It's my way of apologizing." Derek waited for Kathy to go down the counter to the coffee maker, out of earshot. "For what I said the other day."

"We were joking around." My neck went hot thinking about Derek's probing questions in the bedroom with the too-large bed. It was the hottest house visit I'd ever led, and I couldn't get it out of my head, despite how it had ended.

"I'm not talking about that part. I don't regret that," he said.

A man who had no shame about asking flirty questions? Hot.

"I mean the gearhead thing."

Not hot.

The word made my blood run cold, as it always would until the end of time.

"Oh that?" I waved it off. "Just a stupid nickname."

"It's not." He put his hand softly on my arm. "Cary, I'm sorry for using that name. I didn't know the whole story and how it made your life hell. If I had, I never would've uttered it."

He wouldn't let go until I met his eyes. I hated that this story was still alive all these years later. That someone else could know something that personal about me before I could know anything about them. It put me on a forever unequal playing field with others.

"It's in the past," I said, wishing it were so.

"I thought I was being funny. I wound up being an asshole." A tortured look crossed Derek's face.

"You're not an asshole." It was impossible to be mad at Derek. This man could probably get me to walk on hot coals and broken glass if he so desired.

"To be honest, I thought the story was kind of cool."

"Cool?"

"Yeah. Pretty bad ass that you put a whole gearshift in your mouth. It was kinda..." He trailed off, his thought dangling over me just out of reach. Kinda sexy? Kinda weird? Kinda freaky?

"If only our South Rock classmates felt the same way you did." I sighed.

Kathy came back with the coffees in large, clear plastic cups. Three straws stuck up in the air. I unfolded a cardboard cup carrier I'd gotten from Starbucks a while back since Caroline's didn't provide their own. It allowed me to look like a normal person bringing coffee for a friend rather than a mocha java fiend who was double fisting. I put all three cups in my carrier.

"Thanks, Kathy. See you tomorrow." I waved goodbye.

Derek followed behind onto the sidewalk. Flurries fluttered through the air. They weren't the kind that stuck, but rather pretty flakes swirling around giving downtown more holiday ambiance. Derek plunked on his wool hat and zipped up his jacket, looking fuzzy and warm in both. The man was built to be Big Spoon.

"It was a stupid teenage thing. I'd like for it to stay in the past," I said.

"It sounds like things were rough for you. I'm sorry."

"I got through it." The last thing I wanted was his pity. "This guy I had a crush on dared me to do it."

"And then he told people about it? Sounds like a prick."

"I didn't realize that until much later." It wasn't as painful talking about this with Derek as I feared it would be. He had a way of making the memory feel pocket-sized.

"When I was trying to woo my late wife, she talked me into entering a men's wet T-shirt contest."

"That's a thing?" A thing I *definitely* would've liked to have seen.

"Apparently. She took some pictures. I haven't found them yet, but I'm hoping they got lost to time. I would've been mortified if she showed those around." Derek looked out on the bustling downtown and laughed to himself.

"What's with people we care about trying to embarrass us?"

Derek shrugged.

"You two sounded like a great couple. Sounds like you really loved each other."

There was that uneasy look on Derek's face, the one I'd seen when I'd complimented his marriage previously.

"Can I tell you something?" Derek motioned for us to take a seat on a bench, which luckily was one of the benches without the Morris brothers' ugly faces on them.

"What is it?" I asked once we sat down. Derek dug his fingernail into the side of his coffee cup. "You're going to spill coffee on yourself if you keep doing that."

He glanced up at me with a mix of terror and strength. "She was cheating on me."

"Your wife? Late wife?" I kept my response muted rather than bulging out my eyes, which is what I wanted to do.

Derek nodded. "If I hear one more person talk about us as if we were some perfect couple..." The vein in his neck pulsed with contained rage. "Our marriage was crumbling. We were drifting apart, not talking, always fighting. Then I found out she was cheating on me with one of my good friends. Angus."

"She cheated on you with a man named after a hamburger?"

Derek gave me an exaggerated nod. I was surprised he didn't become a vegetarian.

"I saw the texts on her phone. All the times I went to a bar to watch a football game with him, all the times we had him over for dinner, and there I was the clueless fucking idiot because they were going behind my back. Right before I ginned up the courage to confront her, Paula had an aneurysm and died."

"No wonder you wanted to get the hell out of Alaska." I didn't know how people recovered from betrayal like that. That was the risk with relationships. You opened yourself to another person, and they could rob you blind.

"Now I'm left with questions. Why couldn't we work it out? Where did things go wrong? All the while everyone around me is constantly telling me how we were the perfect couple, and I have to play along. It doesn't seem right to tarnish a woman's reputation who isn't around to give her side of the story."

"Does Jolene know?"

He shook his head no. "Thank god for that."

Derek heaved in a breath. I could tell that'd sat on his

shoulders for a long time, the weight accumulating with each passing day. Having to smile and play the mourning widower while you were filled with unresolved hurt sounded like a fresh kind of torture.

I appreciated that he trusted me with the truth. Neither of us wanted to play the victim. I rubbed his back.

"Have you spoken with your allegedly good friend since?"

"Hell no. I want nothing to do with him ever again." Derek turned to me, his face softening just a bit. "Why did you stay in Sourwood?"

"Because I refused to let myself get chased out of town by a stupid name. That, and it's a hot market. And Caroline's coffee, of course."

"Of course." Derek sipped his drink. "This is damn good coffee."

I clinked my cup against his.

"Well, let's promise that we can always be honest with each other. This is a no bullshit zone." I pointed between us.

"I like that." Derek's face split into a jolly grin. "You know what I'd also like? For you to be my agent again."

"What's wrong with Hannah?"

"Hannah's great, but she doesn't try and spin a hole in a roof as being an organic skylight."

"I never said that." I shoved his shoulder playfully... maybe flirtatiously? We were clients and friends with a no-bullshit zone. I had to keep my blatant flirting under check even more.

"Not yet. But it could be a Caryism."

"A Caryism? Is that a thing now?"

"It's definitely a thing." Derek shoved me back. His eyes stayed locked on mine for a few extra tantalizing seconds.

"Let's see...what else...if there's a house without a fridge, then it's an invitation to enjoy rustic living."

"Okay, you did not just come up with that."

"When I'm bored at the firehouse, I'll think up Caryisms to pass the time."

He thought about me in his downtime? He dreamt up Caryisms?

"Oh, here's another one. If there's a house with no windows, you would say the owner has full control over their light intake experience."

A loud laugh exploded out of me, attracting attention.

My lust for this man was quickly being overpowered by a stronger feeling coming straight from my heart. I wanted to jump Derek's bones. That was a universal truth. But was I falling for him?

I focused back on my real estate agent duties to distract myself from that question. "It just so happens that there's a new development being built at the north end of town. Eden Falls. Some of the model homes are available for walk-throughs. I know you were leaning toward an older house, but new construction has its perks. What do you say?"

Derek held out his hand for a shake. "I say we're back in business."

11

DEREK

Cary and I made a plan to see Eden Falls in a week's time, the Monday after Thanksgiving. Between our work schedules and the holiday itself, that would be the soonest we could make it happen. Now that I'd officially started at the firehouse, I was working twenty-four hours on, forty-hours off. It would take me a little time to adjust; thank goodness Cal was there to help with Jolene.

One of the reasons I had us make the move back home now was so Jolene and I could experience the holidays with extended family for the first time in years. In Alaska, it was usually only the three of us–or four on those occasions Angus the deceitful hamburger joined us. Those memories were ruined now.

Cary and I hadn't texted the Monday or Tuesday before Thanksgiving. I was on my shift, and Cary was busy doing back-to-back closings. It wasn't like we needed to talk to each other. We had our plan in place for Eden Falls after the weekend and that was that. But it was weird not hearing from him, like a part of my daily routine that was missing.

On Wednesday morning, I stumbled home after my first

twenty-four shift. Swords of sunlight slashed through the darkness. I was exhausted, using sheer willpower to drive me back to Cal's. The grogginess was its own form of drunkenness, prodding me to text Cary once I collapsed onto the pullout couch.

Derek: Hey

Derek: Happy Thanksgiving.

Cary: Thanksgiving is tomorrow.

Shit. Well, I'd gone ahead and made myself look like a fool.

Cary: But if we were in Australia, it would be Thanksgiving already, so Happy Thanksgiving!!!

It was too early for all those exclamation points, but I imagined Cary's excited face as he typed them.

Cary: Are you just coming home from your shift?

Derek: Yup.

Cary: That schedule is insane.

Derek: I'll adjust. Are we all set for Monday morning at Eden Falls? I promise I won't fall asleep at the showing.

Cary: If you do, there are no extra-large beds in tiny rooms you can crash on. It's an empty house.

I was so tired, at this point, laying on the floor sounded comfortable.

Derek: What are you doing for the holiday?

I held out hope that Cal invited him to the feast. He'd make a great dinner guest, one of those people who would keep the conversation going.

Cary: I'm going to my aunt's house out in Poughkeepsie.

Derek: Poo

Derek: I mean boo.

Cary: Poo works, too.

A smile broke through my tiredness.

Derek: Who'll be there?

Cary: Me, my parents, my Aunt Claire, and my two cousins.

Derek: Older cousins? Younger cousins?

Cary: A little younger, but not by much. They were like quasi-siblings growing up, which was awesome because I'm an only child. We don't see each other as often since they moved away, but when we do get together, it's like we're twelve all over again. This time with cell phones.

Cary: Is this too much information?

Derek: No.

I didn't know why I was asking questions about his cousins. I supposed any little factoid about Cary was interesting for some reason.

Cary: I'll be back on Friday night.

Cary: Just in case there's anything you need to go over with the house search.

Cary: But you'll probably be working at the firehouse.

Cary: So nevermind.

Time was tight, but maybe we could hang Friday night? We could go to a bar, grab a drink...I stopped myself from texting that. That didn't sound like a business meeting. That was a date. I was tired, but I couldn't allow myself to cross that line and risk Cary severing our relationship again.

Derek: This weekend will be tough. But we'll meet up on Monday.

Derek: To see the house.

Cary: To see the house.

Cary: Because you can't buy a house until you see it. Although I did have a client from London buy a house sight unseen.

Derek: That won't be happening here.

Derek: Hey, I'm drinking some Caroline's coffee right now.

I held up my to-go cup and took a selfie. The picture cut off my face under my eyes. Oof, I figured I should cease texting before I really made an ass out of myself.

Cary: We'll have to work on your social media skills 😀

WAS it any surprise that Russ put together a delicious Thanksgiving feast?

Turkey that melted in my mouth. Tangy, sweet cranberry sauce. Creamy mashed potatoes. Pilgrims would rise from the dead to join in.

The boys made turkey-shaped place cards, while Jolene and Cal teamed up to create a festive cornucopia centerpiece. This was hands-down the best Thanksgiving meal I'd had in a while.

Cal clinked his glass to get our attention. "I'd like everyone to raise a glass. As unaccustomed to public speaking as I am–"

"Sure," Russ deadpanned.

"I want to say how grateful I am for everyone around this table. Grateful to have family closer by. Grateful to have energetic, healthy children. And grateful to have a husband who is an amazing cook, but also an amazing father and person. Russ, you and I like to give each other guff, but I love you. Even if the gravy was a scoach too salty. Kidding!"

I was fine being single. Over the past six months, I realized that I didn't want to risk another betrayal, another loss, or worse. Yet when Russ took Cal's hand and kissed it tenderly, the gesture tugged at my heartstrings more than it should have.

I stealthily took out my phone and held it in my lap.

Derek: Thanksgiving Caryisms:

Derek: The gravy isn't too salty. It's packed with extra flavor.

I smiled to myself in that proud way that came with having a running inside joke with someone. I silently cheered when my phone buzzed.

Cary: Meh. 5/10.

Cary: You can do better than that, Hogan.

Derek: Challenge accepted.

I rattled around potential Caryisms while I helped clear the table for dessert. Cal had told Russ to just buy a pumpkin pie, but that was not in Russ's nature. Somehow, he found the time and energy to make a pumpkin and a pecan pie from scratch. It was a good thing he liked Cal nice and round. And it was a good thing I was moving out soon, or else they'd have to grease the doorways to get me out.

Derek: The turkey isn't burnt. It's caramelized.

Cary: Better. 5.4/10

Derek: I didn't set the smoke alarms off. I added a moody ambiance that added mystique to the space.

Derek: The fire in the kitchen will help you cut down on your heating bills.

Cary: LOL

Derek: Was that an actual LOL?

Cary sent me a picture of him laughing. His cheeks bunched up, teeth on display. I closed and reopened it multiple times.

Cary: 7.8/10

Derek: You're a tough judge.

Cary: I take my Caryism scoring rubric seriously.

"What are you watching? Are you on TikTok, too?" Cal asked.

I shoved my phone in my pocket, feeling like I was busted even though I wasn't doing anything wrong.

EARLIER IN THE WEEK, I'd promised Jolene we could go stargazing if the weather held out. Well, I wasn't going to renege on a promise, even if I was stuffed with turkey and it was freezing cold out. I lugged her telescope into the car, and we drove to the playground in Russ's neighborhood. It wasn't as dark as she'd wanted, but it was far enough away from the surrounding houses that they wouldn't limit our view.

I made Jolene wear her thickest hat and thickest gloves before taking the reins of the telescope.

"Dad! I can see Cassiopeia!" she called out from her perch, one eye looking into space. I threw my head back, awed by the sea of stars. Stargazing made me feel both incredibly small and incredibly big. I was but a mere human on this relatively small planet surrounded by an unending array of stars. But I also felt deeply connected to the universe, like maybe me being here wasn't an accident.

"Do you want to see?" Jolene asked.

"Sure, Jo." I leaned over her and put my eye in the viewer. She described the shape to me. Cassiopeia was an upside down girl in a chair, named for one of the Greek myths. "She's beautiful."

"Cassiopeia made the mistake of claiming she was more beautiful than the gods. So they punished her by making her sit upside down for all of eternity."

"Is that punishment? She can be stared at and admired forever."

"But she's all alone."

Weren't we all, I thought. Though I saved that bleak, adult thought for myself.

"Hey," I nudged her elbow. "That was a good Thanksgiving, right?"

"Yeah. I kinda miss mom's cooking, though. I was used to the canned cranberry and canned green bean casserole."

"Canned cranberry sauce is the superior sauce," I said.

"Don't tell Uncle Russ. Remember the year when mom overcooked the stuffing and it came out as one big bread blob?"

"And she just served it on a plate and told us to rip off pieces with our hands."

We devolved into riotous laughter, white clouds of smoke billowing from our mouths. It hurt to laugh this hard with a full stomach.

"It wasn't a stuffing disaster. It was a fresh spin on an old classic that didn't require a fork," I said, my smile getting bigger. "That's a Caryism."

"A what?" Jolene asked.

Then I remembered the whole world wasn't on our text chain.

"I mean, your mom was one of a kind," I said, choosing to remember the good things about her tonight. "But you ate well tonight. I saw you clean off your plate."

She shrugged, choosing not to refute the statement. Jolene adjusted her telescope to find a new constellation.

"Can we go to the storage locker this weekend? Mom had this Disney sweatshirt that was always so comfortable. I loved wearing it even though it was really baggy."

Last year, Paula wore that sweatshirt religiously, even though the sleeves draped down her arm. It was like a wearable blanket, soothing her in the winter.

"When did you guys go to Disney World?" Jolene asked.

"We didn't. We wanted to take you," I said before it hit me. Angus went on a big family trip to Disney a few years back. He'd shown me a picture of him and his extended family in matching Haverstock Family Reunion T-shirts. He probably bought himself a Disney sweatshirt when he was down there. Did he give it to Paula, or did she find it in his closet after one of their...nope, I couldn't go down that path.

"You can order sweatshirts online," I said. "Early Christmas present?"

"I'd rather wear Mom's."

"It'll be so big on you. Your mom was already drowning in it."

Jolene flicked her eyes at the ground for a second. I knew her true feelings. I put a hand on her shoulder.

"We'll go and get the sweatshirt this weekend."

"Thanks, Dad."

"I wanted to do a little snooping around in the storage locker, too," I said. "Hey. I'm grateful for you, Jolene. Doesn't even have to be Thanksgiving to say it."

"Me, too." Jolene gave a slight eyeroll with her smile. Enough schmaltz, she seemed to say. Back to stargazing. She looked into her telescope, getting lost in the stars again.

I did the same.

Or as Cary might've said, "Stars are nature's track lighting."

Eh, that one was a 6.5/10.

12

CARY

Belinda Carlisle famously sang that heaven was a place on earth. More specifically, the heaven she was crooning about was my Aunt Claire's living room sofa.

I was currently relaxing on my aunt's reclining sofa, the kind with cup holders built into the arms, while smothered under thick, hand-knit blankets plural, watching a movie on cable that I would never choose to watch on my own but was very invested in at the moment.

Aka heaven.

The only thing missing was Derek snuggled up next to me. And by missing, I meant something I shouldn't be thinking about at all.

Aunt Claire was a genius because she furnished her house with comfort solely in mind. Her kind of couch would be mocked on Instagram for being unstylish, but it was ridiculously large and comfortable. There was enough room for me and my cousins Harold and Maudrey to lounge without fighting over couch space. Her name was Audrey, but after we watched *Harold and Maude* in high school, how could we *not* call her Maudrey?

This was how Thanksgivings usually went: the kids hanging around the house, the grown-ups talking around the dining table into the evening. It didn't matter that my cousins and I were all over the age of thirty-five. We would forever be "the kids."

Aunt Claire came into the living room with a plate of cookies for us. She looked at the TV and asked what kind of cockamammy movie we were watching, but then stood there for ten minutes watching along with us.

It was these traditions that made holidays so important to me.

"You've been on your phone all night," Aunt Claire said to me while I scrolled.

"Have not," I said.

"Are you watching TV or are you on your phone?"

"I'm a millennial. I can do both." If she chose to ask me a question about the movie on TV, I could've answered her with total accuracy.

She smiled to herself, finding us ridiculous but endearing.

"You kids," she said to a bunch of grown-ass adults with a laugh before leaving.

"You *have* been on your phone all night," said Maudrey. "Like unhealthy, Gen Z-levels."

"There's no such thing." My phone buzzed again. The same surge of serotonin hit my brain and my balls when Derek's name popped up.

He sent me a picture of a black screen.

Cary: Did you butt-text me a picture?

Derek: I tried sending you a picture of all the stars in the sky, but now I see that it just looks black.

Cary: I can kind of make them out.

It didn't matter that it was a black screen. Derek sent me

all the stars in the sky. Stars were inherently romantic. And thus, I had no choice but to swoon.

Derek: How's your night?

Cary: I'm watching a movie with my cousins while I look up house listings in my aunt's neighborhood.

Derek: Are you thinking of moving?

Cary: No. I just like looking at housing listings and prices. You don't do that when you go somewhere?

Derek: Look up house prices? No.

Cary: Oh. You must be normal then.

Cary: At least I can say I'm doing research for my job.

Derek: Research...right...

I imagined him stretching out both of those words until they became growls in the back of his throat. I really had to stop fantasizing about my client. Since I couldn't have Derek, I shoved a chocolate-chip cookie in my mouth instead.

Cary: It's fun. OMG. Look at this listing. Look at those built-ins!

I sent him the listing price for an older house with gorgeous wood built-in shelves around the fireplace, and built-ins in an upstairs nook. It made me want to find the nearest independent bookstore and buy a bunch of books.

Cary: All houses should have nooks. Like English muffins.

Derek: LOL

Cary: Was that a real LOL?

Derek sent me a picture of him being stone-faced. The joke was on him since I got to look at his face.

I glanced up to find Harold and Maudrey staring at me.

"What?" I asked.

"Who are you flirting with?" Maudrey threw a pillow at

me. How could she tell I was flirting? Was it written on my face?

"I'm not flirting. I'm showing a client some houses."

"Texting with a client on Thanksgiving night? That's dedication," said Harold.

"Harold, you've been looking through Tinder all night, so you're not one to talk. I'm surprised your thumb hasn't cramped up yet," I said. Harold was a personal trainer in Miami who spent more time working out than working with clients. This was the first Thanksgiving that he hadn't brought home a girlfriend. Not like any of them had ever made it to St. Patrick's Day. His type was twentysomethings with big boobs and small brains.

"Cary's sexting someone," said Harold, switching to lay on his stomach in full slumber party mode.

"Am not."

"The bathroom in the basement has the best lighting for shirtless pics."

"I don't want to know how you know that, Harold," said Maudrey. She was the smartie of the two of them, using her brains to get a job at a think tank in DC. She'd explained what she did several times before, but it truly went in one ear and out the other. I pictured her as Annette Bening in *The American President* and called it a day.

While we quickly devolved into silliness, we had a solid bond. They had been there for me when all the shit was going down with Gearhead.

I whipped off my blankets and stood up, the cool room temperature air sending a quick chill across my legs. "I'm getting some fresh air."

"It's freezing out!" cried Maudrey.

"It'll be refreshing."

I strutted through the living room to the front door. I

stepped into the night air and threw my head back, awed by the constellations above me. It was prettier and more transfixing than any movie on cable.

I texted Derek a picture of my night sky.

Derek: Beautiful.

Derek: Jolene is turning me into an astronomy geek.

Cary: Better than being an astrology geek.

Derek: What's the difference?

Cary: An astronomy geek studies the stars and galaxies beyond our planet. An astrology geek says things like "It's Leo season."

I was totally an astrology geek, but that was just the Aries in me. Even though miles separated us, it felt like Derek was beside me, and we were having this conversation together.

Derek: Having fun with the cousins?

I sent Derek a picture of me, Harold, and Maudrey taken earlier tonight. We were doing a silly pose. It was impossible not to be silly with them. We were goofballs when we were kids, and we were goofballs now. We'd likely be this silly when we were in our fifties...which wasn't that far off.

Derek: Nice.

Derek: Your cousin is cute.

Cary: Audrey has a really pretty face.

Derek: She does. But I was talking about the other one.

Cary: Harold?

Derek: Yes.

I stared at my phone, making sure I understood. A silence hung over me as I processed what he was trying to tell me. Lots of straight men were comfortable enough with themselves to compliment a guy's attractiveness. But I knew what this was. I could feel it with my gay sense, the quiet release of truth in the dark.

Derek: I'm bi.

Well, there he went confirming it.

Cary: Cool.

I was anything but cool. Fortunately, he couldn't see me, so I didn't have to play cool.

Only now he was FaceTiming me. My screen buzzed urgently with his name.

"Hey," I said. Fuck, Derek looked so good. He was outside, too, silhouetted by moonlight, his knit cap adorably plunked on his head. I wanted to burrow into his beard, let it scratch against my skin.

"Sorry for the surprise. I'd been thinking of telling you, but I didn't know when."

"There's never a right time to come out." Should I say I had my suspicions, enough suspicions to write him a saucy letter? Some guys took that the wrong way. They wanted their coming out to be a total surprise.

I had so many questions, but I didn't know how much I could dig.

"It's something I've known about myself for a while, but never felt a need to explore since I was married."

"Yeah, I get it. The whole adultery thing. Although that's kind of ironic."

"Yeah." Derek huffed out a laugh of cloudy breath.

"Does Cal know?"

"Not yet. So far, it's just you."

I was overwhelmingly honored to be his first...person that he told. That would be the only first I would be for him. Because he was my client. My client who was probably dynamite in bed.

"I won't tell anyone," I said. "How do you feel?"

"Feels kind of weird. Buzzing a little. I can't believe I told someone. Like I said, it's something I've known about myself for a while."

"But now it's in the public record."

"What do you mean?"

"That's how I looked at it," I said. "When I was a little kid, I used to think that God wrote down everything we said and did in some kind of public human record, like a court stenographer. You can think something, but it's not real until you say it aloud." I hoped I wasn't losing him with my weird kid thoughts.

"You can't take it back," he said.

"And you shouldn't. It's great that you know that about yourself and you're comfortable coming out. There may be some initial surprise, but most people will be cool with it." Sourwood had an abnormally high concentration of gay residents. Derek would have no problem fitting in. "It'll throw a wrench in the whole sad widower thing, though."

"Shucks," he deadpanned.

"Have you…explored this side with any other persons?" I asked, trying to stay as relaxed as possible.

Derek blushed slightly. "Once, when I first moved to Alaska, before I met Paula. Then a few months after she passed, I got curious one night and signed up for a hookup app. I was flooded with guys sending me messages like 'wreck me daddy' along with pictures of their assholes."

"That sounds about right." Just hearing Derek say "wreck me daddy" was enough to nearly wreck me.

"I didn't want to hook up with any of them."

"There are good guys out there."

"I know," Derek said, a peculiar twist to his lips. "Do you think Cal will be mad?"

"Cal? Why would he be mad?"

"Am I stealing his thunder by also being queer?"

While that sounded ludicrous, we also knew Cal Hogan, and so it wasn't out of the question. He knew how to make things about himself. The man was an actor, not a sociopath, though.

"You won't. Cal has an endless supply of thunder. Your brother will be happy for you."

"I guess." Derek didn't seem convinced. "Cal and I aren't really close."

"You guys were on different planets in high school."

"And running off to Alaska after graduation didn't help... we get along, but we still feel like we're on different planets." Derek scratched his head. "Sorry, didn't mean to dump that on you."

"It's okay," I said, honored to be his sounding board. "Dump away."

"I'm usually not this talkative. Yet I'm coming out to you and going on about my relationship with my brother. You bring it out of me, Cary."

"Sorry not sorry." I let myself gaze at his face for an extra lingering second. I hovered by the edge of the cliff, but held back from falling. "Unfortunately, my cousin Harold is mega-straight. Matthew McConaughey in *Dazed and Confused* was his dating idol. Harold might be getting older, but his girlfriends always seemed to stay the same age."

"That's okay. He isn't even the cutest guy in the picture."

In the freezing cold air, a surge of warmth zipped across my skin. I didn't know what to say that was more eloquent than "wreck me daddy." So instead, I tipped my imaginary top hat to him like a dork.

"Welcome," I said. "We'll send you your pride flag in the mail."

"Is there a secret handshake?"

"Only in the back rooms of certain clubs. I'm sure you'll

manage it well." And there I went, talking about hand jobs. The flirt in me refused to be tamed.

"I might need pointers."

"I don't mind going above and beyond for my clients." Fuck. Did I just offer my body to be his for wrecking? "I mean, I'm happy to introduce you to other queer men in the area and help you find social activities. I want to make sure you'll be fully acclimated."

I stared at his beard, not his eyes. I was too scared to check if he bought that.

"I appreciate that, Cary."

The way my name rolled off his tongue in his deep voice made me want to melt like one of those phallic-shaped popsicles on a hot, summer day.

"I'm gonna go back inside. I'm freezing. Is it cold up by you?" Derek asked.

"It's incredibly frigid." The weather meant nothing to me at that moment. I existed on a plane outside of mother nature.

"Stay warm. See you on Monday." Derek flashed me one more grin, and I noticed how earnest it was, that underneath the jock, bear, and daddy-capable-of-wrecking layers was just a levelheaded, kind, shy man trying to do the best he could like the rest of us.

I watched the screen go black when he hung up, already nostalgic for our conversation.

"Everything okay?" Maudrey slid the patio door open but didn't dare join me. Harold hung behind her, cookie in hand.

Hmmm...was everything okay? I was doing something I promised myself after gearhead I'd never do again: falling for a guy.

"Remember when we were younger and we used to raid

your parents' liquor cabinet?" I glanced at my cousins. "Could we do that again? Like right now?"

OVER THE THANKSGIVING HOLIDAY, I focused on not lusting or longing for my client. I was full of turkey. I didn't need to stuff myself with heartbreak and fresh rounds of mortification, too.

I spent the weekend running an open house for one of my elderly clients. She refused to make updates to her house before selling, and because of that, interest had been hard to come by. Had she updated her house, it would sell in a heartbeat, and I'd be one step closer to beating the Morris brothers. But forcing clients to do something they didn't want to wasn't my style. I respected her choice, and while it would be more difficult to get an offer, I saw it as a fun challenge. I used Saturday to clean up and restage her house, and the Sunday open house miraculously got some attention, also thanks to a price drop. We ended the afternoon with potential bites.

Derek and I hadn't spoken since that nighttime chat where he came out to me. It was a shame since I'd instantly gotten hooked on staring into his eyes via FaceTime. He was busy at the firehouse, sliding up and down the pole, doing a calendar shoot, or whatever firemen did all day. Still, I'd texted him twice on Sunday: one was a picture of my Caroline's to-go cup, the other was a more businesslike confirmation of our Monday meetup. I received responses to neither. We hadn't been texting for that long, yet that seemed out of character for him. I fought my anxiety tooth and nail not to let myself spiral.

I texted Derek early Monday morning to make sure our

Eden Falls walkthrough was still on for today. Rather than the text thread devolving into our usual banter, he only replied with a thumbs up.

He was probably busy, I told myself. Putting out fires and stuff.

I tried hard to not think that something was up, but my brain was hardwired to cultivate drama from the tiniest scraps.

Eden Falls was on a former field, saplings growing along the sidewalk. I arrived at the home early to make sure everything was in order. It was a cozy, ranch house with all the modern amenities. An open layout, spacious kitchen with island, hardwood laminate floors. Perfect for Derek and Jolene.

My heart sped up as the front door clicked open.

"Greetings! Welcome to your potential new home! Wait until you check out the view from the living room."

Derek didn't move from the front door, though. He stared at me, his face betraying nothing.

"What's up?" I asked, trying to stay upbeat as a sinking feeling washed over me.

He pulled an envelope from his jacket pocket and held it up, the faded edges making my stomach slide into a panicked freefall.

"I found your letter."

13

DEREK

I wasn't actively trying to find the letter.

On Sunday, despite being wiped from my latest shift, I kept my promise to Jolene to take her to the storage locker. She wanted that Disney sweatshirt of Paula's. I knew how much it would make her happy, even though I made a note to buy her one for Christmas.

In the storage locker, we worked our way through piles of boxes. We made a game of it, our twisted version of Christmas morning, because we never knew what we would find. I realized I hadn't properly labeled any of our boxes, so opening each one was a surprise. Kitchen items were found in clothing-labeled boxes. Socks and blankets were found in boxes meant to hold pictures. It was such a mad dash to pack everything up in time that my label strategy had quickly gone out the window.

Jolene and I happily walked down memory lane with each opened box, recalling memories attached to random items. The waffle maker that we only used once but swore we'd use more often in Sourwood. The coffee mug Jolene made in an art class with the chipped handle.

Eventually, we found Paula's sweatshirt in a box labeled books, but by that time, we were having too much fun to stop. There was a whole other side of the storage locker filled with stuff Cal had kept from our parents' old house.

We took the scenic route down memory lane.

Mom and Dad, and by extension Cal, had saved everything. I found old permission slips from field trips, a pre-9/11 history textbook I somehow hadn't returned at the end of the year, a puka shell necklace I'd worn everyday of junior year, my old see-through phone that I had in my room. Yes, I had my own phone line in my bedroom that I paid for, and I was damn proud of it. It was like a history lesson for my daughter. Once upon a time, there were no smartphones. If you wanted to speak to your friends, unless they were baller enough to have their own phone line, you had to call their house and make awkward conversation with their parents first.

At the bottom of one box was an assorted mix of worn school supplies and notebooks. I grabbed a purple three-subject notebook where I'd doodled the Stussy chain logo down the edge of the cover. Just as I was about to flip through the pages to show Jolene that my terrible handwriting had been in place for decades, an envelope fell out somewhere from the second subject section.

An envelope addressed to me.

"Oooh, is that how you passed notes back in the day? Very formal," Jolene had said. "And it's unopened."

I carefully ripped open the sealed envelope and unfolded the yellowed piece of notebook paper. I got a few sentences in before I realized I couldn't read this in front of my daughter.

"What is it?" Jolene was in front of me, still thinking it

was a fun note passed during class. "Someone asking to borrow your portable CD player?"

"Something like that," I said with a strained laugh. I slipped the note in my pocket, where it burned a very hot hole.

When we got home that night, as soon as Jolene went to bed, I retreated to my makeshift bedroom and read the letter in full.

Then I read it again.

Cary hadn't written me a letter defending Cal from my brotherly teasing. He'd had a crush on me all during high school, and he wanted to shoot his shot before he lost his courage. That part was sweet. But then the letter went into confessing all the *very* dirty things he wanted me to do to him should I feel the same way. It was actually impressive what he wrote considering this was back when porn could only be accessed via dial-up internet or deciphering scrambled channels on cable. He certainly had a vivid imagination.

How would teenage Derek have reacted back then? I didn't know. But fortysomething Derek found himself rock fucking hard. Fortysomething Derek had to rub one out before going to bed.

And now fortysomething Derek was face-to-face with Cary, whose face had gone stark white.

"You found it," Cary said softly.

"I think when you put it in my locker, it had fallen into one of my old notebooks." Or even worse, I'd seen the letter was from Cary and shoved it in my notebook because he barely registered for me in high school. Teenage Derek was a dipshit.

"Did you...read it?" His fingers clinging to the wall behind him, as if he were primed to make an escape.

I nodded yes.

"Oh my God." Cary's hands went to his mouth. He stumbled into the dining room, which was empty. He had to dodge hitting his head on the light fixture. "Oh my God."

"Cary."

"Oh my God." He walked to the corner of the room and faced the wall, regaining his composure in real time.

"It's okay."

"It's not okay! Oh my God."

I wasn't sure what to say. Fuck, why did I have to show him the letter? Why couldn't I have read it and forgotten about it and saved him this embarrassment?

Maybe because deep down, I wanted to talk about the letter. I hadn't been able to stop thinking about it, reading it in Cary's voice, my mind going to steamy places with him, a constant, painful erection in my pants.

Since he had been the one to originally bring it up in our first meeting, he'd been thinking of it, too. Hadn't he?

"Cary, can I be honest? I found the letter—"

"Inappropriate." He whipped around, the sense of panic and fear painted over with one of his wide, salesmen smiles. "It was extremely inappropriate. My teenage self was hormonal and out of control. I don't even have a good Caryism to explain this away."

"That's why you were so nervous when we first met. You wondered if I'd read it."

"If you had, you never would've wanted to work with me."

"That's not true. It was..." I wanted to say hot, but I felt that description wouldn't go over well. I wasn't the best with words and searched my mind for a good one. "It was funny."

I regretted the word choice as soon as it left my lips. A

quick look of soul-crushing horror flashed on Cary's face before the salesman came back.

"Teenage Cary was quite ridiculous."

"Funny wasn't the right word. I admire your courage."

"Courage? Yeah, I should've gotten the purple heart for this one. I don't know what I was thinking. I hadn't slept well that night, and my teenage self needed nine hours of solid sleep to function."

Cary put his hands on his hips and looked out the dining room windows. "I was very lonely in high school. All the straight kids around me were hooking up and having sex and talking about having sex. And I couldn't do any of that because I was in the closet. I was just as horny as they were. I wanted to do all those things, too. So these thoughts kept building and building in me. But I couldn't do a thing about it. And I would see you in the halls everyday, and it would only make them build up more. It was like water in a dam."

"And then one day, the dam broke," I said.

"But the dam couldn't break like it could for other kids. I assumed you were straight. Well, mostly straight. It was before bisexuality was accepted. The turn of the millennium was a very binary time."

"You suspected I might be gay. You said 'I have a feeling deep down that this letter will resonate with a side of you the rest of South Rock doesn't get to see.'"

"Oh God. You're quoting the letter."

"It was very well-written. You're a good writer," I said, as if that would help make things more comfortable.

"It doesn't matter." Cary shifted his body ever so slightly, as if he were going to face me but remained staring out the window. "Even if you were openly gay or bi, you wouldn't have wanted your brother's awkward, skinny friend."

"You don't know that."

"I know how the social hierarchy of high school works."

Perhaps he had a point, but I still chose to believe my teenage self would've been open to hooking up with him. Maybe we could've gone to the movies together. What could have been.

"If you believe all that, then why did you give me the letter?"

"I don't know. I guess I wanted to call your bluff."

"Do you..." I struggled to find the nerves to ask what I really wanted to know. "Do you still feel that way?"

He finally turned to me and looked me straight in the eye. "Derek, I promise you whatever crush I had is firmly in the past. It's gone the way of landlines. You don't need to worry about that."

Cary waltzed into the kitchen before I could respond, leaving me with a sinking sense of defeat. At least I had a moment alone to regain myself.

"Derek, you have to check out this kitchen! You are going to freak out over all this counter space!" Cary called from the other room.

I kinda missed landlines and the awkward conversations I had to have with my friends' parents before I could speak to them. Funny how that worked.

14

CARY

That was close.
What the fuck was I talking about? That was a disaster.

A barely mitigated disaster. But a barely mitigated disaster was still a disaster because you were flirting with disaster.

I pressed my hands on the cool, marble countertops as I sucked in a deep breath. Breathing was supposed to help calm us, right? I'd already dropped my professional demeanor today by spouting off enough "Oh my God" exclamations to join the clergy. I had to regain control and forget about the fact that Derek had read my written desire to be his human sex doll. It was difficult telling him that I had zero crush on him, but it had to be done for the sake of my reputation and this business relationship.

There was a part of me that thought he actually liked the letter, that he seemed a little...turned on? Wouldn't a normal person have run away screaming if they'd discovered such a letter? When I glanced down at his crotch (another habit I needed to break), the pants area looked a smidge tight.

But I couldn't take the chance to find out. What if I admitted that I was attracted to him, and he didn't feel the same? Just because the guy was bisexual, a little flirty in text messages, and not horrified at getting propositioned via twenty-year-old letter, didn't mean I had a greenlight. Life had worked out for me in many areas. Not in the romantic realm, though. My batting average was low, so low I was reduced to using sports metaphors apparently.

"You're right. There's tons of counter space." Derek sidled up next to me and smoothed his large hands across the marble. I was jealous of said marble, but I kept it in my pants.

There was a reason why I was in the running to be the top real estate agent in the region. I was damn good at my job, and I didn't let myself get distracted by crushes or cute clients or awkward situations.

"I know you'd said you wanted to do more cooking with Jolene. This is a perfect kitchen for that." I knocked on the marble twice.

"Nice and hard," he said.

"Sturdy," I corrected.

I stepped away from Derek before his manly scent could fully intoxicate me.

"Plus you've got brand new, stainless steel appliances." I smoothed my hand over the microwave, then the stove, like I was a model showing off a prize on *The Price is Right*.

"So we're not going to talk about it anymore?" Derek asked.

"There's nothing to talk about, so no. We're here to find you a house, not to rehash old high school drama. Now will you look at all these cabinets? You have tons of space! You can stock the kitchen of your dreams. Ina Garten could never."

I spun on my foot and led us into the living room. The less direct eye contact I made with Derek, the better.

"We have a vaulted ceiling with a skylight. You rarely see this in these kinds of houses. It really opens up the room, makes it feel bigger don't you think?"

"Is it an organic skylight, though?"

I made the mistake of glancing at Derek as he said it, catching the sly smile forming at the corner of his mouth. Derek was a really cute smiler.

Commission, not coming.

"The flooring is hardwood laminate, which is a great alternative to hardwood floors. You get the look without all the upkeep necessary. You could spill anything on these floors, and it'll come right up."

You could even have dirty sex on them without leaving a mark.

"And the windows..." I pointed to the row of windows looking out onto the street. They were windows. Unspectacular, doing-their-job windows.

"Lots of natural light?" Derek asked.

"Exactly. The front yard has lots of big, mature trees."

So if you did fuck someone on the hardwood laminate floors with the windows wide open, the mature trees would provide some privacy.

"There's a fireplace, too," Derek noted.

"It's gas. Much easier to maintain than wood."

"I prefer wood," he said.

Well, buddy, at this very moment, I unfortunately have lots of it. Why the fuck was I gettting turned on by Derek after telling myself to cool it? This was bodily rebellion. I had to stay in charge and calm.

"You don't have to spend time buying firewood or chopping wood." The image of Derek chopping wood shirtless popped into my mind, and then I ushered it out so fast I gave myself whiplash.

"I love a warm fire on a cold night."

Sex in front of a fireplace...was something I would not be thinking about. Why the fuck did Derek have to look so sexy at a house showing? With his damn black T-shirt and big arms and thick legs. Why did I have to be attracted to men at all? Homosexuality was being very annoying at the moment.

"Excuse me a minute." I darted into the bathroom and splashed cold water on my face. I wasn't a fan of the mauve paint color the builder had chosen, but that could be an easy fix.

The more difficult fix was getting Derek off my mind. It seemed that him knowing about the letter was supercharging my circuits. Sex was in the air thanks to that handwritten missive.

"Pull it together," I whispered to my reflection. "He is a *client*. You are a *professional*."

I splashed more cold water on my face, then realized there was no hand towel. That left me no choice but to squat over the heating vent to air dry.

Nearly twenty years in the real estate game with my own business, and here I was reduced to waving hot air onto my face like a maniac.

I left the bathroom once I looked presentable again.

"Derek?" I didn't see him in the living room.

"Down here," his voice echoed from the hallway.

"Derek?" We were playing Marco Polo, it seemed.

He sprung out from one of the bedrooms just as I reached the door. Our bodies bumped into each other, a quick mash of heat against me, throwing my bathroom pep talk right out the window.

"Sorry," he muttered.

"It's okay." I inhaled his scent, that hint of oil that lingered was manly and dangerous. Working on an oil rig was dangerous work, right? One had to use their hands.

I would gladly welcome climate change if it meant I could feel Derek's calloused hands on my body.

"The hallway's a little narrow," he said.

"It's standard size." It wasn't meant for two bodies at the same time, especially when one is a solid block of man. "But I can…call my structural engineer if you wanted to see about widening it."

I know another narrow hallway you could stretch out.

"It's fine." Derek continued into the main bedroom at the end of the hall.

I checked out his ass, only because I had to see if the hallway really was that narrow.

"Professional," I whispered to myself.

Yet my professionalism faced a major test because for some fucking reason, there was a king-sized bed, complete with bedding and pillows, in the center of the main bedroom. This was the *only* piece of furniture in the house.

"I thought you said it was empty," Derek said.

"This is weird," I said with a nervous laugh. "Why would the builder put in a bed and no other furniture in the house?" They were probably in the process of getting the house staged. I was able to get Derek a sneak peek before the open house. Or the builder was an all-knowing puppet master with an impish sense of humor.

Derek pressed his hand down on the bed's plush comforter.

"Don't touch it!" I said before he could make the mattress squeak. "It's just a bed. You don't need to test it. But see how much room you have here? You can get a king-sized bed in here, no problem."

A bed big enough for two people.

"It looks comfortable," he said.

"Well, it's supposed to. Check out the closet." Fortunately, the closet was small with a sliding door. Not a walk in. I didn't know why that comforted me.

"Nice," Derek growled as he slipped past me, another dash of his body heat sizzling up my spine.

The man is just looking for a house. Stop mentally dry humping him!

He went into the en suite bathroom.

"Marble countertops in the bathroom, too. That's a great find. You don't generally get these types of touches in new builds. It's usually quartz." I hung in the bedroom, turning my back to the bed.

After some painfully long moments where Derek didn't say anything, I peeked my head into the bathroom to see what was going on.

"Ah yes. The linen closet's in the bathroom. Easy storage for towels and sheets," I said.

"I know what a linen closet is." Derek closed the closet door, revealing the large walk-in shower behind us. Big enough for...

"That's a nice shower." I grazed my fingers along the glass wall. "It will get you clean. And it looks like there's a built-in shelf, too! You don't see that everyday!"

I leaned into the shower to get a better view of the shelf. "This really is a great perk. I have one of those plastic shelves that hang on the showerhead, and it sways like crazy whenever I take the shampoo bottle off it."

I tried to step out, but I found myself immobile. A weight pressed on my back. Before I could assess that it was Derek's hands, I was being pushed into the shower, against the cool marble wall. And before I could assess why Derek was pushing me into the shower, he spun me around and mashed his hungry lips against mine.

His beard scratched at my face, rough and prickly. I shoved my tongue between his lips, letting myself fully into his mouth. Our tongues swirled around each other as his salty breath made me fucking purr. Our kisses were breathy, desperate, hungry.

"You're right. This is a nice shower," he said, his oceanic eyes twinkling with desire, face flush with color.

"This is very unprofessional."

"I know." Derek went back to kissing me, and I lost all sense of control and decorum.

I moaned into his lips, grinded my hips against his, wanting him more and more with each second we were connected.

I wrapped my arms around his neck, his buzzed hairs prickling my fingers . The muscles in his broad shoulders tightened and flexed as he pulled me closer.

Kissing Derek was better than my wildest, most vivid, horniest dreams. No dreams could compare to experiencing someone's actual taste, smell, and touch.

"Damn," Derek said as I wrapped my legs around his waist.

I was ravenous. This was decades of pent-up sexual longing exploding out in a model home shower. It was as if I had been fasting for years, then stumbled into a Sizzler.

"Take your jacket off," I commanded.

Without having to put me down, because he is so fucking strong, Derek whipped off his coat, and then he took off his shirt, too.

Dreams coming true. Dreams on dreams on dreams.

His hairy pecs bounced under my touch as my fingers grazed over the hardened ridges of his chest. His back had traces of hair, like light angel wings, which I found incredibly hot. Our society today chastised men for having body hair. Why couldn't we let men be men? There was something primal about Derek's body, untouched by modern beauty standards.

"I put on some weight since my high school days." Derek slapped his stomach, which only made my dick grow harder in my pants.

"You are so fucking hot I can't stand it. If you do one of those naked fireman calendar shoots, I'm buying the first copy."

He grabbed a fistful of my hair and pushed my lips onto his again. I could kiss him forever. Yep, I'd quit my practice and live in this shower full time. I would be totally fine dying of starvation and unrelenting orgasms.

"This is very unprofessional," Derek teased, biting my lower lip.

"So is this." I climbed down from him and got on my knees. Faster than a pit stop tire change, I was undoing his jeans, pulling down his boxers, and shoving his cock in my mouth.

We switched positions so Derek could lean against the shower wall.

"Fuck. Cary." His moans echoed. Just like with singing in the shower, moaning in the shower had a beautiful sound.

I groaned back with my mouth full of him. He was thicker than I imagined, and I took him all the way down. I should've started slow and then sped up, but I was already at a nine on my lust scale. This train had left the station a while back.

I deep-throated him until my nose nuzzled against his

hair. I didn't want this to end, but I also couldn't slow down and savor the moment.

"Keep going. Please don't stop. Fuck." Derek didn't have any witty comments. His groans filled the bathroom. Something about him saying please was very endearing.

I licked up his shaft, slid my tongue over his pulsing head, then dragged it down to his heavy balls. The scent of his musk filled my nose.

I could feel him shift under me, the orgasm building inside him, his balls drawing up. I ran my hand over his furry belly. I would never be able to get enough of him.

"I'm coming." A deep grunt ripped out of him. He tried to pull me away and use his T-shirt for cover, but I wanted it, and I wasn't leaving here without it. I wanted to know what he tasted like.

I sucked him hard, going faster up and down on his thick cock until he unleashed a ferocious grunt and spilled down my throat. I swallowed all of him and fell back onto the shower floor.

Heavy breathing filled the space. We had managed to steam up the glass wall, but aside from that, we'd made no impact on the shower. We'd kept things clean.

Derek gazed down at me, his broad, hairy chest shining in the light, his half-hard cock still hanging out. If he didn't cover up soon, I'd jump him for round two.

"Well, the shower is definitely big enough for two people," he said.

This was so unprofessional. And so worth it.

15

DEREK

"Someone looks awfully happy to be here." Xavier, my fire captain, gave me a quizzical look as we pulled our fire truck into the elementary school parking lot.

"It's my first school visit," I said.

"Get ready for lots and lots of questions and at least one kid who will have a meltdown."

I gave him a thumbs up. I was a fireman. I was used to being prepared for unforeseen circumstances. Like, for instance, getting a blow job while house hunting.

"There you go again. Smiling like a schmuck." Xavier had combed over silver hair and a big mustache that commanded attention.

"Why do you care if I'm smiling?" I shoved him in the friendliest of ways.

He wasn't the first person to comment on my facial expressions over the past two days. It was hard not to smile when I kept flashing back to that shower with Cary. I couldn't stop thinking about what I'd read about in the letter and how turned on it got me. After our shower rendezvous, I went home and reread his letter, this time with a clearer picture, and jerked off into a sock. Luckily, Russ was always doing laundry.

Cary's nervousness while showing me the house was its own form of foreplay. There was this unspeakable sexual tension between us, and I fucking had to do something about it or else I'd never find a house.

Sure, things might be weird between us in the short term, but we were adults. We had to get it out of our systems so we could continue to work together. That was that. The tightening in my pants at the mere thought of Cary would eventually subside.

"We're here," Xavier said.

We all filed out of the truck. Kids watched us from the school windows as if we were superheroes. I stood up straighter and puffed out my chest a little bit more to live up to their expectations.

"I have two ground rules." Xavier rounded us up in a circle and held up one finger. "One, no cursing in front of the kids. That goes for your shits and your fucks, but I also mean hell and damn and ass. Anything you wouldn't get caught saying in church. One time, a guy accidentally uttered *motherfucker* when he was trying to turn on the hose, and it spread through the school like smallpox. I had an interesting conversation with the principal."

We all chuckled at his story. Kids didn't pay attention to ninety-nine percent of things you said, but they had the uncanny ability to hear every curse word. Most of Jolene's blue vocabulary probably came from me.

Xavier held up his second finger. "Two, no flirting with the PTA moms."

"C'mon!" groaned Kelly, the guy next to me.

"I mean it. The last thing we need is one of you getting distracted."

"Is that something that actually happens?" I asked.

"You better believe it, Hogan." Xavier pointed at me. "And you in particular better be careful. A widowed fireman is like spilling droplets of blood in a shark-infested tank. Keep it in the pants. This is a school presentation, not last call."

Obviously, Xavier had these rules in place because of past experiences. Still, I gulped down an awkward lump in my throat. Should I tell him that PTA dads might be more of my flavor at the moment?

We went over the plan for today. Some of the guys on the squad had done a million of these and weren't paying close attention. As a volunteer, I'd only done a handful, so I needed the refresher. We would give kids tours of the fire truck and go over our presentation on fire safety. Depending on time, we would demonstrate how to use a fire extinguisher and even show off spraying the fire hose. These were things we did everyday, but it was fun watching how excited the children got. It reminded me that being a fireman was a cool job.

Classes filed out of the school into the parking lot. Kids' eyes went wide at the truck. We stood in a line behind Xavier who gave a fun introduction. He took on a little bit of a drill sergeant tone, calling the kids recruits that were being entrusted with very important duties. For as much of a hard ass as he could be on the job, the guy was having a ball here.

I also got what Xavier was saying about staying away from PTA moms. They stood in the back, and two were flat-out eyefucking me. Fortunately, as the token PTA dads, Russ and Cal were there, too. Josh and Quentin were mixed into their class. I gave them stealth winks.

We broke out into groups and had classes rotate among different stations. Some of the firemen gave truck tours, some gave fire safety demonstrations, and I was in the group that got to give first aid lessons and use the fire hose.

Our group was the favorite of the kids, naturally.

Xavier and I showed how to properly treat a burn. We demonstrated wrapping bandages and cleaning out wounds.

Quentin's hand shot up. "We already learned this in the Falcons. When can we play with the fire hose?"

Russ tapped his son on the shoulder as a warning. "Quentin, you can never have too much first aid training."

Cal rolled his eyes. "Speak for yourself. We wanna see the fire hose!"

I piped up in my deepest voice aimed squarely at my brother. "Sir, if we have to, we will remove you from fire safety training."

Cal sighed and crossed his arms. I wasn't too old to give him a noogie if I had to.

Eventually, after our demonstration, there was time left and Xavier hooked up the fire hose. We couldn't tease such a thing and then not do it. The kids screamed with excitement. It would probably be the only thing kids remembered from today, but so be it. Precious memories and all that.

Russ sidled up to me while all the students got in line. "Do you see the woman by the fire truck in the white jacket and purple NYU winter hat?"

I turned and carefully followed his eyeline to the woman in question who smiled at me while helping one of the students climb into the truck. She was cute with blond hair that peeked from under her hat.

"She's on the PTA with me. Alicia. She's widowed. She's the absolute sweetest."

There was a natural sweetness in her eyes, like she could've been a kindergarten teacher.

"She's an editor. Smart, but really down to earth."

I knew where this was going, and it made my stomach twist into a knot.

"I think you two would hit it off."

"Because we both have dead spouses?" I shot back.

"No. You're both good people."

I thought I'd have to look out for Cal trying to set me up with someone, but then here came Russ. Alicia seemed like a wonderful woman, and I should start getting back out there. It all made sense on paper.

"I'll think about it," I said.

"That sounds like a no."

"I said I'll think about it." My voice sounded clipped, the knot twisting harder.

"There's a lot going on for you, but I thought it would be a nice thing."

I paused for a beat and remembered that Russ was trying to help, that he somewhat understood what I had been through. He was far less pushy than Cal would've been.

"I know there's a rule about you guys not being allowed to fraternize with PTA moms, which is incredibly sexist. But your fire chief is too scary for me to challenge him on that." Russ pulled a business card from his pocket. "Here's her card. It has her cell phone on it."

"Thanks." I shoved it in my pocket without giving it another look. Why was I so bent out of shape about a fix up? I'd wanted my family to stop treating me like some precious, sad widower.

"Could the force of the water take out a car window?" I heard Cal asking Xavier.

"Oh can we break some car windows?" One of the students asked, an idea which spread like wildfire through the group.

———

THAT AFTERNOON, as I was eating lunch at the firehouse and watching an old *30 for 30* doc on ESPN, Cary texted with bad news.

Cary: The house sold this morning.

Derek: The one we looked at? The one where we...

Cary: Admired the hardwood laminate? Yes. That one.

Derek: We didn't even get a chance to put in an offer.

Cary: That's why you can't wait. If there's a house you like, you have to jump.

Cary: But don't worry. There are plenty of fish in the sea.

I wasn't worried. In fact, I wasn't upset that I lost out on that house, despite liking it. More house hunting meant more time I got to spend with Cary.

Cary: There's another house in that development going on sale. When are you free to take a look?

My dick immediately perked up at the chance to hang with Cary again. I still had residual horniness from our first encounter. I wanted more.

But I also needed a damn place to live. Russ wanted to give me a tutorial on loading the dishwasher tonight.

Derek: I'm free tomorrow afternoon.

Cary: Perfect! Don't give up hope.

Derek: I won't.

As long as we got to spend more time together, I would never feel hopeless.

The rest of my shift flew by. We provided assistance at two traffic accidents which thankfully had no fatalities, just shaken up motorists. I did a workout at our gym. I flashed back to the way Cary stared at my body in the shower like I was the hottest thing on the planet. Nevermind that I had a gut, thinning hair, and an overgrown beard. It made me stand a little taller. I'd worried that I had let myself go and that aging wasn't being kind to me, but Cary helped keep those fears at bay.

It was early the next morning when I left the firehouse. The sun was beginning to rise, painting the sky a pale blue. Two guys with familiar, flat-looking faces were waiting outside holding a warm cup of coffee for me. Their noses seemed distractingly small, as if they were descendants of Voldemort.

"Derek. How's it going, man?" said the one who opted for a neatly-trimmed goatee.

"Here. Have a good morning pick-me-up." The clean-shaven one handed me the Starbucks coffee cup, which I didn't take. Never take candy from strangers.

"Do I know you?"

"Tad Morris," said the goatee.

"Chad Morris," said the baby cheeks.

They each held out their hands. Behind them, I spotted their faces on a bench ad.

"From Prescott Realty?" I asked, giving them each a firm handshake.

"Exactly," Tad said.

"You work with Cary."

They exchanged a knowing look that sent a weird chill up my back.

"We do. We're very fond of Cary. We just had a question," said Chad. "How is your home search going?"

"You came to my work at seven in the morning to ask me how my house search is going?"

"What can I say? We're always there for our clients," said Chad.

"But I'm not your client." This whole conversation was odd from the jump, and I wanted to get to the point as fast as possible. "What's going on here?"

Chad put my coffee back in his holder. He had the debonair confidence of a man that was used to getting what he wanted. "We saw you tried to make an offer on a house in Eden Falls. Unfortunately, our client swooped in."

"They were determined," said Tad with a laugh that I could've sworn sounded rehearsed.

"We know a few people who are getting ready to list their properties. We could get you a sneak peek, let you get in before the rush and have your pick of houses. You're a busy man. Putting out fires and such." Chad signaled at the firehouse behind us. "Thank you for all you do to keep Sourwood safe."

"The last thing you want to do is spend your holiday season going from one house to another," said Tad. "You want that time to spend with family and Jolene."

Hearing my daughter's name out of his mouth ignited a protective urge that made me want to clock these assholes. I didn't like the feeling of being researched. When Cary had talked about Jolene in our first meeting, it came from a genuine place of interest. These guys sounded hollow.

"Are you trying to poach me from Cary?"

"Poach? Who said poach?" said Tad. He and his brother laughed at the same time, as if the cord in their back had been pulled. "We're one big family. We want to make sure all PRG clients are being taken care of. We know that time is of the essence, and Cary's been very busy as of late. We want to make sure you're getting the full attention you need."

Well a few days ago he had my whole dick in his mouth,

so I'd say the answer was yes. Blow job aside, Cary had been nothing but diligent as an agent. I didn't have time for these clowns.

"I'm good." I brushed past them.

"I know this is awkward, meeting up like this." Tad puffed out his chest. "But do you want that to jeopardize finding the right house for your family? It's the most important purchase you'll make, Derek."

Chad handed over the cup of coffee. I took it from him, opened the lid and smelled the roasted beans...before proceeding to pour it out on the sidewalk. A brown puddle formed around their loafers.

"Who the fuck drinks Starbucks? Might as well drink your own piss." I shoved the empty cup into Chad's stunned hands and walked off.

"Those Dumb and Dipshit motherfuckers."

Later that afternoon, after catching up on sleep, I recounted my conversation with the Morris brothers to Cary. We were visiting another house in Eden Falls. It was empty and had a similar ranch-style layout to the first house.

"Those Tweedle Dee and Tweedle Dickheads." Cary paced in the empty living room.

"I'm not going with them."

"Thank you. I mean, it's ultimately your choice, and you need to do what is best for you."

"You can't get rid of me that quickly, Perkowski." I rubbed his shoulders to reaffirm my position and help calm him down.

"Those Mary-Kate and Ashley assholes. If they've approached you, how many of my other clients have they reached out to?" Cary continued to pace. "They know Hannah and I are close to beating them for the year. All their stupid bench ads aren't doing shit to gin up enough new business for them. I'm sorry you had to be subject to such underhandedness. Hell, I'm sorry you had to suffer through a conversation with them."

"They tried to seduce me with Starbucks."

"Of course. Their taste buds are as dead as their souls." Cary strummed his fingers on the fireplace mantel, his mind working through this at warp speed. His body was tight and tense, his tangerine shirt fitted enough to reveal his lean torso. If he was trying to turn me on, he was succeeding.

Cary turned back to me. "I'm not going to let it bother me. I'm the better agent. And more importantly, we are going to find you an amazing house."

"Do you know how sexy you look when you're angry?"

"About that." Cary pressed his finger on the mantel, doggedly making a point. "That can't happen again."

Just the reference to *that* got my dick swelling. "What can't happen again?"

"You *know* what."

"We can't look at houses anymore?" I took a dastardly step closer to him. The way he tried to fight his obvious excitement only revved my engine more. "Or we can't be in a shower together again?"

"That one."

"But what if I need your expertise to determine if it's a good enough shower?" I took another step forward, closing the gap between us, the vibration of energy intensifying.

"Fine. I'll spell it out for you. We can't hook up or have

sex of any kind in a home." His lower lip quivered with uncertainty. And heat. "It's a violation of the real estate agent's hippocratic oath."

"You took a hippocratic oath?" I shot him my best smolder, remembering how I used this look to lure the ladies in high school.

"In my heart I did."

"Cary." I got right up to his face, our lips an inch apart.

"Shit," he whispered before flinging himself on me and mashing our mouths together. I pulled him to my chest, and he wrapped his legs around my waist. Our kisses and bodies were fucking hungry for each other.

"Go this way." He pointed behind me. I scooched us backward, and he reached past my neck and drew the blinds. "This house has brand-new blinds, which are usually a huge cost for homeowners but are included–"

"Cary. Stop talking."

My moves were fast and full of craving. I pushed him against the wall and untangled his legs from my waist. I undid his pants, while he did the same to me. I grabbed both of our cocks and stroked us as we moaned into each other's mouths. Cary tried to help out, but I wanted to do it all on my own. I wanted to feel our flesh rub against each other.

"Oh my God," Cary said over and over again, mumbling in tongues. "I want you so fucking bad."

Watching him writhe and pant from my touch made me stroke us harder and faster.

Cary's moans got more desperate sounding, his voice cracking.

"Gonna come," he said with his last bits of sanity.

In a dash of quick thinking, I pulled my knit cap from

my coat pocket and covered our cocks like they were a live grenade. We spilled our seed at damn near the same time, the milky liquid seeping through the stitches.

When I let go of Cary, he slid down the wall.

"Nope. We definitely shouldn't do that again," I said.

16

CARY

We definitely didn't do that again. Nope, not at all. We definitely did not hook up in two more empty model homes that week. Derek absolutely did not go down on me in a butler's pantry, and I absolutely did not go down on him in a mud room. There was no conceivable way that Derek and I made out like teenagers before and after sucking each other off.

Nope. None of that happened.

And it was all spectacular.

I'd forgotten how great hooking up could be, how my lips could be sore from kissing. I nearly felt the urge to start a LiveJournal to pour out my thoughts. Was LiveJournal still a thing or was that something else the techbro overlords had taken from us?

In all fairness, I was still doing my job and showing Derek houses. We simply hadn't found any he'd liked. And once we crossed a house off our list, it became fair game for fooling around in. We never hooked up in someone's actual home, only completely empty, uninhabited houses.

I tried giving myself pep talks before meeting up with

Derek, reminding myself that I was a professional tasked with helping Derek find a home. But then I'd see him, and he'd smile at me in that way I'd fantasized about every day in high school, and all good sense went out the window. I was a strong, independent man, but there was no better feeling than when a cute guy *looked* at you.

The attraction between us was combustible, and I was addicted. This was over twenty years of pent up wanting and pining set against the backdrop of new construction homes.

There was a brand-new home available in another development, Wooden Crest (seriously, where did they come up with these development names?), that I convinced Derek to take a look at. He hadn't seemed interested from the listing pictures, but I had an idea to get him more on board.

I got to the house fifteen minutes before I told him to arrive. I made sure everything was in order. The lights worked. It was clean. There were no unexpected dealbreakers not seen in the pictures. It was a very nice house with an updated kitchen, brand-new HVAC system, and a giant, clawfoot tub in the bathroom off the main bedroom.

To get Derek more on board, I did what any dedicated agent would do: I stripped naked and got in the bathtub, which also doubled as a Jacuzzi. I didn't turn it on, though. That would've been weird.

Was this insane? Possibly. Would this seal the deal for Derek to buy this house? Possibly. Was the idea of Derek climbing into the tub and having his way with his buck naked real estate agent overriding any sensible thoughts in my mind? Definitely.

I checked myself out in the mirror. I looked good. I was having a good hair day, upstairs and downstairs. Derek would be arriving any minute. To the random outsider, this probably looked strange. But if they knew how it felt to have his hands on my body, they would have no choice but to understand. And if this could help Derek paint the picture for this house, then all the better.

Right on cue, I heard the front door open. My dick hardened at the prospect of Derek walking through that bathroom door, ripping off his T-shirt, and rubbing his hairy chest against me like a loofah. How he would ravage me.

Except, unless the echo was unusually strong, I heard multiple footsteps walk through the front door.

"Check out this coat closet. It's humongous," said a female voice that definitely, absolutely, in no conceivable way was Derek's.

"Shit," I whispered.

Maybe I was imagining things.

"I love the crown molding," said another female voice.

This wasn't happening.

"Mommy! Daddy! This place is huge!!" screamed a little girl.

"Shit," I whispered again. I pulled my knees up to my chest, hiding my most vulnerable bits. I caught a glimpse of my naked self in the mirror and realized just how unhinged I looked. The haze of lust quickly faded, replaced with cold, hard reality.

"Be careful," said a man who I presumed to be the aforementioned daddy. Not the daddy I was expecting. "Don't touch the walls, baby."

"Pastor, this house is less than a mile from your church, too," the female agent said.

I clenched my eyes shut. As if there weren't enough reasons why uber-religious people hated gays. My unclothed ass was going to set the queer movement back thirty years.

"I wanna see my bedroom!" screamed the little girl.

Fuck. I had to get the hell out of here.

I stood up slowly in the tub. I glanced at myself in the mirror. Hmm, I really had been making progress with my squats. My quads looked great. There was nice muscle definition coming in.

For fuck's sake, Cary, now is not the time.

I stepped out of the tub, placing one foot then the other delicately onto the tiled floor. My pile of clothes were stashed under the sink.

Out in the hall, I heard the adults milling about in the dining room with the little girl skipping around in her future bedroom. I opened the cabinet under the sink. My shoes clomped onto the floor, unleashing a slight echo. Fortunately, it seemed the sound was covered up by the hubbub elsewhere in the house.

For the sake of time, I'd have to freeball. No seconds could be wasted on underwear.

I unfolded my pants. My belt buckle clanged against the counter, the metal making an unmistakably loud sound.

"Shit."

"Hello?" yelled the little girl.

"Lizzie, where are you going?" asked the mom as I tried to step into my pants. My legs were shaking with nerves, and I kept missing.

"I heard something! Come with me!" the little girl insisted.

I tried to unfold my shirt and put it on while dealing with my pants. My car keys slid out of the pants pocket and clanged against the floor. Gravity was not on my side, which hurt because I thought Isaac Newton was a homosexual.

"Mommy, come look with me!"

"Did you hear something?" the pastor asked.

"We can go check out the bedrooms," said the real estate agent. Why did she have to kowtow to her clients' requests? Why couldn't she push back?

My limbs were shaking. My heart rattled in my ears. I did not have the coordination to get dressed. I could hide in a closet, but this place had a walk-in that the clients would surely want to check out.

The footsteps got louder. Closer.

Fight or flight took over. I spotted the window over the bathtub.

I balled my clothes up.

"You have three bedrooms. These two will share a bathroom. And then down here we have the main bedroom."

Show them the hall closet! Show them the fuse box! Do your job!

I pushed up the window. Frigid air blasted my skin. I threw my ball of clothes into the open air. A full breath entered my lungs.

"This is going to be your bedroom, Mommy and Daddy!" the little girl screamed, her voice loud and piercing.

In one swift move that should've qualified me for the Olympics, I launched myself out of the window. For a brief second, I was airborne, weightless. And then I landed in a bush.

The prickly leaves broke my fall. I tumbled onto the grass.

I was alive. Naked, but alive.

When I looked up, a familiar truck was parked on the curb. Derek stared at me from the driver's seat understandably confused.

Adrenaline pumped through my veins as I gathered up my clothes.

"Is it cold in here?" I heard the agent say from inside the house.

I crouched down and ran to Derek's truck with my ball of clothes over my crotch. The passenger door was unlocked. I hopped in and slouched down just as the family and agent looked out the window.

Derek gave them a confused wave.

"Drive," I said in a desperate whisper.

My chest unclenched when the car began moving, an extra weight lifting off me when we turned off the street.

I laughed with full relief once we were out of the development, the kind of laugh that tumbled out of people when they escaped death. It took me a few moments to remember that I was still naked.

"Do I want to know?" Derek asked.

"I was trying to paint the picture?"

He pulled onto a wooded dead-end street that had a sign for the beginning of a rigorous hiking trail. Fortunately, all potential hikers were at work today.

"It was a nice house. We should get you in to see it later because I have a feeling that family is going to make an offer." Unless of course their daughter believed it was haunted by a ghost.

"You're actually trying to sell me on a house when you're stark naked? Weirdo."

"When I'm dressed, I'll explain."

I yanked my underwear from my pants pocket. Derek clamped my wrist with his strong hand.

He stared at me with fire and mischief in his eyes. "Now who says you need to get dressed?" he asked as he slid my ball of clothes off my lap.

17

DEREK

I'd had dreams before of hot, naked men coming up to me. Usually, it happened in someplace exotic, like a tropical beach or in some enchanted forest. Not in a suburban housing development.

But hey, I wasn't complaining.

Cary and I had hooked up in heated, quick moments where there was no time to undress lest we get caught. And sure, someone could drive down this empty dead end, but that was a risk I was willing to take.

I finally had an opportunity to see him in his birthday suit, and well...happy birthday to me. The guy was hot. He was trim with a light dusting of chest hair across his pecs, a nice change from the sweater that was on my chest. His arms had a little definition, but he wasn't one of those guys who did shit like watching their macros and lived at the gym. He looked like a natural man, one with perfect imperfections.

"You're staring," he said, crossing his legs in modesty.

"Is that a problem?"

"Is this a good stare or a bad one?"

I grabbed his leg and moved it out of the crossing position. I skimmed through his bush, up his stomach and chest. My dreams never got into this level of detail: the feel of another man's warm skin on my fingertips, his natural, earthy scent coming through the layer of deodorant and cologne. My hand traveled up his neck, feeling the heat pulse off him as I tipped his chin to me and connected our lips in a passionate kiss.

I wanted to devour Cary, but I could stay here for a while, too. He was a good kisser, his tongue playing with mine, moaning into my lips. I leaned over the center console and let both of my hands traverse his body. I tugged at the slight bit of love handle at his waist and gave it a ravenous squeeze. I brushed over his armpit hair as I pulled him closer, intoxicated by the sensation. His nipples were hard jabs under the pads of my fingers. Even with a polished guy like Cary, there was a ruggedness to his body.

"Derek," he gasped out.

"Is this okay?" I realized I was kind of taking advantage of him since he desperately ran into my car naked.

"Uh huh. That Derek meant 'keep going.'"

"Don't mind if I do."

I bent over the center console and took his hard cock into my mouth, my beard brushing against his soft thighs.

I savored every inch of Cary, of which there was plenty. My tongue swirled around his head and slid down his shaft, the salty taste of him cresting in my mouth. My hairy forearms were a stark contrast against his smooth legs.

I tipped the seat back, getting better access. Cary bucked his hips up to meet my mouth. Something new hit my tongue with a rough texture, an odd sensation. I started chuckling, the kind of laughter kids would try and hold in during class.

"Are you laughing mid-blow job?" Cary asked.

"Sorry."

"What's so funny?"

I pulled a piece of bush (actual plant bush, not personal bush) from his inner thigh.

"Oh dear lord," Cary said.

"It's a good thing they didn't plant cacti out there," I said. "I keep thinking of watching you tumble out of that window buck-ass naked. I hope I never forget that image."

"Please do. Go on and forget all about it."

I began to chuckle again, and this time, Cary joined in.

"Your beard is ticklish."

"Is it?" I rubbed it against his thigh and drifted down to his taint, making him scream out a high-pitched, clown laugh. "What the hell was that?"

"You hit a sensitive area."

"Do you use that laugh to scare small children at birthday parties?" Listening to that wild cackle escape his clean-cut lips was too irresistible to only do once. I rubbed my beard down there again.

Another clown laugh filled the car. Cary threw a hand over his face.

"That's so embarrassing. I can't even be cool when I'm getting a blow job."

"You are very cool, Cary Perkowski."

"I'm not, but I appreciate the sentiment."

"I love that crazy laugh," I said, my eyes beaming straight into his. And I meant it. I loved all of his noises and awkward pauses. Cary was a book I couldn't put down.

"You're just saying that."

"I'm not. But I promise I won't do it again on purpose since it makes you uncomfortable."

I lowered myself back down to his crotch, but he pushed me back up.

"I have another idea," Cary said, in a rapid, cat-like movement, he climbed over the console and straddled me. His hot body pressed on mine? I wasn't complaining. I pushed my seat back to give us more room.

We made out like horny teenagers, heat and breath pounding between us. He rubbed his hands through my beard then slipped down my back. They pressed just under my arms.

"Wait, are you trying to tickle me?"

"Maybe," he said.

It didn't work, but it still made me laugh. We kissed and laughed at the same time, the heat and smiles overlapping with each other. I didn't know that was possible but it turned this into something special. There were no boundaries with Cary, no barriers to hold back my awkward self. Yes, bears could be awkward.

I snorted a laugh when he found my tickle spot on my side.

"Okay, now we're even," I said.

"You're still clothed, so this is not an even playing field." Cary pulled off my Smashing Pumpkins T-shirt and rubbed our chests together, flooding my system with more lust.

"Do you only own band T-shirts?" he asked, flinging it into the backseat.

"Do you only own brightly colored dress shirts?"

"Touché."

All of this rubbing and laughing and kissing and searching for my tickle zone had made me so hard I could barely focus. My body went into autopilot dry-humping.

"Cary, I have to tell you something."

"If that sentence ends with the phrase 'I have a boyfriend,' I will be very perturbed."

"It doesn't. I, uh, went to the store this morning." In a surprising show of flexibility, I reached one arm into the backseat and pulled out a plastic shopping bag. Cary reached inside.

"You bought condoms and lube?" He pulled out the contents, amazed at what he was holding.

"It seemed like something I should have, considering... all the houses we were seeing." We were on a natural progression to move beyond oral sex, and I wanted to be prepared. Although, nothing could've prepared me for a naked Cary running at me full speed.

"Did you want to?" I asked. "I don't want to push anything or pressure you."

"As the real estate bros in my office say, let's fucking go." Cary leaned down and kissed me softly, an unexpected move considering the heat building between us. "I want you inside me."

I groaned in response. I needed Cary in that moment like I was a swimmer coming up for air. In an even more surprising amount of flexibility, Cary rolled the condom on my dick with his hands behind his back. He was shockingly good at it, but I wasn't going to explore that thought. I slicked up my aching cock and plunged my lubed fingers inside his hole.

"Fuck," Cary said.

Same. Damn, he felt amazing. Hot and tight.

"You ready?" I asked.

He nodded, unable to speak. Something shifted in his eyes. Gone was his sarcastic shield, revealing a tender man.

We locked eyes as he sunk down on my cock.

"Yes," he whispered out.

"Your letter is coming true," I said.

"It's so much better." Cary wrapped his arms around my neck and moved up and down slowly, as much as the car dimensions would allow. It was glorious torture. I wanted to fuck the hell out of him, but taking it slow let me savor filling him up, let me watch his face change from pain to pleasure as I entered him.

"Derek," he whispered into my neck.

"Is that a *keep going* kind of Derek?"

I felt him nod against me, his body tight and coiled, his cock rubbing against my belly. He dug his fingernails into my back.

"Don't stop. Please don't stop."

I arched my hips up to get deeper inside him. I pulled him close, our foreheads together, breaths coming out in strained gasps.

"Not bad for a couple of fortysomethings?" I flashed a grin.

Cary couldn't reply with a witty retort. He was flush, hot, too in the zone. Watching him lose the control he desperately clung to pushed me to the edge.

Our lips met. He huffed out short breaths as his body shook.

"Derek, don't stop. Yes. Yes." He buried himself in the crook of my neck and held on tightly as his whole body tensed.

"Oh, God. Derek," he pleaded. Goosebumps prickled down his back as hot jets of come burst onto my stomach.

"Baby, that was so hot," I whispered.

"Come inside me," he commanded, heavy-lidded.

I didn't need to be asked twice. I thrust into him with a strong slam and emptied myself into the condom. Cary groaned with delight as the warmth made contact with him.

He collapsed onto me, and I collapsed back onto my seat. We lay there for a moment, me rubbing a hand up and down his back, until our bodies could be mobile again. I was going to be sore for the rest of the day, and it was fucking worth it.

Eventually, Cary managed to untangle himself from me and return to his seat. Car sex wasn't the best spot for post-coital cuddling, which sucked because I was still craving the closeness of his body.

A heavy moment hung between us as it usually did post-coming. A dip of longing formed inside me. Usually, once we came, we parted ways until next time, and the next time always seemed achingly far away.

Cary wiped off my stomach and himself with his boxers. I pulled a blanket from the backseat to cover him.

"Not that I don't want to keep seeing you naked."

"I've been naked enough today." Even with the heat on, it was cold, so he got dressed, expertly maneuvering his legs and arms into his clothes. His shirt was rumpled, hair askew. He was a shaggier version of himself; I was grateful to be one of the only people who got to see it.

Before Cary could break the tension with another funny comment, an idea came to me. We were in the most tender moment of our relationship thus far.

"Whether it's tickling or whatever, you never have to feel embarrassed around me, Cary."

I shifted to hover over the center console, hovering just above the gear shift.

"Derek...what are you doing?"

I sucked in a breath. *Here goes nothing. The things we do for others.* I disappeared the gear shift into my mouth, getting it all the way down to where it met the car. I only lasted a second though before gagging and pulling up. My jaw would be sore for the rest of the day, but again. Worth it.

"Now we're both weirdos." I smoothed back Cary's hair and gave him a peck on the lips, a kiss of solidarity.

I couldn't read Cary's expression. It was a mix of confusion and deep thought.

"Is everything okay?"

"Yeah," he said, preoccupied with something. Had I crossed a line?

"I'm actually impressed you were able to do that," I said, clearing my throat. "My jaw hurts. The shape is—"

"It's a lie," he blurted out.

"What's a lie?"

"Gearhead. It never happened."

18

CARY

"Gearhead is a lie?" Derek asked, his eyes squinting. He was really cute when he was confused.

The truth had sat tucked away in a dusty corner inside me, but I could always feel its weight, no matter how small a box I put it in. Opening it, I had to be feeling what Pandora felt when her box was opened. I prayed there was hope at the bottom of mine.

"Is it okay if I start at the beginning?"

"Of course." Derek raked a hand up and down my arm.

I heaved out a breath, a light breaking up the darkness lodged in my chest.

"The year after you graduated and absconded off to Alaska, I found another closeted athlete in our school. What are the odds? We were lab partners. We bonded over dissection." It almost sounded sweet, like something I might've read in Maudrey's *Seventeen* magazine. "I also wrote him a letter. Not steamy like yours, but outing myself to him and wondering if he wanted to talk. And he did."

"Who was he?"

"Let's call him Gaston."

"From *Beauty and the Beast*?"

"I don't like to use his real name." Calling him his real name made him real. It was easier for me to picture him as a Disney villain. It minimized his power over me. Plus, I didn't want Derek tracking him down. I hadn't spoken to him since high school, and I preferred to keep it that way.

"For the record, my desire for him wasn't anywhere near what it was for you. But I'd shot my shot with you and missed, and he was here." My hands got sweaty as layers of memories unpeeled themselves. "We started hooking up. A lot. He wasn't interested in having a deep connection, just getting off. I did that stupid thing where I mistook hooking up for something more and imagined that we could be an actual couple one day."

I glanced up at Derek, wondering if he was ready to bolt. His hot hookup was sounding more pathetic by the second. Yet his eyes remained kind and alert, and that gave me just enough confidence to keep going.

"We'd meet up. We'd hook up in his home while his parents were working. And it was exhilarating. *One time*, we drove out to a field a few towns over. And while we were fooling around, in the heat of things, I...stroked his gear shift. And I might've kissed it. Kinda like there was a third person there. *He was into it*. It really turned him on."

I dipped my head into my hands.

"I get it," Derek said. "People do lots of weird shit in bed."

"Exactly! When you're intimate with someone, you do and say weird shit because you trust them, and you know they won't judge you. Think of all the wives whose husbands ask them to stick their finger in their asses during sex. They don't want their golf buddies to know about that."

I hated myself for trusting him. All these years later, that was the one thing I couldn't get over. As a closeted gay kid, I thought I'd been good about keeping my guard up.

"I didn't go down on a gear shift. I stroked it for less than thirty seconds, put my mouth on it for less than ten. Gaston had zero stamina so things rarely lasted that long."

Derek threw his head back and let out a loud, hearty laugh, taking away a few bits of Gaston's residual power. He quickly calmed down and got serious again.

"Why would he tell the whole school that? Did you dump him?"

"Not quite." I steeled myself for part two. "One night over Christmas break, Gaston drove over to my house drunk after a party. He wanted to have sex. And I said no."

I was still amazed at my response, all these years later. I was grateful that my teenage self had enough brains to listen to the tiny voice of reason inside him.

"I mean, yes I liked him, and I thought that this was all leading somewhere real. He'd tell me how cute I was, how funny I was, how nobody really got me like he did. But I don't know...I didn't want my first time to be some drunk, spontaneous thing. And I think on some level, I knew I didn't want him to have all of my firsts." I let out a sigh. "I watched him sour on me in real time. The intimate connection we'd been building over those months instantly vanished."

I could see his face, clear as day, practically growling at me like an attack dog. The features that I loved most about him, like his thick eyebrows and pouty lips, turned against me.

"When I returned to school, I learned that he used the rest of his vacation to share the story of how I sucked off a gearshift to seduce him. And because I was uncool and powerless and closeted and my family wasn't wealthy, I had to take it. I tried to tell people it wasn't true, but nobody believed me. I didn't want to out him because...honestly? I was scared of how he would retaliate if his secret got out."

Deep down, every gay guy lived with a sense of danger, a tiny alarm blinking inside all of us that violence could be one misstep away. We were only a few years removed from Matthew Shepherd back then. It was still true today.

"I thought it would blow over, but gearhead really took hold. People who claimed to be my friends used the nickname behind my back."

"Did Cal?"

"Never. He was one of the only people who stuck by my side." But I would only let him get so close. I wondered if he and I could've been better friends, but a part of me always held back because what if something happened and he became an enemy? I watched how quickly Gaston turned on me. I knew what people were capable of. I never wanted to label myself a victim, but I couldn't deny that the whole gearhead thing fucked me up.

"Cal must've believed you. He's loud. He could spread the truth," Derek said.

"I didn't tell Cal the truth. He came up to my locker when everything broke and said he didn't care what happened, he wouldn't stop being my friend. He believed the story without hearing my side. If he believed it, then so did everyone else. There was no point trying to tell the truth. It was a salacious piece of gossip. The truth was boring. So I smiled and nodded and tried my very best to laugh with them. I wouldn't let myself be the punchline. I'd be in on the joke. Bullying 101: bullies don't find joy in bullying when their victims laugh along with them."

Words I'd been wanting to say for decades poured out of me, and I had a hard time stopping.

"And you know what the worst part was?" My voice cracked with raw emotion struggling to get out. "My mom and dad drove Gaston home that night. I told them my *friend* had driven to our house drunk. They were in their pajamas and tired after a long day of work, but my dad drove him home in his car, and my mom followed behind them. I still feel immense guilt that they had to do that." The image of them taking this creep home while wearing their pajamas made me ignite with anger. Anger at Gaston. Anger at them for doing the responsible thing. Anger at myself for being a bad son who put them in this position.

"Do they know about..."

"No. By the grace of God, they never found out about gearhead. They wondered why I barely went out in high school or why my grades plummeted junior year. I couldn't bear to tell them the truth, so I made up stories, did whatever I could so they wouldn't have a different opinion of me."

I was used to keeping this secret. I knew how to live with the weight. Letting it go was like walking in zero-gravity for the first time. I was wobbly and couldn't find my footing with Derek.

"I wished none of this happened. I was never that into Gaston. The highs were never that high. But...I was so lonely, and dammit I just wanted someone to love me. Even if it was only an approximation, at least it would be mine. I went to school every day with straight kids who were falling in love and breaking up and hooking up and flirting, and I had to stand on the side watching, neutered, hiding. I would take the fake version of a relationship over not having anything at all."

Derek stared out the windshield in a daze, as if he was

the one who just told this story. A million thoughts swirled in his dark eyes, but I couldn't decipher a single one.

"I didn't mean to bring the party down. At least I waited until after sex, right?"

"This isn't funny," he snapped through gritted teeth.

Before I could break the tension with another awkward joke, he punched the steering wheel so hard I thought he was going to put a hole in his truck.

The silence thickened. What could one say after watching someone punch an inanimate object?

"I'm sorry."

"You're sorry? You have nothing to be sorry for." He punched the wheel again. "Fuck. *I'm* sorry, Cary. I'm sorry that happened to you. I'm sorry I wasn't there..."

"What would you have done?"

"You could've trusted me with the truth."

I wanted to believe him. I really did. But I was invisible to him back then. He would've believed the story and laughed along like everyone else.

"Who is this guy? I'm going to serve him twenty years worth of justice."

"How will that make things better?" It was the same question I asked myself whenever I had a hankering for revenge. When I last checked, Gaston lived in Dallas with a wife and kids. They would feel the brunt as much as him.

"You didn't deserve this."

"I know," I said softly.

Derek grabbed my hand and gave it a strong, supportive squeeze. His eyes were glassy, on the verge of watery. "Thank you for trusting me with the truth."

"I didn't want you to be the only person with a secret you couldn't tell others," I said. My body refused to be serious. Serious was scary. I craved levity in this moment.

"You're a good person, Cary." Derek pulled me to him and kissed the top of my head. Maybe this was where I let out all my crying and hurt, but I'd gotten too good at holding it in. So instead, I listened to the rhythm of his heartbeat.

We stayed like that, me in the crook of his arm, Derek nuzzling against my head. Somehow, it was more intimate than everything else we'd done.

19

DEREK

Xavier and I worked out at the firehouse during our shift. His drill sergeant demeanor pushed me to move more weight than I thought I could. I might've been hitting the cusp of middle age, but I still got it. Mitch was hounding me about joining the recreational hockey league with our old teammates. At first, I wondered if my middle-aged body could handle the sport, but the fact that I could keep up with Xavier's workout regimen was a good sign.

The exercise room was located on the top floor of the firehouse with the tall, arched windows overlooking a small park currently being used as the latest filming location for *A Mountain Man Christmas*. The Mitch and Charlie lookalikes sat on swings reading through their scripts as hair and makeup touched them up. I could've sworn that was Mitch's exact jacket.

"How much longer are they filming this shit?" Xavier asked while doing pull-ups.

"I think another week or so?" I stood in front of the mirror doing goblet squats, which would help me if I ever had to lift someone from the floor. "You don't like Christmas movies?"

"Too sappy for me. *Die Hard* is the only Christmas movie I care about."

"*Die Hard* is very romantic. McClane gets back together with his wife." Also, *Die Hard*-era Bruce Willis? Very hot.

"Not before he kills a bunch of guys and blows shit up." Xavier struggled to hit the last two reps, his arms shaking and neck straining to get over the bar.

I couldn't help staring out the window in between reps. There was something compulsively captivating about film shoots, the way they created a fake reality right before our eyes. The actors put away their scripts and blocked the scene with the director. By the looks of their closeness, it was going to be a big one, maybe their first kiss.

"The action's in here," Xavier said to me, snapping me back to my job. "Row with me."

He led us to the rowing machines. Two of our squadmates finished using them and wiped off their seats. Xavier and I got to it, cutting through imaginary water with full force.

"Have you and Jolene been to the Rutherford Observatory? It's at the college. They have a big telescope. You can see lots of constellations."

"Chief, I didn't take you for a stargazer," I said.

"I took my wife there on a date there years ago." A saddened look washed over his face, yet he didn't give up any of his speed. "It was one of the few romantic things I actually did."

"I doubt that." Xavier seemed like a big romantic at heart.

"It'll be sixteen years next month that she's gone." He stared at the wall, wistful. "Still miss her."

"I'm sorry."

"How about you? How are you holding up?"

"I'm getting through." The answer sounded accurate, even if I was probably doing much better, a fact which gave me some guilt. Even though Xavier and I could bond over being widowers, our situations were much different. He and his wife were deeply in love and committed. And for me...it would be forever complicated.

"I'd rather keep moving forward, you know? It's what she would've wanted. For our daughter's sake," I said, hoping that didn't make me sound like an asshole. Paula had been ready to start a new chapter of her life. It was what she wanted. "Can I ask you a question, Chief?"

"Uh huh." Xavier pulled the rowing cord so hard I thought it was going to snap off.

"How long until you felt comfortable dating again?" Xavier was currently in a long-term relationship with a lovely woman. They didn't have a desire to get married, but they planned to be with each other until the end.

"Honestly? A lot sooner than I expected. A helluva lot sooner than my friends and family expected, too. I loved Celeste. But there comes a point where your grief can tip from being a process that you work through to a state you're stuck in. I've seen it with others. They spend so much time in mourning, they can't move on. Knowing when it's time to move on is different for everyone."

I didn't expect such soulfulness from Xavier. It was like my mom used to say: let people surprise you. His steely eyes swirled with an emotional undercurrent laying plain his whole journey to finding love again.

He raised a curious eyebrow, again, without losing speed. "Is there someone new for you?"

"Maybe." I tried to keep up with his speed, yanking the rowing cord as hard as I could. "I know it's soon."

"There's no mathematical formula. People who move on sooner love their spouses as much as people who are in mourning for years."

"Thanks, Chief." A small weight lifted off my chest. I wished there was a proper path for mourning, but at the same time, I was grateful that we could go at our own speed.

We stopped rowing. Xavier checked my total knots. He barely beat me, and a gloating smile muscled its way onto his lips. We got water from the cooler. A bright constellation of colorful lights shone through the window.

We walked over and watched as the actors filmed their scene. The one who looked like Mitch, played by Lucien, had decked out the playground in Christmas lights, and turned them on when the one who looked like Charlie, played by Skip, approached. It was a cliché, but I found myself entranced.

Lucien and Skip closed the gap between them and exchanged some dialogue that was likely corny and over-the-top. And then they kissed as fake snow fluttered over them.

It was movie magic, and watching it made me long for a certain real estate agent. Ever since he told me his heart-breaking, enraging story, I couldn't stop thinking about him. All I wanted to do was hold him in my arms. He could show houses while I was hugging him, and I could probably work a firehose one-handed. We'd make it work. I took a picture of the filming to text to Cary.

Thinking of you, I started to write before deleting. Was that too mushy for Cary?

You can have Hollywood right in your backyard, I texted. I mulled over if that was the best Caryism I could come up with.

Sourwood is the Hollywood of the Hudson Valley, he texted back.

THE NEXT NIGHT, I took Xavier's advice and planned a trip to the observatory with Jolene. Unfortunately, I didn't do my due diligence. They were closed for a private event that night, some corporate Christmas party.

Dad fail.

Fortunately, my daughter was infinitely smarter than me, and she had us pack her telescope in the trunk, just in case.

We stopped off for gas at a station outside Sourwood.

"Can I get a snack?" Jolene asked.

"What are you thinking?"

She pinched her face in thought, looking as adorable as ever. "Something chocolatey."

"Twix?" I asked. It was her favorite. She had a process of taking a bite of one, then the other, and trying to make her bites as even as possible.

"I don't *always* get Twix," Jolene protested. "But a Twix does sound good."

"Get me some kind of chip. Something crunchy. And a water, too."

She gave me a salute then went inside the store.

I began filling up my gas tank when I heard a familiar voice muttering out expletives. I eased my head to the other side of the dispensing station.

"What the fuckity fuck? I already gave you my credit

card." Cary stared at the machine, as if he were waiting for an answer for why it was acting up.

The commercial on the screen advertising Gatorade blared up.

"I don't think it's going to respond," I said. I swung around to his side, leaning against the dispenser. Cary lit up when he saw me before returning to frustration.

"Hey."

We had a weird moment where neither of us were sure how to greet the other. I wanted to pull him close for a kiss, but that wasn't the best idea, especially since Jolene would be out in a minute.

"What's the problem?" I asked.

Cary raked a hand through his hair. "It's not taking my credit card."

"Is there something…"

"There's nothing wrong with my credit card."

"These machines can be sensitive," I said.

"Then they should see a therapist."

I cracked a smile. At least Cary never lost his sense of humor.

"Here. Let me try."

"I know how to use a credit card."

"These machines can be wonky. Let me help," I insisted.

"I think the thing is broken." The machine prompted Cary to insert his credit card. He was about to jam his card inside with his typical manic, impatient energy, when I clamped my hand over his.

"You need to leave it in there." I pushed our hands against the machine, keeping the card inside, my body too close to his but unable to pull away. "Gentle."

"We're…still talking about my credit card, right?" Cary

said. I could feel his heartbeat vibrate against me. Damn, he smelled good. Crisp and clean.

Before I could answer, the machine beeped its approval and signaled Cary to remove his card. With my hand still over his, we pulled it out slowly.

"I hate chip readers," he said. "I miss the days of sliding your card. It was like a rush of adrenaline."

"You have to be gentle and patient with these machines." I handed his card back to him, letting our thumbs touch, a rush of heat in this cold, cold air.

"I should've known. Your fingers do have the magic touch, whether at the gas station or on my—hello there!" Cary's face went white. I followed his eyeline to my daughter standing behind me.

"Hi," she said awkwardly. I stepped away from Cary and tried to keep a stern look on my face that gave nothing away.

"You must be Jolene!" Cary's high-pitched voice only added to the weirdness. "I'm Cary. My name is Cary. I'm your dad's real estate....something."

"Agent," I said.

"I decided on Cheetos." She handed me a bottle of water and a bag of chips.

"Do you know that the Frito-Lay company has a giant mechanical mouth that tests the crunchiness of their chips?" Cary's smile was so big that it was about to fall off the sides of his face.

I put a calming hand on his shoulder. "Thanks, Cary."

"I'm gonna go pump gas." Cary hooked the nozzle to his gas tank. He shot me a quick apologetic look for his verbal disaster.

"I say we just go home," Jolene said to me. "It's a clear night. We should be able to see something."

"Are you going stargazing?" Cary popped his head to our side of the vestibule.

"We are," I said.

"You should try Renegade Park. There's a hill there that would probably be a great place to look at stars."

I remembered Cary mentioning the spot in our initial meeting. Jolene turned to me, intrigued by the idea. "That could be fun," she said.

"I remember going there on summer nights and just staring up at the sky. I was never good at picking out constellations, but I liked that feeling of infiniteness." Cary shrugged.

"When you look up, everything feels so vast," Jolene said.

"Exactly!"

"Let's do it. Renegade Park." I nodded.

Cary returned the gas nozzle and turned on his car. The sounds of Taylor Swift flooded from his speakers.

"You're a Swiftie?" Jolene asked.

"Yes. Technically. So here's what happened," Cary began, and I loved that he had a story for everything, including this. "I would hear her songs on the radio or out and about, and I liked them. But I never actively sought her music out. And then my cousin who lives in DC got tickets to her latest concert on a whim. She was supposed to go with her friend, but her friend broke her foot when her treadmill malfunctioned. She's currently suing the manufacturer, and it's in active litigation. Oh, and the lawyer for the treadmill company is her ex-boyfriend. It's a whole thing. The point is, I wound up going to the concert, and it was a religious experience. I was converted into a middle-aged Swiftie." Cary danced in place and mouthed along to whatever this song was.

"That's so cool! I didn't know grown men were into Taylor Swift," she said.

"We're out there. Taylor is an inspiration. She has been mocked and maligned her entire career for being a maneater or boy crazy, yet when male artists write songs about girls, they're romantics. The media only wants to talk about her in relation to men in her life, but she's persevered and refused to let them write her narrative. She's shown everyone that she is an icon all on her own."

After what he went through in high school, I could see how Cary found Taylor to be a beacon of light for him.

Cary kept mouthing along to the song and dancing in place, ignoring looks he was getting from people getting gas. Jolene began shuffling in place, the music slowly taking over her. He went into his car and turned up the volume.

"What are you doing?" I asked them.

Cary took Jolene's hand and spun her around during the chorus, both of them belting out the words like they were in the shower.

"Uh, we're in public. Let's keep it down," I said.

So what did they do? They sang even louder, right at me. Cary danced around me, using my body as a prop in a choreographed dance.

"We're going to get kicked out," I said.

"Or invited back." Cary bopped his hip against mine. I refused to take part. "Jolene, does your dad ever dance?"

"What do you think?"

"Hey! Traitor." I raised an eyebrow at her.

"Derek, you work at a place that has a pole and you don't dance?" Cary shook his head. "Criminal."

Jolene took her Twix bar and sang into it like a microphone. Cary bent down and joined her at the mic.

I had secondhand embarrassment for both of them, but damn if it wasn't sweet watching Jolene cut loose.

"What's this?" Cary pointed at my shoe, which had begun to tap.

"It's not tapping," I said.

"It's tapping to the beat."

The song faded out, cutting me a break.

"Let's go. In the car." I pointed to the door, giving Jolene no option. I couldn't be caught dancing to a Taylor Swift song. The security camera footage would probably go viral.

"It was great meeting you, Jolene! Never forget that your dad kinda sorta danced to a Taylor Swift song."

"Hey." I brushed against Cary's arm as he turned to go. "Did you want to join us at Renegade Park?"

Cary looked to Jolene who nodded her eager approval.

"It'll be fun!" she said. I feared for my hearing if they were going to sing more Taylor Swift songs, but I was willing to take that chance.

Cary shrugged his shoulders. "Sure."

Jolene clapped her hands excitedly, but I might've been the more excited one.

20

CARY

Back when I was in high school, Renegade Park was a patch of riverfront dirt with a janky, rusty playground where kids used to get high or experiment with setting plastic lighters on fire. But as Sourwood had gotten more upscale, some might say bougie, Renegade Park also got a makeover, too. The janky tetanus magnet was replaced with a colorful, state-of-the-art playground area with multiple sections for different ages. Instead of kids falling onto jagged wood chips, the ground was a bouncy material. Trails were updated through the woods, and a walking path with benches was put in place along the river.

I was surprised that Renegade Park wasn't deserted when we arrived. Who was coming out here at night? It was so cold. I was only here because a lovely preteen and her hot stack of a dad, who I wasn't crushing on because we were just having sex and that was it, invited me.

A group of teens hung by the water, but instead of getting high or causing mischief, they were on their phones. Though to be honest, I wasn't one to judge.

"We're going to see Mars tonight," Jolene told me, a glow

on her face, as if Mars was a Taylor Swift concert. (Taylor in space? Here for it.)

"Like the planet?" I asked.

"Yep," Derek said. He set up her telescope. Watching him put stuff together was a weird kind of turn-on. He had major dad energy, and like Taylor in space, I was here for it.

I offered to help, mostly by sticking out my hand and pulling it back a few times. The only stargazing I did was in *US Weekly*. I still couldn't get over that Jennifer Garner and I ate the same brand of yogurt. We were so in sync.

"Isn't it like far away?" I asked of the red planet.

"Usually yes. Mars has a wider orbit than Earth. It spends years behind the sun, but it should be visible tonight." Jolene got to work positioning her telescope. A big, goofy smile took over her face when she found a constellation. I wished I'd had academic interests like her when I was young, or that celebrity gossip could be considered academic interest. In a way, celebrity worship was the modern version of Greek mythology.

"Is this your first time looking at the stars?" Jolene tucked her red hair behind her ears.

"I've never astronomied before," I said.

"Have you ever seen the Big Dipper?" she asked.

"Uh...isn't that the one that looks like a measuring cup?" I hadn't thought about constellations since I was a little kid.

"Go and check it out." Derek put his hand on the small of my back, sending shivers over my skin that rivaled the freezing temperatures.

I looked into the telescope and saw a cluster of nondescript stars. Weren't there supposed to be lines connecting them?

"Very cool," I lied.

Jolene and Derek shared a look that called bullshit on

my response. I loved how they arched their eyebrows in the same way, the left moving higher than the right. In moments like this, seeing that Derek had imprinted himself onto another human being, I had a pinch of regret about not having children. (Although, being a single gay man, it wasn't like it was really an option unless I was fabulously wealthy.)

"I'm sorry. I just see stars." Funny enough, I also saw stars the last time I was with Derek, specifically when he was fucking me in his truck.

"You don't see it?" Jolene asked. "You have to find the North Star. It's the brightest star in the sky."

"Jolene, not everyone is an advanced astronomer like you. Give Cary some grace," Derek said.

I felt bad. Jolene was trying, and all I could come up with were lazy jokes about measuring cups.

"Here. Let me help. It's a clear night. We can do this with the naked eye," Derek said. Funnily enough, I was also naked the last time I was with him.

Derek stood behind me, the hairs on his beard dancing dangerously close to my neck. God, this man's scent was addictive. A sense of peace, and a hint of lust, came over me when I inhaled.

Must not get boner in front of preteen daughter, I reminded myself.

Derek stretched an arm in front of me pointing into the darkness. "Follow my finger."

"Gladly," I said, not intending that to be a double-entendre but oops here we were.

My eyes traveled to where he was pointing, a star that did seem brighter than the others. It didn't try to fit in. It marched to the beat of its own drum.

"That's the North Star," he said.

"I like it."

"So that's the North Star. And then you follow it straight up. Here." Derek took my hand. Even through our coats, I could feel his warmth. He led our hands above the North Star to two stars on top of each other.

"That is the start of the Big Dipper," Derek said calmly, owning the moment of being my celestial tour guide. "You have the square–"

"Trapezoid," corrected Jolene.

"Trapezoid of the cup." He traced the edges of the cup with our hands, then down to the handle. "And there it is. The Big Dipper. All for you."

"There it is," I said, a bit starstruck by the beauty of the sky and the man lighting the way for me.

Maybe Derek had made it all for me. Maybe he made me feel complete. Or maybe I was getting buzzed from our *Beautiful Mind* ripoff.

"It's cool, right?" Jolene asked.

"Yep." I could've stayed like that all night.

"I bet using the observatory would be unbelievable. I can't wait until I get to college."

"Why wait?" I asked her, sitting on a blanket Derek had laid out.

"She still has a few years before she leaves the nest," Derek said, the adorably protective father.

"No, I mean why do you have to wait to work at the observatory? I'm sure they take interns."

"College interns probably," Jolene said.

"Probably, but not definitely. You should reach out to them."

"They likely want to stick with college students," Derek said. I took a brief pause from perpetually lusting and longing after him to be angry at him.

"You don't know that for sure. And Jolene knows more

than most students in that program." I turned to Jolene, who I could tell was intrigued. "You should email, or better yet call, a researcher at the observatory whose work interests you and ask if you could intern with them a few hours per week."

Jolene's eyes sparked with possibility.

"I don't know." Derek said. I put my hand on his chest to shush him.

"Well, *I* know that if you don't ask, you don't get. Simple as that. And what's the worst that can happen?" I crossed my arms. "This isn't a rhetorical question. What is the worst that can happen if you inquire about an internship?"

"They...say I'm too young?" Jolene asks.

"Right. And if they say that, then you know. But let somebody else tell you no. Don't tell yourself no." If I had listened to my doubts about entering real estate, then I wouldn't have this successful career. Sure, the market was flooded with other agents. Sure, I was young and on the shy side. But I didn't let that stop me. It seemed I only held myself back when it came to relationships, but that was more out of self-preservation.

Jolene and Derek absorbed my TED talk in silence. She looked up at her dad.

Derek curled his lips into a satisfied smile aimed at me, one full of unexpected sweetness. "You got it, Jo."

———

DEREK and I hung on the blanket chatting while Jolene was having a field day with everything she could observe in this freakishly clear sky. It was nice not having a conversation around real estate or past traumas. I was happily interrupted by Jolene whenever she wanted to show me a constellation during her hunt for Mars. I loved that her enthusiasm could stretch from Taylor Swift to Ursa Minor.

"Wait, hold up. You're joining a hockey team? Aren't you a little old for that?" I asked, half-jokingly and half-concerned when Derek brought it up. "Can't you take up golf or tennis?"

"I'm not that old. I can handle it. I'm in good shape." Derek slapped his gut and laughed, which I found oddly hot. "I have to work out regularly at the firehouse."

I quirked a quasi-lusty eyebrow at Derek's physique. Underneath his gut was solid muscle. I knew he was strong. He could lift me up and spin me around like I was one of those signs guys held up on the side of the road.

"I remember watching your games," I admitted, hoping it didn't make me sound too pathetic. "I had no idea what was going on, and I didn't get why everyone kept fighting. But you looked really cute in your uniform."

I used to dream about Derek coming up to me after a game, picking me up in his arms, and skating us around the rink. My fantasies with him apparently either went super-dirty or super-romcom.

"I found Orion's belt! It should point the way to Mars," Jolene called out, one eye firmly affixed on her telescope.

"Does his belt match his shoes?" I asked.

Derek snickered.

"I hope you don't mind that I encouraged her to look into an internship at the observatory. I realized after the fact it would be you driving her there and picking her up. My excitement got the better of me. I've seen *Working Girl* too many times, so I'm hard-wired to help women fight for their careers." Derek's firehouse schedule was already a mess. I shouldn't have added to his plate without asking.

Derek cracked a warm grin. Most of my pop culture

references likely went over his head, but they seemed to entertain him nonetheless.

"You're great with her," Derek said, gazing at Jolene.

"She's so cool. Seriously." Although, it was no surprise that Derek wound up raising a cool daughter.

Derek rubbed my back as a thank you. "Paula and I would have disagreements about raising her. She was very protective of Jolene because she was always on the small side and very sensitive. Paula was always wanting to do everything for her, but I wanted to prepare her for the world because I knew she could handle it. Now I feel like I've gone in the opposite direction, and she doesn't really need me that much."

"You got what you wanted."

He sighed. "I know."

"She can handle a college-level internship," I said with zero hesitation. "Most college students are hungover or recovering from crabs. She'll run circles around them. And I can chauffeur her if she gets it. Make your life a little easier."

"Thanks." He rubbed my back again to say thank you. A guy could get used to this. "A part of me will always worry about her. She's going into high school next year, and teenage girls can be vicious to each other."

"Not just the girls," I said, reminding him of my high school experience.

"I remember what high school boys are like, too. Now I get why some fathers joke about locking up their daughters until they're eighteen."

"Notice how nobody ever wants to lock up their sons?" I arched my eyebrow. "It can be a cruel world out there, but there's good people. Jolene will find her crew. She'll be all right."

Derek peered at me with his dark, intense eyes. "How did you get through it?"

It wasn't until he asked me this question that I actually thought about it. All we knew how to do was move forward, letting one day turn to the next. "I used to be terrified of getting made fun of. There'd be this constant knot in my stomach. I was closeted and not the butch kind of closeted like you. I wanted to blend in. But then the whole gearhead shit happened, and all my worst nightmares came true. And you know what I realized?"

"What?"

"They weren't nearly as scary as I imagined."

A faint flicker of relief washed over his face for just a second, then it was gone. Maybe that was what being a parent was all about. Very temporary moments of relief and joy interspersed with persistent fear.

"I went through hell with gearhead. Laughed at, stared at, whispered about. After a while, it started to roll off my back. I developed callouses. I survived hell, which means it actually wasn't hell. Or that I'm secretly a witch."

I also had the enormous good fortune to go to high school before the age of social media. But even with that, I had a good feeling Jolene would be okay. She wasn't Derek's fragile little girl anymore. She was stronger than he knew. We all were.

"You know, you were right before. About having the courage to let someone else tell you no. Because there's something I want to ask you." Derek reached for my hand, intertwined his fingers with mine. The stars provided romantic lighting.

He kept looking at me, then looking down. I could feel the nerves coming off him. I knew what was coming. And it caused me to panic. I could hear the beeping in my head that my car makes when I'm about to crash.

Those closest to you can turn on you.

"There's a house I want you to see. It'd be perfect for you and Jolene. It just came on the market." I turned on my most professional voice, the kind I used when I gave a presentation at a real estate conference. "We've seen a lot of houses, Derek. There's a good one in there. If you see too many houses, then you'll never make a decision."

Whatever sweetness and hope crested on his face melted off in real time. My heart sank at his reaction.

"Yeah, sure. Let's go see it," he said in a mumble.

"Great! I actually need to get home." I hopped up and dusted off my pants. The beeping alarm in my head wouldn't subside until I was in my car, driving away.

"Wait! I'm just about to find Mars," she said.

"Can we take a raincheck on Mars?" I asked.

She nodded yes, but shades of disappointment ringed her eyes.

"Next time," I promised.

That was the thing about calluses. They made us stronger. They helped us survive the harshest parts of life. But they never went away, no matter how hard you pumiced.

21

DEREK

I was so busy on my next shift that I had no time to think about Cary and the awkward moment we ended on. The roads were slick after a freeze, causing a few accidents, and an elderly woman tried to light her cigarette on an electric stove and caused a small fire in her kitchen.

By the time I saw Cary next, he was showing me a house that was supposed to be my dream house. He seemed adamant that I lock down a house soon. I didn't want to be looking forever. I wanted to close and move in with minimal disruption to Jolene's school schedule. But did buying a house mean I wouldn't see Cary again? That was the weird vibe I thought I'd picked up while stargazing with him.

He was definitely allocating way too much time to my search, and he did have a business to run with other clients. It wasn't like he was waiting for all of them in bathtubs in the nude.

I pulled up to the house and parked behind Cary's car. This house wasn't in a new development. It sat on an older street where the houses had larger front lawns and giant mature trees in the yard. I'd driven by this street a million times when I used to live here. It was another anonymous road on my way to somewhere, but it turned out to be a winding path of hidden gems.

It was an older ranch with a brick exterior and blue shutters. A little rundown, but nothing that some TLC couldn't fix. Cary liked to say that all houses had personalities. I hadn't seen that with the new builds, but here, I could tell this beauty had a story.

"Welcome," Cary said from the front door. Fully clothed, it should be noted. "Did you find it okay?"

I wanted to lean in and kiss him hello, but I stopped myself for some reason. Blame the awkward moment rearing its ugly head.

Cary held open the door for me. I caught a whiff of his citrusy cologne before being enveloped in the scent of the house, which could only be described as homey: the smell of going over to your friend's house and his mom is cooking dinner, the quasi-stale smell of your grandparents' house that made you feel safe.

The current residents had been there a while judging by their older furniture and clutter that took over every flat surface. They had tried to clean up as best they could, organizing their mess and keeping it off the floor. It was a valiant effort, like when Jolene tried making me birthday pancakes as a little girl that was more of a soupy bread blob.

Flowery wallpaper lined the walls and the only sign of post-2000 life was a flat screen TV in the living room.

"It's on the older side, but the house has great bones," Cary said.

I believed him. An old house like this could double as a bomb shelter.

"And wallpaper can easily come off. I think a nice cream would open things up." Cary wiped a sprinkling of dust off the sliver of coffee table not covered with magazines. They tried to arrange the magazines like a fan. Bless them.

"And despite the old look of this house, the HVAC and roof were replaced within the last five years. That will save you tens of thousands of dollars. Oh, I love this little nook." Cary strummed his fingers on a breakfast nook with stools, the nook and stools covered in papers. "I told the agent repping the house to have his clients clean up, and this was the best they could do. But before you move in, I know a—"

"Great cleaning service." I knew all of Cary's stock answers by now.

"They will make this place sparkle like brand new."

I realized I wasn't looking for brand new. I wasn't a brand new kinda guy. Like with Cary's body, I was enjoying all the imperfections that made it feel real. New houses were too sterile, trying too hard to blend in.

"There's a stone fireplace, too," I said.

"You don't see those very often."

I loved building fires in my old house. Listening to the crackling of the flames was my version of a relaxation bath. Jolene had introduced me to a fireplace YouTube channel, but it wasn't the same. A real fireplace didn't pause every few minutes for a commercial.

Maybe Cary and I could have sex in front of a roaring fire. Unless those dreams were long gone.

He wasn't giving me much to go off of. Cary was all business, his back stiff and straight. He entered the kitchen and turned to me, a chasm of empty air between us.

"I know it's a hard left from the houses we'd been seeing, but I think it's very you. I think this is the first house I could see you in."

"You said that about every house we've seen."

"Well, it's most apparent with this one."

And this time, I had to agree with the man. I wished we hadn't spent all that time in brand new sterile homes. Although, it was worth it for all the hooking up, something I'd never do with him here. People lived here. I didn't want to risk wiping a come-drenched hand on their fanned out magazines.

"The bedrooms are down that hall. Now, there's no en suite bathroom to the main bedroom, but since it's just you and Jolene, that shouldn't be a problem," Cary said.

He pointed to the hall, essentially telling me it was a journey I'd have to do on my own.

I checked out the three bedrooms, only one of which had a bed in it. My parents might've had that floral comforter. The rooms were on the small side, the closets not as spacious, and yet they gave off a welcoming warmth.

"What do you think?" he asked when I returned to the living room.

"The bedrooms are smaller than I expected, but a small bedroom means I'll sleep cozier." I cracked a smile, hoping to see one from him in return. "That was a Caryism."

"Good one."

"Eh, it was a five out of ten."

"No. It was at least a five point three." There was that smile that I'd been missing. "Come check out this kitchen. It has great potential."

"I believe you."

"You're going to take my word about one of the most important rooms in your house?"

I closed the space between us with my answer: a kiss. I pulled his body against mine. God, it was like I'd already forgotten how great he tasted, the perpetual hint of mint mixed with his warm breath.

"Derek." He stepped back, sliding a rickety, unbalanced

kitchen chair between us. "Maybe we shouldn't be doing this. You're my client."

Who would've thought the word client would sting this much. "You still think of me that way?"

"No. I don't. It's...complicated."

"Complicated," I repeated. Complicated was the necktie of words. It sounded fancy, but it served no purpose but to take up space.

"There's a great backyard, too. Perfect for grilling outside." Cary opened the sliding door. Cold air hit me in the face, a nice distraction from the turmoil turning in my chest. We'd had this incredible breakthrough in my car. We told each other things we'd never told anyone else. And now he wanted to go back to business only?

The backyard stretched out behind us. I never would've suspected a yard this big when I pulled up to the house. A small garden box sat by the deck. In contrast to the older feel of the inside, the deck looked to be fairly new and in great condition.

"The deck was recently updated. The people living here have been very savvy with their updates. A recently updated HVAC, roof, and deck are things you won't find in most other houses." Cary leaned against the railing of the deck before hopping off a second later. "Oh, there's a shed, too! You don't see those too often."

"That's part of the house?" I asked. "They're not taking it with them?"

"Nope."

We strolled across the lawn to the shed in the back corner of the yard. It was like a lone sign of life in unsettled land. Overgrown grass stuck around its edges. Its color matched the blue shutters out front, albeit with peeling paint.

The Fireman and the Flirt

Inside, the shed was empty save for a lawn mower and gardening supplies tucked in the corner. It was a bit bigger than an outhouse.

"It's small but it gets the job done," Cary said. "Doesn't have too much of a serial killer feel." He turned to me. "What do you think?"

"I'll take it," I said.

"I was asking about the shed, but you'll take the house?"

"Yeah. Let's put in an offer."

"You shouldn't have a problem. It's been sitting on the market for over a month," he said, minus the enthusiasm I would've expected from him. "I'll begin to draw up the papers."

I thought he'd be thrilled about this. I was having flashbacks to Paula and the confusing hot/cold way she acted as our marriage unraveled.

Cary is not Paula, I told myself.

"Okay. Was there anything else you wanted to see?" Cary asked, visibly nervous.

I crowded the exit from the shed, and being this close to him was doing something to my head. Both of them, actually.

"Nope. Can we close on the house today?"

"Today? I wish the banks worked that quickly."

"Well, how soon can I stop being your client, Cary? Because if being your client means I can't kiss you or hold you or fuck you, then I'm ready to sign the papers today."

The professional veneer Cary wore this entire visit began to crack, and the Cary I remembered and was falling for shined through. He could handle any client question except for one, apparently.

"Derek."

I took a step toward him, fully plunging us into the shed. Shards of light slipped through the windows.

"Cary, I want to keep seeing you. In fact, I'm glad I won't need to have an excuse of a house listing to spend time with you."

The turmoil that churned within him flashed on his face.

"Why is this complicated?" I asked, making a supposedly complex situation very, very simple. I was a grown-ass man. I'd been through so much in my life already. I didn't want to waste more precious time playing games.

"I'm not good at this," he said softly, his voice cracking.

"I'd say you're doing a pretty bang-up job."

"I've never been in a successful relationship. If my boyfriend track record were my sales numbers, I would've left the real estate game years ago."

"I've only been in one successful relationship, and it turned out it wasn't that successful because she was going behind my back with my friend." The fear of that happening again would always live inside me. It was like those people who'd been through horrific accidents. Statistically, they knew it couldn't happen again, but that didn't stop them from worrying, from the worst case scenarios creeping in.

"If you wanted to keep this just sex, I'm cool with that."

I caressed his cheek with my hand, feeling the tiny nicks and grooves in his seemingly smooth face. "I want more."

I could tell he did, too. In the way he nuzzled against my hand like it was sustenance. In the way he closed his eyes and heaved out a tiresome breath that'd been cooped up too long. He had trust issues. So did I. I never thought I'd consider dating after Paula died, and I certainly didn't think I'd fall for a guy. But like the house I was about to make an offer on, in my gut, I knew this was right. Maybe, despite the odds, we could be made of more than hurt. Maybe we could be something pure in this world that only wants to shovel shit on us.

"Cary..." I slid my hand to his chin, tipped it up, waited for him to meet my eyes.

"Fuck it," he said. And with that, he pushed me against the wall and kissed me.

22

CARY

This wasn't supposed to happen. Derek was a client. Derek was my best friend's sad widower brother. Derek was a crush, someone to be desired and admired from afar. He wasn't supposed to notice me and want me.

When this was fooling around, it was easy. It was fun. But the way we kissed in that shed confirmed what Derek was telling me right before I launched my body on him. That this was more.

I could handle Derek when he was a fantasy, but when he was real? Nightmare memory flashes of bad boyfriends leading all the way back to my gearhead origin story spliced into my head in between swooning over Derek's lips on mine. I had trouble remembering my social security number, but unfortunately, I would always remember the ruthless glare of Gaston when I rejected his ask for sex. It truly was a thin line between love and hate. Why did our brains hold onto these memories and let the happy times fade away? I believed it was for self-preservation, that despite letting myself fall for Derek, I always had to be on my guard.

"You seem very deep in thought for someone who's half-naked," Derek said.

Oh, right. He'd unbuttoned my shirt and slid it down my arms, letting it fall onto the dirty floor. In fairness, he'd also pulled off his T-shirt. We had twenty more minutes left of our showing before the homeowners could be back. Why the hell was I letting my anxiety take over? Why was it impossible for me to live in the moment?

"Sorry," I said. "Sometimes I wish I could turn my brain off."

"I like your brain."

"Metaphorically, of course. If I turned off my brain completely, then I would have no bodily functionality. I would be a vegetable, and you couldn't have sex with a vegetable. Well, you could but that would be ethically–"

Derek rightly shut me up with a kiss. Our chests rubbed together, his furry pecs overpowering my more waifish body. He rested his forehead against mine.

"Stay with me, Cary." His stern but caring voice shut up the squabbling in my head. "We only have so much time."

"Right." If I kept babbling, then the moment would die.

Derek picked me up and twisted us around so my back was against the wall, the uneven grain in the wood digging into my skin. I would gladly risk a splinter for good sex. I loved how he maneuvered me so easily, his biceps flexing with my weight.

"You are so fucking hot, you know that?" he growled into my ear. "Were you this hot in high school?"

"I was skinny and pimpled and used way too much gel in my hair."

He bit his lip and grunted in uncontrollable heat. "Hot."

"It was not hot."

Derek kissed down my neck. His calloused fingers

pinched my nipple, eliciting a gasp from me. "I had sideburns that were too long, pants that were too baggy, and frosted tips. Frosted tips, Cary. I wanted to be like Mark McGrath from Sugar Ray." He laughed into my shoulder, his deep chortle vibrating in my chest.

When he said it like that, he sounded like a total loser, but trust me, Derek made all of it, including the frosted tips, unbearably sexy. As Sugar Ray might've sang, every morning when I woke up there was a boner in my Abercrombie jeans.

"It was hot," I said, palming the erection in his non-Abercrombie jeans. "We've learned from our teenage mistakes." Although, I wondered if in twenty years, we'd look back on our outfits now and cringe with embarrassment.

Derek kept laughing into my chest while still tweaking my nipple. He curled an arm behind my back and let his hand drift southward to my ass crack. I had to admire his ability to multitask.

"Now I have Sugar Ray in my head," Derek said as his finger lodged itself deeper into my crack.

"Which song?"

"*Fly*."

"Oh yeah. I loved that song. You know what's an underrated song of theirs? *Falls Apart*." I shook my head, getting some fucking sense in there. "Derek, what the fuck are we doing? We're supposed to be having sex, not talking about frosted tips and ranking the best Sugar Ray songs. Your hand is in my ass, and my hand is on your dick. This is no time for shooting the shit."

"We can do both." A shit-eating grin cracked his lips. "You make me laugh and you make me hard. The two aren't mutually exclusive."

I'd never had this much fun during sex. Correction: I'd never had *any fun* during sex. Like, sex was a great time, obviously. But was it fun? I was always trying to put on a performance of the kind of man the other guy would want to fuck. With Derek, I was just...me. And Derek was Derek. And it was all so remarkably easy.

"Cary," Derek said, snapping me back to the present, where he'd undone my belt and pushed my pants and underwear to the floor. I stepped out of the legs, then returned part of the favor. I only undid his belt and opened his fly, wrapping a hand around his thick cock.

Derek stroked me back as our lips tumbled into each other's, kissing and smiling and laughing over nothing in particular. Our cocks brushed together, sword fighting in the chilly open air. Derek spat into his hand and grabbed both of our dicks in his strong grip. He reached behind me and continued playing with my ass. His finger circled my hole, teasing me and setting my skin on fire. Because he was a gentleman, he didn't try to enter me without some kind of lubrication.

"What are we going to do about sex?" I asked in between catching my breath. I didn't want to derail our sexytimes with more talking, but there were logistical questions to work out.

"I gotcha covered." Derek winked at me, stripping me naked all over again. He yanked his pants off the floor and pulled a small bottle of lube from the front pocket. I'd seen the bulge in his pants (yes, of course I glimpsed when I first saw him. I was only human.). I'd assumed it was lip balm. I was so glad to be wrong.

"You brought lube to a showing?" I asked.

"Yeah. I fucking did. Have you met us?"

Us. He called us an us!

He turned me around, pushing my face against the wall. A few tantalizing seconds later, I felt him spread my cheeks and flick his hot tongue against my pulsing hole. I wanted to scream with delight, but these walls were so not thick enough.

"You're a natural," I said as Derek's tongue did wonders to my ass. His beard prickled against my taint, sending new sensations fizzing over my skin. He was gentle and curious, sliding two slicked fingers inside me. "This feels so good."

If I didn't control myself, I would finish right here and now.

"You are so fucking hot, Cary. I can't wait to fuck this ass."

"No waiting required." I gave it a little doggy wag, which I instantly regretted for being too weird. But then I realized, fuck that. Derek liked my weirdness. And so I wagged my ass again.

He gave it a hard slap of approval. I could feel the red of his hand burning on my cheek.

"Turn around," Derek ordered, his voice husky.

I turned and raised my leg, thinking he was going to eat me out from another angle. Instead, he gave me head. Derek was going full gay today, and I was happy to help him fully step into his bisexuality.

I nearly lost consciousness as my cock disappeared into his mouth, his tongue slinking down my shaft. He grabbed my dick and stroked me as he sucked, his firm, slicked-up grip making me turn to jelly. Or jam. What was the difference? Actually, now was not the time for those kinds of existential questions.

"Jesus Christ, you're good," I said through moans.

"I didn't take you for a religious person."

"Girl, I don't know what half the things are that come out of my mouth during sex."

He winked at me, sending another current of lust through my system. Derek took me to the base, the heat of his mouth pushing me closer to the edge. He spat on my cock and slapped it on his tongue.

"How does it taste?" I asked him.

"Like you," he said, then licked at my sack. I dug my fingernails into a shelf above me that fortunately was empty. I thought I had known pleasure before this moment, but I had been mistaken.

I quivered from the tips of my toes to the strands of my hair. I needed him against me. I needed his heat inside me or else I was going to scream and alert the entire neighborhood to our whereabouts.

"Derek, fuck me. You have to fuck me. Please." Maybe down the road, we could experiment with switching positions, but right here right now, I had a deep down, primal, aggressive need to get my ass fucked.

"Baby," he grunted, seeing how serious I was. He took a condom from his pants pocket.

"We can do it without," I said, speech interrupted with desperate gasps for air. "You're the only person I've...in a while...and you...widowered..."

"Works for me." He tossed the condom behind him.

I looked up at the boards making up the roof, basking in the glimmers of light breaking through the cracks.

"Derek..." *Derek, I'm falling in love with you. I think I want to be with you forever. You've exceeded all my trivial high school fantasies.*

It was all on the tip of my tongue. But fear choked me at the last minute.

And then he was inside me, and my brain ceased transmission of anxious thoughts. I wrapped my legs around his waist, his thick cock plunging into the deepest parts of me.

"You're so tight," he said.

Low-grade anxiety kept me permanently clenched, but I kept that tidbit to myself.

"Don't stop." My head banged lightly against the wall.

"You okay?" Derek cradled a hand behind me while holding me wrapped around him. Again, the dexterity.

"Your fingers are going to get scraped up," I said.

"Worth it." He kissed my neck, then rested his head there as he huffed out ragged breaths and fucked me.

I threw my arms around him and pulled him closer, my cock rubbing against his stomach. The laughter stopped. His crystal eyes turned a dark shade like a storm brewing on the horizon.

"Let's try a different spot." Derek moved us to the opposite wall with a window. It wasn't comfortable having my head against the glass, but it was better than a splintery wall. And it was better than leaning down in a car's front seat. This was going to be our thing, wasn't it? Sex in tight quarters.

Derek rested his forehead against mine, never taking his eyes off me as he pummeled into my opening. The orgasm built inside me, heat and lust and heart brewing an overpowering cocktail that raced through my veins.

Our sweaty limbs intertwined. My hands scratched across the prickly buzzed hairs at the base of his neck, and the hairs nested on his shoulders. I inhaled his heady scent of sweat and thanked my lucky stars that I got to have sex with men and relish all of these details.

"You feel so good, Cary. Need you," he said through a strained breath that told me how close he was.

"Come inside me." I wanted to feel his warmth completely.

"Yes. Yes. Yes." They were half-grunts, half-words. Then he unleashed a final, bellowing groan as he emptied himself in my hole.

After he finished, he kept going and stroked me. "Are you close?" he asked.

"Uh huh."

Derek plunged his half-hard cock fully inside me and stayed there. He jerked me fast, and before I could feel guilt about not helping out more, I was coming all over his stomach.

He pecked me softly on my lips as we came down from our high. Goosebumps spread across my body while he slid out of my opening. The chill of the wintry air filled the shed.

"I'll draw up the offer," I said, grasping at some type of reality to pull me out of our cloud of sex. I had to drive after this, after all.

Derek dipped a thumb in the mess on his stomach and tasted it, which was so hot it had to be unholy.

"Cary," he said, his voice as warm and creamy as a hot chocolate on a snowy day. "I really like you."

And despite my fears and reservations and oppressive need for self-preservation, I said it back.

23

DEREK

"You know the rules. No drinking. No drugs. No parties. No orgies. These are the babysitting commandments I expect you to follow." Cal stood over his babysitter going over the rules.

Except, the babysitter was his husband.

"Are we clear?" Cal said to Russ.

"As clear as the glassware you incorrectly load into the dishwasher despite my multiple tutorials." Russ gave his husband a sweeter-than-sweet kiss on the cheek. "Have fun you two."

Cal and I were grabbing a brotherly bite to eat before meeting up with our friends at Mitch's bar. Apparently, he ran this weekly event called Musical Mondays where they played clips from musicals on the TVs and people sang along. Not usually my cup of tea, but we'd see how the night went.

"Thanks for watching the kids tonight. Don't tell anyone, but you're kind of the best." Cal cocked a loving eyebrow at his husband. He took his hand and squeezed it tight. "And bless your heart for thinking I actually paid attention to any of your dishwasher tutorials."

"Derek...he's all yours."

I drove us to C&J Pizza, which was a few blocks away from Stone's Throw Tavern. Cary was right. Their pizza remained primo delicious. Salty, buttery tomato sauce, hot cheese dripping with oil, and a crust that had to be folded, as pizza was intended to be eaten.

"The Hogan brothers. Back together. Causing trouble. Should we hold up a liquor store?" Cal asked.

"What?" I truly did not understand how his brain worked, but bless him for playing to the beat of his drum.

"I'm thinking of fun things straight guys like to do."

A fresh layer of sweat covered my hands. My heart began to amp up like a roller coaster clicking to the top.

"About that..." I put down my pizza, took a sip of soda. "Cal, I gotta tell you something."

"What is it?" he asked, fully serious.

"It's not bad," I clarified, though I appreciated his concern. "I'm fine. So is Jolene."

"Did you need help with the down payment for the new house?"

"No. I'm good on that front." Our offer was accepted on Sunday evening. Cary texted me with lots of emoji. "The owners wanted to get this done fast, so I think we can close by the end of the month."

I didn't know how the hell they were going to pack up and move out all their shit by then, but that was their problem to solve. And more importantly, I was stalling.

"Cal, I'm bi."

"You're by what?"

"No. I'm bi. Bisexual." It felt weird to say it out loud, to permanently give myself a label. Like any nickname, it would feel more comfortable the more I said it.

Cal was on a three-second delay as he processed the news. His response was more muted than I expected for a guy who preferred playing to the rafters on a daily basis. His mouth opened slightly, but he chose to stay quiet.

"Good. That's good."

"Surprised?" I asked jokingly.

"Uh, yeah. Kinda. Yeah." I wasn't used to Cal holding in his thoughts. It was unnerving and against the natural order of things.

"It's something I've known for a while, but I hadn't acted on it since I'd been with Paula."

"How long have you known about it?"

"If I'm being honest, probably high school. I definitely noticed some of my teammates' bodies in the locker room more than I should have. So I guess I knew about it on some level, and as time went on, I became more sure of it." And because I was in a sharing mood, I added this whopper: "And Cary and I are dating."

"Dating? Cary, as in my friend and your real estate agent?"

"Uh huh. It's new. And wonderful. We wouldn't have met were it not for you pushing me to buy a house. You've always wanted to be a matchmaker."

A pause fell between us, a very uncommon thing when talking to Cal. We had a relationship where we preferred constant noise to silence.

"Are you cool with this?" I was compelled to ask.

"Yeah. Yeah, of course. Just...processing." Cal was lost deep in thought. I wasn't used to my loud brother keeping everything in. This was not how I planned for any of this to go, and we hadn't even gotten to the Cary part yet.

"Cal, what's wrong? You're scaring me."

"Nothing's wrong. I'm sorry. I...I'm sorry that you didn't feel comfortable telling me earlier." A lash of pain creased his forehead.

"I guess I was worried about upstaging you."

"Were you?"

"I didn't want to steal your thunder." I cracked a smile, but Cal wasn't laughing. "I'm joking."

Then, something happened that I definitely did not, under any circumstances, expect. Cal's eyes watered up, and two fat tears trickled down his face.

"Hey. Hey, what's wrong?" I gave his hand a playful punch. "Cal, what's wrong?"

"I'm sorry. I'm being such a bitch. This is your big coming out moment, and I'm the one upstaging you. I'm sorry." He wiped away tears, and fresh ones came. They were tears that wouldn't listen to logic, that had to come whether we wanted them or not.

I handed him a napkin, then the napkin dispenser.

"Derek, having you back in town has made me realize how much I missed you all these years. You know, when we were younger, we were in two different worlds. And then right after graduation, you left for the other side of the country. I feel like I learned more about you from Mitch and Leo than from living under the same roof as you. And sure, we kept in touch with a call here or an email there, but it wasn't enough. I see that now. It wasn't enough. We weren't there for each other. There's this twenty-year gap in our relationship, and we can't get that time back. And the fact that you've known you were bisexual this whole time and didn't feel comfortable talking to me, your gay brother, about it... I'm sorry that we didn't have the kind of relationship that we should have."

Cal's teary face dared to break me. But I was the older brother. I had to stay strong. He was right. Having him nearby, being able to talk with him and joke with him has added richness to my life. I was getting to know my brother for the first time in our lives.

"It's my fault," I said. "It's difficult being the older sibling. Mom and Dad had no idea what the fuck they were doing. They made all their mistakes with me so that they could have their act together for you." My teenage years were filled with memories of arguing with them, of hearing them argue. I tried shielding Cal from it when we were little kids. While I loved our mom and dad, and they were good parents overall, I got the feeling they didn't want to be parents, but that was the only path forward for them. That was all they knew. "I wanted to get the hell out of Sourwood and forge my own life. I didn't mean to leave you behind."

"I think I was mad that you left, and so I was resolved to be on my own. And…it was hard. I made a lot of mistakes in my twenties. I'm so grateful for Josh and Russ because without them, my life could've gone in some really terrible directions." Cal fiddled with the napkin dispenser. "There were times when I could've used my big brother."

"I'm sorry." There were times when I could've used Cal. Loneliness was like looking up and realizing you were in a hole you couldn't climb out of. "It's water under the fucking bridge. I'm here now. We're still young…ish." I handed Cal a napkin from the dispenser, but he preferred to use his sleeve, just as he did as a little kid.

Cal nodded, getting himself under control. I reached across the table and squeezed his hand, letting him know I was here and I wasn't going anywhere. I never realized how much I needed family until I was back. It wasn't merely being with Cary that had made returning to Sourwood so special.

"And just so I'm clear," Cal said, sniffling away the last of his tears. "Aside from Cary obviously, I'm the first person you told? Not Leo and Mitch?"

Leave it to Cal to always be clambering for a starring role in something. He made me smile.

"I was going to tell Leo and Mitch when we got to the bar."

Cal's face lit up for a moment. "You do you. You come out on your own timetable and to whom."

"Like I wasn't going to tell you first."

"I'll still pretend to be surprised." Cal practiced surprised reactions, ranging from complete shock to more of a *Huh. Interesting* before settling on a supportive head nod. "How was that?"

"Perfect, Cal. You were perfect."

THE REST of the week was a whirlwind, and Cary and I didn't get a chance to meet up, which sucked because I could not stop thinking about him. Our texting back and forth was an extended foreplay, even before you added in all the peach and eggplant emojis we wound up sending each other. Cary was working to ensure we closed on the house before the new year. He and Hannah were also scrambling to track down new leads. The hustle never stopped.

With the first substantial snowfall this week came an uptick in car accidents as well as people using their fireplaces for the first time. It kept us at the firehouse busy. When I reached my days off, I relaxed for a little bit before Mitch dragged me to my first hockey practice in decades.

It wasn't as painful as I feared. We were all too old to be playing competitive hockey, and none of us had the speed or energy of our teenage selves, but it was damn fun being back on the ice. The cold of the rink smelled the same and instantly transported me back to my glory days. It took me a few plays to get into my old grooves, but it came back to me shockingly well. I glided around the rink, skates slicing through the ice, the cold brush of players whooshing by me amping my adrenaline. We shittalked each other, roughed each other up a little. We were all back on our bullshit.

After practice, a few of us went out for drinks at a pub next to the rink. We would've gone to Stone's Throw Tavern, but the space was rented out for a company Christmas party. Bill, Des, Hank, Mitch, and myself crammed ourselves around a high-top table, just as we'd crammed ourselves into a booth at Caroline's during our lunch period all those years ago.

The pub was crowded with mostly a younger crowd. A big square bar sat in the center. Multiple TVs played ESPN. We were all sore, but a good sore, one that reminded us that our bodies still worked.

"It's so odd coming here on a weeknight. Different crowd," said Hank, our goalie. When we were in high school, he would grow out his hair into a wild mane during the season. We used to call him Fabio. Seeing him bald today was a stark reminder of the passage of time.

"How so?" I asked.

"It's filled with young professionals," he said with disgust at the crowd's youthful energy. "On weekends, this is the best spot to pick up divorcées."

Hank rubbed his hands together. He was recently one of them. He and his ex-wife shared a fifteen-year-old son who was smarter than all of us put together.

"Hank, I don't have enough alcohol in me to hear about your recent dating adventures," said Bill.

"Well, we can talk about your dating adventures for a change. Oh wait, one must actually go on dates to have stories to talk about." Hank tossed a peanut into his mouth.

Bill rolled his eyes at the implication, and something told me this was far from the first time Hank had brought it up.

"You need to step into your divorced dad power. These women spent decades in unfulfilled, sexless marriages. They're wild in the sac," said Hank, who turned to Des. "They'd even love you and your one ball."

Des punched his arm back, playfully but with force. "Me and one ball could run circles around your pair."

"Then come back with me on a Saturday night, dude!"

Des rolled his eyes. He was a hell of a defenseman who was like an attack dog on the ice. He'd beaten testicular cancer a few years ago, and he'd already cracked a few jokes tonight about having one ball. He'd told me that humor was a necessary element to fighting cancer. He was truly indestructible.

"Why does every conversation come back to Des's one ball?" Bill asked, a no-nonsense look etched on his face. He was our captain, just as he had been in high school, a natural-born leader who'd been grizzled even as a seventeen-year-old. He'd had a rough family life and channeled that frustration into being a ferocious hockey player. Having a daughter had softened him, but only a little.

"One ball to rule them all," Des said, smiling into his beer.

"I'd rather hear about that than Hank's sex life," said Mitch.

"And I'd rather hear about Hank's sex life than *A Mountain Man Christmas*," I said.

"Me, too," groaned Mitch. "That actor Lucien McDipshit broke an aged bottle of Glenfidditch on his last day of shooting."

"Was he trying to spin it *Cocktail*-style?" Des asked.

"No. He was holding the bottle in a scene and dropped it. He said he overmoisturized his hands that morning."

The film shoot was a month of hell for Mitch, but on the bright side, it would provide hilarious stories that would last a lifetime. It felt good laughing with buddies. I'd missed the camaraderie of teammates.

"Back to the business at hand." Bill wrapped his knuckles on the table. "We need a name."

"What about the Has Beens?" Hank asked.

"Who said we were has beens?" I asked in mock offense. "We're just getting started."

"Speak for yourself." Mitch rubbed his leg, old injuries from high school coming back.

"All those in favor of being called Has Beens, raise your hand," said Bill, although by his tone, we all knew where he stood with that name. None of us, not even Hank, voted for it.

"Where are your bright ideas, Bill?" asked Hank.

Bill shot him a glare that dared him to ask that again.

"What about the Comebacks?" I tossed out.

Instantly, a silence took over our table as the guys mulled it over.

"That's not half-bad," said Des.

"I don't hate it," said Hank.

Mitch nodded along.

We all looked to Bill. He was the decider, unofficially.

Bill raised his glass. "The Comebacks!"

We clinked pints in the center of the table.

We spent the rest of the time catching up. Mitch had to leave early on as his daughter Ellie was coming into town with his granddaughter. Hank talked with pride about a math competition his son had competed in, even if he couldn't explain what kind of math it was. We chatted about sports, about old teachers and memories of past games. Time whizzed by and also rewound, as if we were chilling in the locker room after a day of classes.

"So are you still staying with your brother and his family?" Bill asked me.

"Yeah, but not for long. I'm in the process of closing on a house for me and Jolene."

"Get ready to sign a million documents at the closing. I've never signed my fucking name so many times in my life," said Des.

"I'm impressed you could spell your name." Hank laughed at his own joke.

"Hank, you are the least qualified person at this table to be saying that." Des arched a thick eyebrow. "Do you remember what you got on your SAT's?"

"Ketchup," Hank deadpanned. None of us were academic all-stars, that was for sure, Hank the least of us.

"I might be looking at selling my place next year. Who did you use?" Des asked.

"Cary Perkowski at Prescott Realty." A smile quirked on my lips. I'd forgotten there was a time when Cary was simply my real estate agent. "He was good. Very diligent."

I debated telling the guys we were dating. That would drop the whole "I'm bi" bomb, and I might've needed another drink in me for that to happen.

"Why does that name sound familiar?" Hank asked.

"He went to South Rock," I said.

"Isn't he that gearhead guy?" Hank flicked another peanut into his mouth.

"Gearhead? What the fuck are you talking about?" Hearing the name ignited a match of fury in my chest. I tried playing it off like Hank was crazy and changing the subject. "Where are you thinking of moving to, Des?"

"I think I remember hearing about that," Des said, ignoring me. "Wait, what happened?"

"He tried to have sex with a car? Something like that?" Hank cocked his head.

"It's bullshit. Drop it." I didn't want to flip out on my newly reconnected teammates, but I wanted to convey I was serious. Unfortunately, that only seemed to egg them on.

"He went down on a gear shift, I think," said Hank.

"How the hell is that possible?" asked Des.

"Well, it obviously wasn't in a Chevy. Here, he probably did something like this." Hank grabbed a cocktail napkin and a pen from his pocket.

"Hank, what the fuck are you doing? Seriously, drop it." I grabbed for the pen, but Hank used Bill's back as his surface for drawing.

"There." Hank handed it to Bill, who showed it to Des. While crude, it accurately showed a guy's mouth taking the bulbous gear shift.

"Shit," said Bill.

"That's impressive. And weird." Des arched an eyebrow.

"What the fuck is your problem?" I dove across the table, yanked the napkin out of Bill's hand, and shoved it into my pocket where they wouldn't dare reach. "It didn't happen! It was a dumb, made up story that Cary has had to live with ever since. How would you like it if some asshole made up a story about one of your kids?" The guys hung their heads. I'd ruined our night, but I didn't care. "He's a good guy, and he doesn't deserve to have this shit follow him around forever."

I bolted out of my chair and grabbed my coat. Maybe it was a bad idea reconnecting with these guys. Was this what Cary had to deal with on a daily basis? Constant fear that this story bubbled under every interaction he had? He didn't deserve this, any of this.

"And by the way, he's not just my real estate agent. He's my boyfriend. I'm bi, you fuckwads."

24

CARY

Christmas was around the corner, but Hannah and I were already thinking of next year. We spent our morning putting together an invite list and email invitation for a kick off party to meet new potential clients.

That was the thing about sales. You could be on top, but when the ball dropped on January first, we'd be back to zero. And we'd be ready to push that boulder up the hill all over again.

We weren't celebrating yet. We were still working on Derek's closing and aiming to have that done by the twenty-ninth. Once it was a done deal, then we'd officially end the year on top.

And the next stop, Bali.

But we weren't thinking of Bali yet. We weren't counting our chickens before they hatched.

"How is the invitation coming?" I spun my chair to her side of our cubicle and looked over her shoulder, where I did not see an email invitation being typed out. "Hannah, are you looking up swimsuits?"

"Maybe. We're taking a family trip to Florida in February?"

I cocked a dubious eyebrow her way. Those swimsuits with plunging necklines weren't for visiting her in-laws in Florida. They were for lounging poolside with cocktails and no kids in Bali.

"Let's concentrate. We don't have it yet." Who knew what kind of last minute shenanigans the Morris brothers could be pulling right this moment.

"You didn't hear?" She licked her lips. Juicy gossip incoming.

"Hear what?"

"Tad and Chad were all set for their clients to close on a luxury condo, but the deal fell through because their clients were caught lying on their mortgage application." Hannah gave a real Grinch-like smile, and I'd allow such pettiness. The brothers Morris deserved it for all their underhanded practices like trying to steal clients and pushing people to buy way more house than they could afford.

"That is...a shame. Mortgage fraud is a serious problem," I said, straining to keep a straight face. But hell, I couldn't keep a straight anything.

We burst out laughing, and watching each other laugh made us laugh even more. We dabbed at the happy tears prickling our eyes.

"So, who do you think you'll take with you to Bali?" she asked.

"Uh...not sure." I hadn't told her that I was fucking my client, and that it wasn't *just* fucking with me and Derek. At least, I hoped it wasn't. There was a lot to catch her up on, and now wasn't the place to do it.

But as luck would have it, Derek strode through the front doors of PRG a little while later. My heart raced when the office admin let me know he was waiting in the lobby. What was he doing here? And why did my mind immediately assume it was something bad?

Derek lumbered through the sea of cubicles in our office. He looked very out of place, his large, bulky body figuring out all these right angles of corporate America. He was my rugged man, and no building could box him in.

"Hi Derek!" Hannah said when he got to our cube.

"Good morning. Thought you would like these." Derek handed me a large cup of Caroline's coffee and Hannah a large cup of Starbucks.

"Derek, you spoil us." Hannah gulped down a huge sip of her gross, overcommercialized coffee. "To what do we owe this honor?"

"Just wanted to say hi." He flashed his eyes to me, setting my chest afire. Was this what it felt like to be with someone? Knowing they could pop in at any moment to say hi and dazzle you with their gorgeous smile? I was here for it.

"Hi," I stammered. I was still getting used to Derek noticing me.

"I was in the neighborhood. How's all the closing stuff coming along?" he asked.

"Good. I've scheduled the inspection for this week." I could feel my face turn red. Could Hannah feel the sexual vibes between us? Could I not feel them and go back to being my professional self? Would I ever reach out a point when I wasn't full-on googly eyes for Derek Hogan?

"Well, about that. I've actually decided to work with the Morris brothers. Yeah, I thought about it, and it would be best."

I didn't know where the hell they came from, but Tad and Chad popped up at the mention of their name.

"What's this?" Tad asked.

"Derek. Good to see you again, bro!" Chad clapped him on the shoulder.

"Nah. I'm just fucking with you guys." Derek smiled and shook his head.

The broad shoulders of the Morris brothers slumped. They slunk away, presumably under the bridge where they'd been hiding.

"Couldn't resist doing that." Derek entered our cube and sat on my desk. Usually, I would invite him into a conference room, but we'd broken down so many client-agent walls already.

"Derek, do you know anyone who might be thinking of buying or selling a house in the new year? We're having a referral party," Hannah said.

"Not off the top of my head. But I'll give it some thought." Derek glanced at me while he spoke. The sexual tension flared between us, but also something more romantic. "That's a nice shirt, Cary."

"Thanks. I bought it myself."

"You have good taste."

"I know I do."

"Someone's cocky this morning," Derek said, his voice dropping to a growl.

"Okay. That's it." Hannah put down her coffee. "How long has this been going on?"

"What?" I asked, feigning innocence.

"Oh stop. People don't banter like this unless you've seen each other naked." Damn, she was good. Hannah had the ability to suss out the truth from her small children with only a stern look. It seemed those powers transferred here, too.

"We're not breaking any rules," I sputtered out. "I'm allowed to have sex with my clients."

I clamped a hand over my mouth. There were times when I could be smooth and operate in the real world. This was not one of them.

Derek rubbed my back. "What Cary means to say is that yes, we've been intimate."

Hannah's eyes burst open in surprise. "Cary!"

"I'm sorry. It just happened. Over and over and over again."

"If it's any consolation, Cary tried his best to resist." Derek interlocked our fingers. "I couldn't. Your business partner is just too damn cute."

I gazed up at him, and he gazed back. And the offices of PRG melted away for a moment.

Hannah's face softened.

"Are you mad?" I asked her.

"Are you still planning to close on the twenty-ninth?"

"Yes."

"Of course I'm not mad!" She playfully smacked my arm. Playfully, but with some force behind it. She probably was also relieved that this didn't mess up the sale.

"Would it be all right if I borrowed your business partner for a second?" Derek massaged my shoulder, his firm grip soothing me.

Hannah nodded yes. "In between all your fawning all over each other, think about anyone you know who might be in the market for a house."

"I will." Derek leaned down close to my ear. "Is there a conference room we could go to?"

"Uh huh." My first thought was that we were going to fuck on a conference table, but then I realized my life wasn't a total porno. Only occasionally.

I walked us down the hall with a feeling that Derek was

checking out my ass the whole time. I might have put in an extra shake in my step to give him a show.

We entered the conference room where once upon a time he'd been a potential client and I'd been his potential agent. Derek shut the door behind us.

"We are not having sex on this conference room table," I blurted out. What was with me blurting out comments about sex today? I had forgotten how to play it cool. Fortunately, Derek was amused. "There were rumors that two associates had sex on a conference room table during a holiday party, but I don't know if it was this one. And I don't know how it's relevant to whatever we're about to discuss. And I don't know why I'm still talking."

Derek shut me up with a soft kiss, a kiss that was full of warmth but would not be a gateway to sexytimes today.

"It's a good thing I love the sound of your voice because you talk a lot," he said.

"Thanks?" I smoothed out my shirt and gestured for Derek to take a seat, which he did not. "So what's up?"

"Are you free tonight?" he asked.

I mentally checked over my schedule, which included binging a new show that everyone was talking about while scrolling on my phone. I had a very active social life.

"I am."

"Good. Because I want to take you on a date."

"Uh. Sure. There's a good restaurant that people rave about..."

Derek shook his head no, a smirk hitting his lips. "I have something else in mind."

"Oh? Like what?"

"You'll find out tonight. And to answer your next question, it's not sex. Or just sex."

"I didn't suspect that at all," I lied.

Derek wrapped his fist on the table twice. "I'll pick you up at six."

"You'll pick me up? So this is like a date-date?"

"As opposed to just a date?" he asked.

I didn't know why the idea of a date seemed so strange. Perhaps because our only encounters had been fucking in model homes and one stargazing session. People went on dates with the intention of forging a relationship. Derek and I were working because we'd done our own thing. Were we going to ruin it with a proper date?

Derek peered at me, as if he were actively reading my mind. But it didn't take psychic abilities to see that underneath the great wardrobe and professional competency, I was a mess.

"Are you sure you don't just want to fuck on the conference table?" I shrugged.

"Cary, I like you. And when people like each other, they go on dates." Derek rubbed my arms. "Why are you hesitant?"

"What if I'm like...a bad date?" It was a statement that made perfect sense in my head but wasn't as solid when said aloud.

Derek gave me a sweet eye roll. Bless this man for putting up with my anxiety. "Cary, I hate to break it to you, but you're wonderful. I like you, and I want to spend more time with you."

I felt myself blush. Compliments would always be weird. But I said fuck it and let myself trust Derek.

"Pick me up at six fifteen," I said.

"Deal." Derek took my chin in his rugged hands and planted another soft kiss on my lips, which despite it being chaste, made me think about all the hot things we could do on this conference table.

AT SIX FIFTEEN, Derek pulled up in his truck. Did anyone else find men in trucks super hot? Or did I, an east coast suburbanite, have some kind of country boy fetish?

Derek wore a gingham button down under a navy blazer with pressed jeans. My guess was Russ did the ironing. He was a few steps up from his usual attire, and his beard was nice and trimmed. I couldn't wait to feel it on my inner thighs later.

"You clean up nice," I said.

"Just trying to keep up with you. Get in." He nodded his head for me to join him in his big, honking truck. He curled an arm behind my headrest and drove off.

The first stop was an Italian restaurant that overlooked the water. But the Hudson River couldn't hold our attention. Derek and I looked at each other the whole time. We talked about...I didn't even know what. It was one of those nights where the conversation poured out of us, like one of those champagne pyramids spilling from one topic to the next. I knew that I could talk, but so could Derek. He had a lot to say. I wondered if people were so used to assuming he was the strong, silent type that they didn't try to engage him that much.

"Are you full?" he asked as he signed the check.

"I'm satiated. Italian food can sometimes put me into a food coma, but not tonight." I didn't want to be in a food coma and miss anything with him. And also...I wanted to be prepared for any activities that might come later.

"Good. Because now we're onto the physical part of the date."

My dick shot up in my pants. Even though we'd had sex

multiple times, there would always be a part of me that felt like each time was the first with him.

"You don't beat around the bush. I like that in a man." I held up my wine glass and raised an eyebrow, apparently channeling the great Samantha Jones.

"I brought hoodies for us to stay warm."

"Oh...wait, huh?" Was hoodies slang for condoms? How much of our changing lexicon was I missing not being on TikTok?

Derek closed the check and gave me a wink. "Let's go, Perkowski."

"I'm actually confused now. Where are we going?"

"You'll see."

25

CARY

"Why are we at a hockey rink?" I asked when his truck pulled up to the warehouse-looking building.

"Welcome to the physical part of the date. Ice skating."

I blinked at him. Derek hadn't known me long, but I thought he would've inferred that I had zero athletic ability outside of an elliptical.

"We're going ice skating?"

"Yeah. It'll be fun." Derek pulled two ratty South Rock hoodies from his backseat. Hoodies were not slang for condoms. They were actual hoodies, and they would keep us warm on the ice.

Because we were going ice skating.

"Derek, it shouldn't be a surprise that I suck at ice skating."

He tipped his head at me, amused at my comment, the outside lights catching his face just right.

"You don't suck at ice skating. You merely haven't done it enough times. Oh, hey. That was a Caryism!" He gave himself a tiny fist pump, which was very dorky and very adorable. "When was the last time you did it?"

"When I was at Cory Washington's birthday party in sixth grade. I was the kid who clung to the wall and took baby steps on the ice, and then when I finally built up the confidence to glide, I instantly fell on my ass."

"I won't let you fall."

Such a swoontastic line. Why did it have to be in the context of ice skating?

"I'm going to pass," I said, staring down the building, waves of humiliating childhood memories hitting me like a supersized hurricane that had become all too common nowadays.

"What size shoe are you?" Derek said, blatantly ignoring me.

"Can't we take a leisurely stroll instead?"

He interlocked his fingers with mine. "Cary, do you trust me?

I squeezed his fingers. Derek had come up with this lovely date for us. I wouldn't let my neuroses ruin it. They would have to chill in a mental waiting room for a few hours.

"Let's ice skate," I said, trying to play the part of a cool date.

The building was dark and empty when we entered.

"This is how horror movies start," I said.

"One second. Stay right here." Derek kissed my hand and then walked off somewhere, leaving me alone in the dark.

"This is definitely how horror movies start," I shouted. I used my phone's light to scan my surroundings. I was by a wall with a bulletin board covered in flyers offering lessons and advertising different leagues. I might as well have been in a foreign country. This was pure athlete territory.

All of my hesitation and fear about ice skating vanished when the lights turned on. Twinkly lights had been strung around the perimeter of the rink. A disco ball reflected color across the ice. Disco balls belonged above ice rinks—not above beds in creepy *Shrek* shrines.

And there, in the center of the ice, hands in his pockets, looking as good as he did in the halls of high school, was Derek, skating toward me.

"Did you do this?" I asked, not wanting to blink. I wanted to file the image of Derek set against glowing lights away in my core memories. "Are we trespassing?"

"I know the rink owner. Same guy who owned it years ago."

"Is this where your old guy hockey team is practicing?"

"I decided not to join." A pained look crossed his face. "Too much of a time commitment."

With his crazy firefighting schedule plus caring for a daughter, I couldn't imagine how he did anything. It made me extra grateful that he carved time out for this date.

"Cal helped me string the lights."

"Now I'm really impressed."

"I hope you don't mind, but I told him about us."

"Wow."

Telling people about us meant he was serious, something that I technically already knew, but had to keep reminding myself of. While I appreciated my mind's fierce self-preservation, I wished I could make it back off at times.

"I would drop leaflets from the sky if I could." He skated closer, dipping his hands around my waist. I fit perfectly inside his bushy forearms. "I like you, Cary Perkowski."

"I like you, too."

"I know." He winked at me before glancing back at the rink. "Shall we?"

I wanted to kick myself for being a baby about skating. I wasn't going to be on the ice alone. Derek would be there beside me. He was right. He wouldn't let me fall.

"Let's skate," I said.

Derek grabbed me a pair of skates. He offered to lace them up for me, but I could do it myself. I wasn't the damsel in distress in this relationship. He did help me stand up, though. My wobbliness made me regret not getting into rollerblading when I was a kid.

He played music from his phone, a playlist of Throwback Thursday '90s jams. I breathed in the scent of him on the hoodie I was wearing. We held hands and skated around the rink. As expected, I was spastic and tried to take baby steps on the ice.

"Sorry," I muttered. I was really trying to concentrate and not make a fool of myself.

"Push off with each foot." Derek left me stranded so he could demonstrate. He glided across the ice with the burly hunch of his back that all hockey players had. I was too distracted by how cuddly he looked in his hoodie to pay attention to his feet.

"Now you try it."

Here went nothing. I closed my eyes and channeled my inner Adam Rippon. And then I thought about how wonderful his friendship with Gus Kenworthy was during the Olympics. It was a rare example of gay friendship in the media. Were they still friends?

"Cary?"

I blinked my eyes and remembered I was supposed to be skating, not having parasocial thoughts about gay Olympians.

As predicted, as soon as I pushed off, I fell over. I didn't even have the grace to fall on my ass. I belly flopped onto the ice, a sheet of freezing cold residue slicking my Derek-scented hoodie. My fingers burned from the frigidness of the ice.

Derek squatted next to me and offered a hand up. How he was able to squat while ice skating was a feat I could only dream of mastering.

"Why is there a blade at the front of the skate?" I asked, pointing at the jagged metal.

"It's a toe pick. It helps you to stop."

"Mission accomplished."

"Let's try it again. This time, I'll help you."

Was Derek into me being an oaf on the ice? I preferred being someone who had their shit together, who could pull himself up.

"What are you doing?" I asked as Derek spun around to face me.

He held out his hands, a sweet smile greeting me when I stood up. I could stare at that face all day.

Derek held my hands and skated backwards, slowly pulling me around the ice. I felt like I was floating, my body having no control over my limbs. I gazed into his dark, swirly, warm eyes. They kept me safe.

"Doing good, Cary."

I built up a whisper of confidence, and I used it to try pushing off again. This time, I kept my foot straight, not pointing down, so I didn't toe pick onto my ass. And I did it. I was floating *and* gliding! Derek pushed off in time with me. We were dancing. We were flying. My heart pounded in my ears.

I could do this forever with him.

My fears and reservations slipped away as I pushed off,

moving further and further from the scared, lonely man I'd been for most of my adult life.

Derek slowed down, and I sped up so I could get closer to him, so I could kiss him. This was a moment meant to be seized.

"Oh, shit," he said just before our lips touched.

I followed his tender gaze to our hands clasped together. Only one of them was covered in blood.

"Shit!" I yelled.

Drops of blood had dripped onto the ice, leaving a breadcrumb trail of red around the rink.

"Shit," said Derek, the word of the moment. "I think this is how horror movies end."

"Not to make things even creepier, but is this your blood or mine?"

When we pulled back our hands, I found the culprit, a cut on my ring finger. I must've cut myself when I fell. Or maybe when I laced up my skates. The cold and the adrenaline rush of being with Derek kept me from feeling the wound.

I looked down and, because I was incapable of embarrassing myself at every turn, discovered a dotted trail of blood down my pants.

"It's a good thing we're not in the ocean, right?" I joked.

"Let's get you bandaged up."

"I don't even feel it!" I said, as if that would make this better.

Derek cracked a wide smile and chuckled to himself. "The red of the blood really pops against the ice."

"A Caryism? When I'm mutilated?"

"You'll be fine." He took my clean hand and skated us off the ice. He found a first aid kit and had me sit on the bench.

Derek proceeded to clean out and bandage my cut, which was surprisingly minor despite what it produced.

"I'm sorry about getting it on you." I nodded at the red stains on the sleeve of his hoodie.

"We'll throw it in the wash."

"What about the rink?"

"They use the Zamboni first thing every morning to clean the ice. You should see some of the bloodshed hockey games produced. This is nothing."

I was relieved but also concerned for all hockey players out there.

———

MY MEDDLESOME FINGER didn't ruin the night, though. There was still a buzz between us as Derek drove me home.

He parked in front of my house. A plethora of thoughts circled through my always-buzzing mind. Make that a myriad. Tonight was magical. Usually, my time with Derek was limited, like there was a running timer on our interactions. But tonight, we could breathe. We could luxuriate in each other.

I really liked Derek. I thought that I wasn't built for relationships, but he was proving me wrong. This was the greatest night I'd ever spent with another man. Maybe I wasn't a lost cause with love.

Love? Did you just use the L-word, Cary?
Maybe I did...

"I had a great night." He kissed my bandaged finger.

"Me, too. Not even blood could ruin it."

He turned my hand over and kissed the center of my palm, unlocking an erogenous zone I didn't know existed.

"Did you want to come in?" I asked. Even though we'd

seen each other naked plenty, my heart pounded with nerves.

"There's something I want to do tonight." He kissed my wrist and moved upward. My arm was all his. "I want to make love to you in a bed."

I laughed at the remark for a second before I realized that we had never done it in a bed. All of our sex had been heated and rushed in cramped quarters.

"I don't want to worry about someone barging in. I want to take my time with you." He kissed up my arm. I didn't have the patience to wait for him to hit my shoulder, then neck, then mouth. I pulled his face to mine and locked our lips in a heated kiss.

I led us to my door. It was whatever the opposite of the walk of shame was. Derek followed behind.

A few minutes later, we were in my bedroom, taking our time undressing each other. I made myself slow down so I could enjoy seeing Derek's body come into view. There was no invisible timer counting down, no boiling pot of sexual tension spilling over. This was something different.

"This does feel nice," I said when I sat on my bed. "Bathroom tile is not forgiving on the back."

"That's for damn sure." Derek gazed down at me, this big man making me feel pocket-sized and protected.

I unbuttoned his shirt and buried my face in his nest of chest hair, breathing in his manly scent. I could live here. Derek shucked off his shirt. I kissed down his chest and stomach. Fuck six-pack abs. The little belly Derek had was much sexier. It was real. It was him.

His erection pressed through his jeans. Yes, we were supposed to go slow, but when a beefy dick was literally staring me in the face, there was only so slow I could go.

Derek ruffled his hand through my hair, letting out a

deep groan above me as I pushed down his pants and boxers.

"Take it, Cary," he whispered.

His hot cock filled my mouth, hitting the back of my throat. Derek grunted above me in all his primal glory. His hand behind my head lightly pushed me forward, but I didn't need any direction. I could do this all by myself. I moaned against his dick, our sounds and bodies perfectly in sync. My fingers grazed the hair of his meaty thighs, before moving behind and grabbing onto his ass.

He thrust into my mouth. Looked like I wasn't the only one unable to go slow.

I pushed back and caught my breath. Derek bore into me with heavy-lidded, heat-soaked eyes. He pushed me backward. He undid the buttons of my shirt, his thick palm sliding down my chest.

We quickly got my pants off. Derek lay on top of me, our naked bodies stacked, dicks rubbing together. He kissed me deep and hard, exploring the contours of my mouth.

"This feels so good," he said, rolling back onto the bed. He let out a comfortable sigh as he dug into the springs of my mattress.

"Are we having sex or shopping for a new bed?" I asked.

"This is a really nice bed. Better than the pull out sofa I've been sleeping on."

"I sprang for a top-of-the-line mattress. I spend one third of my life in bed, so I better be comfortable. There's a great mattress store just off the highway—wait." I sat up. "Why is this happening again? Less talking. More fucking."

"Get over here." Derek threw me back onto the bed, tossed my legs in the air. Then, just as I dreamed about during dinner, his bearded face found its way to my soft thighs, then to my hole. His prickly hairs rubbed against my sensitive opening as he flicked his tongue inside.

"Yes. God, yes." I sounded like such a damn cliché, but when one received this much pleasure, one's verbal skills plummeted. Heat and lust built inside my core as his slippery tongue slid in and out of my ass. His rough fingers dug into my thighs. I balled the comforter in my fist. His mouth went from my ass to my dick, hitting me with one bolt of pleasure after another. I was dizzy, lightheaded, doing my absolute best to not explode. Derek took my cock like it was nothing. (And it wasn't nothing!) The hairs of his beard prickled at the tops of my inner thighs.

"You are leaking like crazy," he said of my dick.

"Gee, I fucking wonder why."

"I can't wait to fuck you and make you come," he said in a raspy growl that was part-promise, part-threat.

I wanted him to fuck me right off my uber-comfortable bed.

Derek sat up and pulled me onto his lap. I grinded against his cock, my hole aching to be filled. The teasing of his head pressing against my opening was even more exhilarating than the actual deed.

"Need you inside me," I gasped out.

He had the audacity to crack a smile.

"What's so funny?"

"You."

"Not something I want to hear during sex."

"I love how you make me laugh, Cary."

He said love and Cary in the same sentence. It got me wondering...could he love more than my laugh? Was I someone who could be loved, genuinely loved, no-holds-barred, take-me-as-I-am loved?

Derek reached behind me and opened my nightstand

drawer where I kept my lube. I was about to ask how he knew it was there, but where else would it be?

My cock got harder just listening to him slick up his erection, just knowing that soon he would spear into me. I wrapped my arms around him and kissed his salty lips as he pressed two lubed-up fingers inside me. I rocked back, letting him go deeper. If I kept this up, I would come before he got a chance to plant his flag.

"You're fucking begging for it." His bearded cheeks bunched into a smile.

"I'm being sexy. Stop smiling."

Then, because he was pure evil, he ran his fingers along my neck, hitting that one spot that could make me scream out laughing.

"No tickling when you're about to enter me."

"Fine." Derek's eyes got lost in me, staring into my face with a mix of amusement and deep care, like he was committing these moments to memory with each passing second. "I can't wait to wake up with you tomorrow morning."

I was about to ask who was watching Jolene, but I trusted he had a plan in place. I forced myself to get the fuck out of my head and live in the present, where gearhead and anxiety and my horrible track record with love didn't exist. All that existed was Derek and me.

I threw my head back with abandon as Derek entered me. His thrusts were deep and slow, drawing every last drop of agonizing pleasure out of our connection. He didn't take his eyes off me as we fucked. We'd kiss, then stare at each other, kiss some more, gaze some more. I didn't know it was possible to give myself this completely and freely, to let myself be this vulnerable and trust it would be okay.

"Derek..."

He nodded, his calloused thumb stroking my cheek. "Come for me, Cary."

I collapsed onto him, and he held me tight as I emptied onto his furry stomach. He pumped into me until he came himself, a loud grunt tearing through the silence.

We lay there in silence for a moment. I hugged him tight, listening to his heartbeat.

This was more than the best date ever. It was more than a perfect evening. It was everything.

I woke up early the next morning, tangled in Derek's arms. It was dark outside. While there was no place else I'd rather be, my bladder had other ideas. I extracted myself from his grip and tiptoed to the bathroom.

After, I went into the living room and found our coats on the floor, thrown there as we'd made our way into the bedroom. I relived those moments in my mind over and over, goosebumps littering my skin each time.

Even though I wanted to get back into bed with him this instant, I couldn't very well leave our coats on the floor. I wasn't a neat freak, more like a neat weirdo. I picked up Derek's thick jacket and threw it over the sofa. A cocktail napkin fluttered out.

When I turned it over, my past collided with my present, a pounding car crash that jolted me out of my afterglow.

As much as I tried to outrun it, gearhead was alive and well.

26

DEREK

I pulled Cary closer to me, a salve of warmth on this cold, cold morning. But there was no Cary, only his pillows, which were plush. But they weren't him. Shooting rays of yellow sun slashed through the blinds, catching my eye.

Cary did seem like an early riser, one of those guys who didn't sleep that much yet were always refreshed. My dick hardened at the thought of us being awake again, so that we could go again. God, I wanted to wrap him in my arms, smell his skin, feel the thick comforter around our naked bodies as I slid inside him.

I slipped on my pair of boxers and headed into the living room. My morning wood was ever present, but I didn't try and hide it.

Cary was hunched in front of the fridge. I wrapped my arms around him and let my dick poke him hello.

"Morning," I said.

"Morning," he mumbled back, no reaction to my hug or my poke.

"What's for breakfast? Did you want to go out?"

"Don't you have to get home to Jolene?" He kept his head in the fridge searching for something way in the back.

"She's going to the children's museum with Russ, Cal, and the boys. I don't have to be at the firehouse until noon." In other words, we had time for breakfast and more fucking and lots more cuddling. I didn't want to take my hands off Cary until the last possible minute. "You probably know some cute brunch place."

"Not really feeling brunchy today."

"Fuck it. Let's just go to Caroline's."

I kissed the spot where his neck met his shoulder. Cary stood up and shut the fridge, orange juice in hand. Oddly, his head was still turned away from me.

I spun him around and kissed him good morning. There was a coldness on the other end, like when I was mid-sentence on the phone before I realized the call was disconnected, something that happened a lot in Alaska, land of the dead zones.

"Good morning." I kissed him again, hoping that was a fluke and the bright, spunky Cary would return.

Yet his eyes darted anywhere but at me, looking for an emergency exit.

"I have some toast if you want it, but I can't do breakfast today. I have so much to do," Cary said. I might've been out of the dating scene for over a decade, but I still knew a blow off line when I heard one.

What the hell was going on? Did we have different nights last night?

"I'm good on the toast," I said, waving it off when he offered me the twisted up bag. "Are you okay?"

"Yep. Just have a lot to do."

I began to lean in for a kiss since he was close, but he took a small step backward, then pivoted around me to grab a glass from the cupboard. He was in constant motion, something very noticeable in this small kitchen.

He poured himself orange juice. He'd only taken out one glass.

"I had an amazing time last night. It was a date for the ages." I winked at him.

Cary nodded tensely, as if he were trying to get through polite conversation. What in the actual fuck?

"How's your finger?" I went to lift his hand, the ring finger swaddled in a bandage, but he reached for his glass of orange juice instead.

"Good. Fine. It was only grazed by the blade. It'll heal nicely." Cary took a tentative sip of his drink. Tension stifled the room. Something was *off*.

Flashbacks rocked my head. This was how Paula acted the final few months of our marriage. I was too tired, too busy, too willfully ignorant to see the signs, but they were there. The distance, the coldness, the mood swings. Her attitude toward me would change on a dime. Things would be fine until I set her off for some unknowable reason. She would be polite but not much else until she was tired of even doing that.

Was that how things would be here between us? Cary would act like he loved me one night and then push me away in the morning?

"I'm going to get showered and dressed," Cary said, not meeting my eyes. He went to leave the kitchen, but I blocked him with my arm thrown across the entrance.

"I'm not moving my hand until you tell me what the hell is going on." I was too old, I'd been through too much, and fuck, I was still too tired to deal with this shit.

"Nothing."

I shot him a steely look. *Don't you even give that passive-aggressive bullshit.*

"Cary, I had one of the best nights of my life with you. And I know you had yourself a good time, too. If I did something wrong, we can talk about it. But right now, I am really fucking confused."

He sighed, as if the energy to play this game was wearing him out. He removed a piece of paper from the pocket of his robe and handed it over.

That was when I realized it wasn't paper. It was a napkin, a familiar napkin.

"Shit. Where did you find this?"

"It fell out of your coat pocket. I wasn't looking for it."

The crude gearhead drawing stared back at me.

"I didn't draw this."

"Then why was it in your coat pocket? Why were you holding onto it?"

"A guy on the hockey team drew it when we were out. I grabbed it—"

"Why was he drawing it?"

"He was being an asshole." Hank, Bill, and Des had each texted me to apologize about the other night. They'd seemed sincere, but I wasn't sure if I could let it go.

"You said you weren't joining the hockey team, but you went out drinking with them?"

"It was before—one of them brought up—but I shut it down." I couldn't unravel the story in my head. Words failed me. Cary's questions were sharp pinpricks keeping me on edge.

"What did they say?" He was a cop grilling a witness, wanting to get every detail. "Let me guess. I was that weirdo who fucked a car. Because my fucking reputation always precedes me. And there was probably a team member who didn't know who I was, but wanted to hear the gearhead story because it's so crazy. And what better way than using visual aids?"

"I told them to shut up! I told them it was bullshit. I ripped this out of their hands the second I realized what they were doing," I said of the napkin, balled in his fist. "I would never make fun of you."

"If you heard about this story back in the day, you would have."

"Maybe I wouldn't. I don't know what I would've done, and neither do you. But you keep bringing that up like it's some trump card you can use to push me away when you get scared."

I wanted to believe I would've stood up for Cary in high school. We weren't in that timeline, though. We were here, in this moment, and right now, I was watching the man of my dreams pulling away.

Cary shook his head, his jaw tight, fury blazing in his eyes. I'd never seen him angry like this, like all his nervous energy had caught on fire. "Still. Twenty years later. This story, this lie, is my scarlet letter, and no matter what outfit I put on, it's there, following me around. I can tell people the truth. I can laugh it off and play the good sport. I can tell people to shut up. It doesn't matter because it doesn't go away. Even after I found someone, someone who made me start to believe I wasn't meant to be alone...the scarlet letter remains." Cary waved the napkin in the air, almost as if it were a white flag.

"I'm sorry, Cary." I wished I could take this pain away from him. I wished I could endure it for him. "I would never let anyone talk about you like that. Please believe me."

It was like I was stretching my arms as far out as they

could go, but he was just out of reach. He wouldn't meet my eyes.

"When you look at me, do you think of gearhead?" he asked, his voice raspy with old wounds infused with new pain.

"No. I think of the man I want to be with."

"I hate that they were talking about me."

"If anyone ever brings it up again, I'm going to body check them so hard, they'll be praying for the penalty box." I put a hand on his shoulder. Contact. He didn't shrug me off. "Cary, it's okay."

He looked up at me, tears clouding his eyes. "I don't know if I can do this."

My heart plummeted through the floor. The thought of having a wonderful future yanked away from me was a gut punch.

"Cary...please..."

"Am I overreacting? I don't know. But what if you want to meet up with them again? What if they bring it up as a joke, and you laugh along?"

"I would never do that."

"You say that, but what if you're having some beers, having a good time, and a laugh escapes your lips? What if you share some new embarrassing story about me? What if everything is going great between us, and then it takes a turn, and you get mad and want to lash out? People already think I'm a weirdo. They'll believe anything you say."

"Cary. What? No. Where is this coming from? Do you think I would do any of that?" His anxiety had taken his mind hostage. All I wanted to do was save him.

"You say that now, but things can change."

"You can trust me."

Cary bit his lip, fighting back tears that begrudgingly rolled down his face.

"Cary, you can trust me."

The silence was deafening, eating away at every magical moment we shared.

I wanted to break down that wall hardened around his heart, a wall put up to protect himself after past attacks. I could bang at it with a hammer all day and night, but maybe it was too strong for me.

I had a daughter to look out for. I'd managed to keep the dissolution of her parents' marriage from her, saving her the added heartache on top of losing her mother. Even though Jolene had a good head on her shoulders, she was barely a teenager. Maybe it was wrong of me to risk bringing Cary into our lives when he could run away in a flash. She'd already dealt with one parent's abrupt departure.

"I never meant to hurt you, Cary. If you want to live with your worst case scenarios and shut me out, I guess I can't stop you." I kissed him on the top of his head where his cowlick split.

I tried to make it work with Paula. Tried and tried and tried. But I learned too late that love was a two-way street. I couldn't use force of will to make a relationship work. Not then. Not now.

27

DEREK

With one week to go until Christmas, I continued to keep myself busy so as to not think about Cary. I helped Jolene with her homework, which mostly consisted of checking her work and finding no errors. I put together a science kit for Quentin and Josh. I ate family dinner and smiled along with Cal and Russ's lovely bickering and hid the crease of hurt that came from knowing I wouldn't have that with Cary.

For Christmas Eve, Russ cooked an absolute feast. Turkey, potatoes, sides galore. I lost track of everything he cooked, but I ate it all. Smartly, I didn't wear a belt, which allowed my stomach to expand. Like with Thanksgiving, I was incredibly grateful to be spending a holiday with family at a large, warm table.

"I'm surprised you didn't invite Cary," Cal said as we loaded the dishwasher together after the meal. Unlike him, I had watched Russ's tutorials which were...surprisingly informative.

"Things have cooled on that front," I told him. It was

nice to be able to share this stuff with him now. I couldn't keep holding it in.

"Oh no. Why?"

I shrugged, lost for an explanation. The shock of losing Cary so suddenly still had me turned around.

"I've got Jolene to worry about. A new house, a new job, newish town. I can't be messing with a boyfriend."

Cal loaded in a salad bowl, which I reversed in the opposite direction to make more room.

"Take it from me: don't use your child as an excuse not to have a romantic life," he said. "I did that for the longest time. I told myself I was being a good father. I was very good at lying to myself."

"She's had a lot of upheaval over the past year. I don't want to add a bisexual dad and his new boyfriend."

"She's not porcelain. Hell, she probably knows more about the spectrum of sexuality than you and me combined. Sure, it'll be an adjustment, but she'll adjust. Let people surprise you."

Jolene had continually surprised me, showing she was much stronger than I sometimes allowed myself to believe. I was forever conscious of wanting to protect her, but I never wanted to shelter her. Finding that balance was the constant struggle of parenting.

"Maybe give Cary a call?" Cal shrugged, his face bunching up with hope.

I tossed a pair of forks into the silverware holder a little harder than I should have. "It didn't end well."

"Is it over? Or is there still hope?"

My heart refused to give up on the idea of us completely, even though all the evidence pointed that way.

"I know it may not be as strong as what you had with Paula, but give it time." He handed me a plate to load. I held it in my hands, staring at it, finding the courage to say the truth.

"Cal, me and Paula...we weren't the happy couple you think. I mean, we were at first, but then she changed." I held back from telling him about the cheating. I wanted to leave her with some dignity since she couldn't defend herself. I didn't want him to think poorly about her despite how everything went down. "We grew apart. Things were very rocky in the months before her death."

Cal's mouth dropped open slightly, genuine shock rather than a reaction he was milking. I unintentionally rocked his world.

"That sucks. I'm sorry. I always thought you two..."

"Me, too." I shrugged. Like with Cary, I didn't have any grand insight into what went wrong. Perhaps I let myself ignore the space that had grown between us. I was too scared to face it head on. "Maybe I'm meant to be a single guy."

"Or maybe you have your head up your caboose."

"Do you want me to shove you into this dishwasher, Calvin?" We might've been grown-ass adults, but he was still my little brother.

"Is that what you want? Not the shoving me into a dishwasher. Being the single guy. No Cary."

"Things will be quieter." I smirked to myself. Cary loved to talk. He could talk forever about nothing. Yet all that nothing added up to something.

"Things will be quiet once you're dead. Life is about noise!"

As if on cue, a loud crash followed by the high pitch yelling of the aforementioned two boys came from upstairs.

"Boys!" Russ yelled, his booming dad voice taking over the house. "What did you do!"

"Quentin did it!" yelled Josh.

"Only because Josh dared me!" Quentin yelled back at a pitch that would make dogs howl. They devolved into a cacophony of yelling, punctuated by Russ yelling over them to get them to stop.

"Trust me, Derek." Cal slammed the dishwasher shut. "Learn to enjoy the noise."

AFTER WATCHING *A Christmas Story* for the third time today, this time through the haze of a food coma, I wandered upstairs for another night of sleeping alone. Light peeked out from under Jolene's bedroom door. Unsure if she were asleep or not, I turned the knob slowly to check.

"Oh. You're still up," I said. She sat on her bed watching a Taylor Swift interview on her tablet.

"I'm still digesting." Russ wasn't one to use low fat ingredients when he cooked. Jolene patted her stomach the same way I did. All these little things she learned from me.

"You're young. At least you don't have to worry about heartburn."

Jolene peered up at me with her sunflower eyes, which seemed too big for her head. "Did you have a good Christmas?"

"I did." I didn't sound very convincing. "It was great being with you, and your cousins, and your uncles. And Uncle Russ's food is top-notch, although…"

"It can't compare to the canned stuff."

"That's my girl." I kissed the top of her head. I didn't know if she actually preferred the canned food, but I appreciated being humored.

"Dad, are you sure you had a good time? You seemed..." Jolene shrugged her shoulders.

"What?"

"Quiet."

It was true. I didn't say much at dinner. Fortunately, Cal filled any and all silence, as did Quentin and Josh with their rundown on their latest video game obsession.

"I was too busy eating to talk."

Jolene studied me for a minute, as if she were peeling back the lie layer by layer.

"I'm tired from work. All those long shifts are catching up to me."

She opened her mouth to say something, but stopped herself.

"What is it, Jo?"

"Did you and Cary have a fight?"

A sharp pain hit my stomach at the mention of him. I was prepared for Cal to bring him up, but not my daughter.

"No..." I began, stammering for an answer, and hating that lying to my daughter was my go-to choice.

I could feel the thoughts vibrating in her head. I appreciated how transparent her emotions were at this stage because I knew that wouldn't always be the case. She shut her eyes and exhaled a nervous breath through her nose.

"You miss him, Dad. You miss him like you miss a boyfriend."

And there it was. The room shifted just a little, a new reality being born. All my worrying about how to come out to Jolene when she already knew.

There came a point in every child's life when they realized their parents were flawed, imperfect individuals. I'd wanted to be her strong, wise, all-knowing dad forever, but I had to let go of that dream, let myself be human, and hope that she still loved me.

"I do," I said. "I miss him. We liked each other. We liked each other a lot."

"You guys texted all the time, and you *hate* texting. And when we were looking at the stars, you were totally flirting with each other." A giggle trailed her observation. "I'm in middle school, Dad. I know what flirting looks like."

I could feel my eyes crinkle with a bright, relieved smile.

"I know this is a surprise. It's a new side I'm discovering about myself. Sometimes, a man who has had feelings for women his whole life one day starts to have feelings for another man."

She rolled her eyes. "Dad, I know how being bisexual works."

"You know what that is?"

"Yeah. We learned about it in health class. Plus a bunch of kids in my grade are queer."

Man, times had changed. If only Cary could've gone to school today. He wouldn't have felt so isolated, so alone. Hell, neither would I.

"And apparently, there's a bunch of gay teachers in the high school. Like an abnormally high amount."

"So you're okay with this?"

She nodded yes. "Of course, Dad. You need to be you."

I pulled her into a smothering hug.

"I like Cary. He makes you happy. Happier than you were with Mom."

"What makes you say that?"

"You and Mom seemed distant before she died."

We tried our best to hide our arguing and anger away from her. We didn't want to expose Jolene to it and ruin her homelife. Turned out Mom and Dad's dislike for each other could only be hidden so well.

"And then...I found this." Jolene pulled a folded-up letter from her nightstand.

Oh God. Was it Cary's letter?

She handed it over. I unfolded the weathering paper and instantly noticed Paula's clean handwriting.

The letter was written to Jolene from Paula. Each sentence was a gut punch, making my back cave in:

Paula telling our daughter how much we loved her but that sometimes, marriages didn't work. Paula explaining that sometimes, mommies fell in love with someone else, like daddy's best friend. Paula praying that one day, her daughter would understand, and that this would be a good thing in the long run.

If Paula hadn't died, I had no idea how we were going to break the news of our impending divorce to Jolene. Paula had already thought ahead.

"I found it when I was going through her stuff in the storage locker," Jolene said. "I guess she was going to give it to me when she...when she left."

Her bottom lip trembled, and that was all it took for the tears to fall. From both of us.

"She loved you with all her heart," I said. "She wasn't leaving you. She was leaving me. She was crazy about you. I promise you that."

"Wasn't Angus your friend?" she asked.

"He was." Reading the letter made me see how serious Paula was with him. She was in love if she was going to share that detail with Jolene. It meant she expected Angus to be a part of her life. For the first time, I felt a twinge of sympathy for my former friend and wondered how he weathered the past year.

"Is it okay if I miss her?" Jolene asked.

"Of course. I miss her, too."

"You do?"

"She gave me the best gift I could ever receive. You." Paula and I would forever have a complicated relationship without closure. But we produced a fantastic daughter, and that was worth all the strife and heartache.

"Dad, I've been worried about you this year. I'm happy that you and Cary found each other."

I hugged Jolene, smelling her hair and feeling eternally grateful that I got to call her my daughter.

"Are you guys going to get back together?" she asked.

"I don't know about that. Cary's pretty mad at me. I messed up."

"Have you tried winning him back?" She sat cross-legged on her bed as if we were in the midst of girl talk at a sleepover.

"I don't think he'd like that."

"What would Cary say?" Jolene cocked an eyebrow my way. "If you don't ask, you don't get. What's the worst that can happen?"

"You're right."

"That wasn't a rhetorical question. What is the worst that can happen if you tell Cary you want him back?"

"He says no?"

"Right. And if he says that, then you know. But let somebody else tell you no. Don't tell yourself no." Jolene had a pleased smile on her face. She was absolutely right, and she knew it.

28

CARY

And just like that, we were back in Poughkeepsie for Christmas. My family turned the holiday into a two-day celebration. We went up for eve and stayed through the day. When we were younger, my cousins and I would turn it into a fun sleepover, each of us taking shifts by the fireplace for Santa sightings. The spirit of the tradition remained into adulthood, even if our staying up late was fueled by insomnia rather than excitement over Santa.

"Forget Derek," said Maudrey. She passed me her fork and the pecan pie, still in the tin. As God is our witness, we were going to finish it off by sunup.

"He sounds like an asshole," said Harold, pouring himself a shot of eggnog, a drink I would never find appealing. In his lap was his phone open to Tinder. He was always looking for a last minute stocking stuffer.

"He's not an asshole," I said. I had told them what happened with us. The great date followed by the not great napkin and even worse argument.

"He was making fun of you to his jock friends." Maudrey scrunched up on the couch, tucking her legs under her.

"Why did he have that drawing in his pocket?" asked Harold, swiping left on a woman who committed the unforgivable sin of being over thirty.

"He acted this whole time like he didn't know shit, but he did. You're right, Cary. How can you trust him again? Do you have anything of his that we could burn in effigy?" Maudrey asked, fired up. The last time we tried that, she singed her eyebrows.

"Just sell him his house, get your coin, and get out." Harold added a sassy finger snap. His last hookup had them regularly marathon *Real Housewives*.

"No, you're right," I said. "But was he an asshole?"

My cousins gave me confused looks.

"Maybe I was too quick not to believe him about the napkin? Maybe he did yank it away and tell them to shut up. That seems like something Derek would do."

To their credit, Harold and Maudrey were trying to support me. I told them what Derek had done and how it had made me upset, and they were taking my side as loyal cousins.

Then why didn't I find the same joy in it this time?

"Did I push him away because I got scared?"

"Well, you do have major trust issues," said Maudrey, immediately hopping from the prosecution to the defense.

"And Derek has given you no reason to not believe him," added her co-counsel Harold. "He's seemed like an honest, decent fella up to this point. And sure, he might've made fun of you in high school if he had the chance, but you don't know that."

Maudrey turned to him. "Cary's probably using that as a flimsy excuse to push him away."

"Right, right. Because of his trust issues."

"He was bound to find a reason to push away Derek. This was inevitable when you think about it."

"Hey, I'm still here!" I said. I wasn't a character on a TV show meant to be analyzed in a weekly recap.

Harold reached for the pecan pie, but I pulled it back.

"You're supposed to be on my side," I said.

My cousins exchanged a look, recalculating their strategy.

"Derek's an asshole." Maudrey said, now back with the prosecution. "You were right to get out of this toxic sitch before he could keep hurting you."

She turned to Harold, waiting for him to jump in. Too bad her co-counsel was ensconced on his phone.

"Hey, would it be weird if I messaged this girl when I hooked up with her twin sister over the summer?"

I turned my attention to the fireplace. Maybe Santa would have some sage advice for me. Or maybe he could whisk me off to the North Pole so I could stop thinking about Derek.

———

SOMETIME AFTER THREE, my cousins faded off to sleep. My insomnia beat theirs, leaving me to wait up for Santa. The man hadn't visited yet, and considering all the places he could be that weren't Poughkeepsie, I didn't blame him.

I went into the kitchen and found the crudités wrapped in plastic in the fridge. After all the pie and rich fixings, my body craved vegetables. I tried to eat softly, but celery and carrots were loud no matter how one crunched.

"Any sign of Santa?" Dad came into the kitchen, wearing the baby blue robe I got him for Christmas years ago. It had his initials sewn over the heart. I'd gotten my first big commission check and decided to treat him and Mom to swanky, luxurious Christmas presents.

"Santa is making a Starbucks run."

"He drinks Starbucks?" Dad made the same face I made at the coffee chain. Starbucks disdain was in our DNA.

He sat at the kitchen table and munched on a celery stick. Dad invited me to join him rather than hover over the fridge.

"How you been, Cary?" he asked.

"Good. Same as always."

"You sure? Because you seemed a little down tonight." He tipped his head. Parents had a supernatural power to tell when their kids were upset. Dad could always see through my brave face.

"I'm not used to eating so many carbs."

"Don't you have a cupboard full of individual mac n cheese cups?"

"Guilty." Darn him and his exceptional memory. "Dad, am I going to be alone forever?"

When I used to get scared during thunderstorms, I would crawl onto Dad's lap. I knew there wasn't much he could do to control the weather, but his warmth and his Old Spice smell had a way of comforting me. I wished I could get away with this as a fortysomething man.

"You're not alone. You have me, your mom, Harold and Audrey, your friends."

"You know what I mean."

He patted my hand, his eyes sleepy but alert. "There's a special guy out there for you."

We'd come a long way for him to be able to say that. I had worried that coming out would permanently damage my relationship with my parents, but through time and love, we had emerged a stronger unit.

"There is," I admitted. Things with Derek had been as close to perfect as could be. "But I let him go."

"Now why would you do a knuckleheaded thing like that?" asked Dad, ever the romantic, apparently.

"I know I haven't shared much about my dating life. That's because there hasn't been much to share. It's been mostly tragic." I didn't want my parents feeling sorry for me. I didn't want all their worst fears about having a gay son to be true. "Dad, do you remember in high school when you had to drive one of my friends home?"

I felt nauseous referring to Gaston as a friend. Even now, all these years later, I was still trying to minimize the shame.

"Vaguely. He'd driven over drunk, and your mom followed behind?"

I nodded. A lump formed in my throat as I remembered he and Mom in their pajamas, tired from long days, shuffling into their car. Yes, in the grand scheme of things, having them drive home a "friend" wasn't a big deal, but for some reason, it broke my heart. It made me feel like a failure of a son.

Tears fell down my face, a dam finally breaking.

"He wasn't my friend, Dad. He was...we did stuff together."

I waited for it to click in Dad's mind. I wouldn't give Gaston the courtesy of calling him my boyfriend or my lover. He fulfilled neither of those roles.

"There were certain things I wasn't comfortable doing, and he didn't like that. So he made up a story about me and told the whole school. And everyone believed it. He was mean to me."

And that was the hardest part to admit. That he was mean to me. That I was the victim, no matter what kind of self-empowerment lens I chose to view it through. That I allowed myself to feel weak.

I wiped away my tears. Why was I rehashing this? I always thought it would be better if my parents didn't know. They had enough on their plate. But shielding them only made things tougher on me. It only made me learn to push people away.

"He sounds like a real asshole." It was a charge of relief to hear Dad call him an asshole.

"He was."

Dad fiddled with a carrot stick, the wheels actively turning in his head. "I think I know what the story was."

I met his eyes, and without having to say a word, the squeamish pinch of his face told me we were thinking of the same story.

"Does Mom know, too?"

Dad nodded yes. Fresh waves of shame and humiliation poured through me.

"I'm sorry," I said. "I'm so sorry."

"Why are you sorry?" Dad stroked my thumb, giving me a hint of that security from being in his lap as a kid.

"Because I embarrassed you. Because you've probably had people gossiping about me behind your backs, and they probably made assumptions about you and Mom as parents. I brought shame to this house."

"You brought shame to this house? Are we the royal family? We're better than them. They're all a bunch of inbred wackos who've never held down a real job." Dad massaged his palm across my back. "I didn't care because I knew the story wasn't true."

"You did?"

He nodded confidently, a detective who'd seen all the evidence.

"You'd never do something like that. You have a fear of opening your mouth too wide and unhinging your jaw." A soft chuckle left his lips.

The man was right. In addition to my litany of weird anxieties, I had a fear of eating big pieces of food. I'd once heard my jaw click when taking in a bite of seven-layer cake, and it freaked me out for good. I preferred small pieces of food, small bites, or just sticking with liquids as much as possible.

The gearhead story icked me out when I thought about the oral mechanics. I let out a soft chuckle myself.

"So you've known about the story the whole time?"

Dad nodded yes.

"And you didn't care that people were talking about it?"

"I had some concerned adults ask me if I heard. I told them it wasn't true. And that was years ago, around when you were graduating. I didn't say anything because you didn't seem bothered by it. You went about your life, head held high. I admired how you took it in stride. You were a mature kid. You didn't need your mom and dad to fix your problem." Dad scrunched his eyebrows together, finding fault with his statement. "I didn't realize that you were just very good at hiding your pain. That's on me. I should've been more aware."

"No. I was very good at hiding things from you and Mom. You both worked hard. You didn't need to get dragged into my high school bullshit."

Dad put his hand over mine and squeezed, a steely, papa bear glint in his eye. "We gladly would've been dragged in. You didn't have to fight this battle alone."

I wanted to be a good son. I wanted to be successful. I wanted to prove the haters wrong. I thought that could only happen if I accomplished it all solo, but like Catherine Zeta-

Jones memorably sang in *Chicago*, I simply couldn't do it alone. Maybe it was okay to need people. It wasn't weakness. Letting myself be vulnerable for someone else was a sign of strength, a sign that I knew when to let my guard down.

Then, I uttered a sentence out loud that I'd been too afraid to say my whole damn life, but once it came out, the statement was freeing.

"I don't want to be alone anymore."

I imagined that was what it was like in AA. Admitting you were an alcoholic was the first step to not being one. Once the words were in the air, they were real and less scary. They weren't a boogeyman, but rather something that could be conquered.

"You're not alone, Cary. You never were." Dad held up a carrot stick. I held up my celery stick. We toasted to me, to us, to family.

29

DEREK

Closings weren't exciting. It was a shit ton of documents that you had to sign. Make that a metric shit ton. I remembered when Paula and I bought our house, we signed so many documents that our hands cramped. I didn't know what the hell most of them were, only that at the end, we'd get the keys. For all I knew, we could've signed our lives away.

This time, I was nervous. I was going to see Cary for the first time since our fight. I had expected Cary to text me over the Christmas holiday to inform me that Hannah would be taking over, but that never happened. When I asked if we were still good for today, he gave me a thumbs up.

A thumbs up was a frustratingly neutral emoji.

I got to the title office a few minutes early. The closing agent at the title company and the real estate agent representing the homeowner were seated at a large conference in a meeting room that had the generic, vaguely interesting art usually found in hotel rooms. I sat across from the agent and leaned back in the chair, twiddling my thumbs.

"He should be here any minute," I said of Cary.

The real estate agent was a middle-aged woman with spiky blonde hair, thin glasses, and heavy eye makeup. Beside her was a keychain lanyard of a Catholic school overflowing with keys and smaller keychains. It was a miracle the thing fit in her purse. If a guy tried to put that thing in his pocket, his pants would fall down.

"That's a lot of keys," said the closing agent, an older man in a short sleeve button down with a solid blue tie.

"I have a busy life."

I wasn't sure what she meant by that, but was afraid to ask.

That was the extent of our chitchat. Fortunately, Cary bounded into the conference room before the silence became too much. His shirt was a deep purple that provided a much-needed dash of color to this drab room.

"Oh no. Were you waiting for me? I was stuck behind the slowest driver. That's the problem with living in a quaint small town: one-lane roads. It's all fun and farmers markets until you're trying to get somewhere."

He slipped into the chair next to me, his body somewhat tense. I wasn't sure where we stood after our fight. Was this solely a business transaction to him? I didn't want to make him uncomfortable, so I figured it was best to keep things professional.

"Hi." He gave me a quick nod of acknowledgement and turned to the pile of papers on the table.

There was so much I wanted to say to him. I wanted him to know that I missed him, that I didn't want this to be the last time we saw each other. But all that came out of me was a quick nod back.

"You ready to become a homeowner again?" he asked me while thumbing through the stack of papers.

"Yep. Let's get this over with." I managed a half-smile. It

was painful enough to be sitting next to him and not able to hold his hand or joke with him. Each minute that passed would be compounded torture. It was best I got out as soon as I could.

"Okay." His face dropped slightly, surprised at my directness. "We can do that."

"I have to get back to the firehouse," I lied.

"Duty calls." Cary nodded again.

"We'll make this quick and painless," said the closing agent.

"I also have places to be." The female agent fiddled with her keys. What kind of adventures was she off to after this? Did she have to attend to the multiple people she had locked up in her clients' houses?

The closing agent handed Cary the first document, who then slid it over to me. Cary gave a cursory explanation of what I was signing, then pointed to the X where my signature was required. He offered me the option to read through, but if I did that, we'd be here all day.

"This one is the initial escrow statement, which outlines what will come out of escrow for taxes and insurance in your first year." He slid the paper my way, and I got a whiff of his cocoa butter hand cream.

I signed my name.

He passed me the next document. There was a rigidness to his movements that made me wonder if he was just as anxious to get out of here. Maybe he really had put me in the past.

"This one is the deed to the property, officially transferring ownership to you."

I could've been signing my soul to the devil himself for all I knew. I scrawled my name and passed it back.

So this was how it was going to end? The man who

made me believe in love again and cracked open my heart was going to fade away in a whimper of signed documents?

All because of one fight over a stupid rumor from decades ago?

What we had was real and deep-rooted. The gearhead story was trifling in comparison.

Yeah, like with Paula, things could go south with Cary out of nowhere. Or things could be amazing and Cary could still drop dead right in front of me. Such was the risk in being alive. We had to cherish the highs because we got less of them as we got older.

I wasn't giving up without a real fight.

"Derek?" Cary pointed at the X on the document. He could barely look at me.

Instead of my John Hancock, I wrote this instead: *I love you.*

I shoved it back to him defiantly.

And Cary absent-mindedly slid it over to the closing agent before yanking it back at the last second, his eyes bulging out of his skull. I could always count on him for cartoonish reactions. His face was adorably elastic.

"Um..." Cary stared at the declaration, then at me, then at the closing agent. The struggle to keep on a professional expression was real.

"Is something wrong?" the closing agent asked.

"What? Um, no..."

"You know what? I missed the part where I was supposed to initial," I said, finding a perverse glee in Cary's reaction. I snatched the document back and found the space for my initials.

I wrote this instead: *I want you back.*

Oops.

Hell, they could always print off a fresh copy.

I slid the paper back to Cary. "Did I miss anything?"

A smile peeked at the corner of his mouth. "You missed one here."

He turned the page and pointed with a shaky finger to the final signature line.

"Sign and date," he said, clearing his throat.

"Sign and date. You got it." I signed my actual name this time. For the date, I put this: *Seriously, I am in love with you.*

"Are you writing out the date in words?" asked the female agent.

"Did I do that wrong?"

"Can I actually have a minute outside to speak with my client?" Cary asked, turning the same shade as his shirt.

"Don't take too long. We want to get this wrapped up soon. I need to pick up my daughter from gymnastics and my son from basketball practice," she said in her nasally voice that made my balls jump up into my body.

"Just one minute, Pat," Cary said. "Derek."

His eyes urgently insisted I stand the fuck up and follow him into the hall.

Cary shut the conference room door softly behind him. He glanced around. It was only us. I got a good look at his beautiful, confused, scared face.

I crossed my arms, refusing to take back what I'd said—or rather, written.

"Derek." Cary paced in front of me. "We are in the middle of a closing, arguably the most important closing of the year for me. Buying a home is a major life event. Those are important documents in there and..." Cary stopped, out of breath. He put his hands on his hips. "And...you said you loved me."

"I did."

"Twice."

"Uh huh."

"Did you mean it? Or were you trying to get a reaction out of me?"

"C," I growled. "All of the above."

"Oh thank god." Cary jumped into my arms and smothered my lips in a passionate kiss full of relief. He grabbed on so tight I didn't know how I'd ever get him off me. Not like I wanted to, but I did have a house I needed to buy.

Our mouths parted. Cary heaved in breath. Our faces were so close it was as if we were meeting under the covers in bed rather than in a bland office building lobby.

"I was so scared I pushed you away for good," he said.

"You didn't." I kissed him again. "I'm right here."

"I'm sorry I was an asshole. I trust you, Derek. I know you didn't draw that napkin. I'm so fucking done with gearhead. I'm done with it being this dark cloud over my life. I'm done with it making me keep people at arms length. If people want to talk, let them talk. I have a fucking life to live with this sexy fireman. I love you."

Our foreheads rested atop one another. I'd hoped to hear these words, and they sounded sweeter than my dreams.

"I shouldn't have walked out that easily," I said. "I'd been burned in the past, but that doesn't mean I'm going to get burned now."

"I'll never burn you. And if I did, you're a fireman so you can extinguish yourself."

There was that Cary humor I'd missed. I was a serious guy. I needed someone who could bring levity to my life.

"I've been telling myself that Paula's affair came out of nowhere, that she changed overnight. But I'm tired of telling myself that story. There were signs. I didn't want to see them."

"Let's put our sob stories behind us, shall we?" Cary smiled on my lips. I savored the cherry flavor of his lip balm.

Pat, the real estate agent with a plethora of keys, cleared her throat behind us. The closing agent stood beside her. Unlike her, he seemed won over by our show of affection.

"Am I still wrapped around your waist?" Cary asked me in a stage whisper.

"Uh huh."

"I know this looks unprofessional..." Cary hopped off me. Fortunately, my flannel-lined jeans were thick enough to hide my erection, or so I hoped. "We were discussing whether Derek should get a home warranty plan."

"Right. Shall we?" Pat rolled her eyes and went back into the conference room. A part of me was pissed that she'd be earning a commission check today. Then again, I got to leave this building with a new house and a hot boyfriend, and she had to go to gymnastics practice.

"Let's get back in there." I patted Cary's ass as I ushered us inside.

It was a professional ass pat.

30

CARY

I used to roll my eyes at all the people who were obsessed with finding someone to kiss on New Year's Eve. In the words of my Jewish brethren, why was this night different from all other nights?

New Years was just another night. Our society made this huge deal out of it. *Live it up! Send the old year out with a bang! Go to a bar and pay marked up prices for watered-down drinks!*

But now that I was going to have my first New Years kiss, and that kiss was from Derek, I got the appeal. A kiss on New Years was pretty wonderful. Although, a kiss from Derek any day of the year was a magical experience.

It finally happened. I became one of those mushy people.

It had only been a few days since I'd climbed Derek like a tree at the closing, and yet I was already in heaven. There was nothing quite like being with a guy who cared about you, who you could trust completely, who could make you hard with the tiniest curl of his upper lip. The small voice in my head warning me that he could deceive me and humiliate me at any moment began to subside, and I found that I could just *be* with Derek. No performance. No anxiety. And definitely no performance anxiety. By golly, we were single-handedly keeping Astroglide in business.

For New Years, I went over to Cal and Russ's house. The kids were staying up late to watch the ball drop, and Russ had made artisan popcorn and from-scratch chocolate molds of the ball drop. Cal bragged that he picked out the napkins.

I'd had much more exciting New Years spent at Manhattan nightclubs and exclusive parties thrown in abandoned warehouses. But spending the evening watching TV on the couch tonight was easily my favorite.

Derek and I kept our PDA to a minimum. I kept looking over at Jolene trying to read her expression, but she was nothing but smiles. We watched Taylor Swift perform in Times Square and dissected her performance, all the while Derek had his arm around me. Jolene didn't flinch or have any negative reaction. I wanted to ask if she was cool with this, but I decided to ride the wave and not rock the boat.

With thirty minutes to go until the year ended, I went to the kitchen for a refill on popcorn. Russ insisted we use the New Years-branded cups to hold our popcorn lest kernels tumble to the floor. Cal wasn't following that rule. He ate directly from the large bowl.

"Is your kink disobeying your husband?" I asked him.

"I think it might be." Cal scooped a handful of popcorn from the bowl and cupped it against his chest. I couldn't see behind me, but I assumed Russ was peeved. "Listen, you are my dear friend, but Derek is my brother, so it goes without saying that if you break his heart, I will hunt you down and sell your organs on the black market. And I won't tell you which order I sell them in."

"Um...understood? And you don't have to worry about that."

"Oh, I know. But I wanted to say it anyway." Cal shrugged, always finding ways to amuse himself.

"Well, if you break Russ's heart, I will hunt you down."

"But you're not his brother."

"I know, but the man is a really good cook." I swiped another chocolate mold from the platter. I'd heard that people gained weight in relationships. I was ready to join the club.

"Hey, can we talk about something serious for a second?" Cal asked. He looked over my shoulder to make sure nobody was coming into the kitchen.

"Sure," I said, caught off guard by the tone shift. Cal and I weren't the type of friends to have heart-to-hearts. Though, most of that was because of my whole keeping-people-at-arms-length schtick.

"Cary, I want to apologize to you." A pained expression creased his face. I could tell he wasn't putting on an act this time. "I'm sorry I believed that rumor about you and that I never questioned it."

"It's okay." My New Year's resolution was to finally put gearhead firmly in the past. "What made you think of this? Did Derek say something?"

I glanced over my shoulder. Derek was busy throwing Josh and Quentin onto the couch over and over.

"He did, and I'm glad he did. I feel terrible. When people would mention it, I always told them to shut up. But I should've gotten your side of the story. I really am sorry for hurting you, Cary. You got a raw deal, and I was complicit."

A lot of people did a lot of terrible things in the wake of the gearhead story. Cal's was minor. I was ready to move on.

"Thanks," I said.

"Better late than never, right?"

He had a point. The fact that I brought it up to Derek all these years later meant it was still on my mind. It was a tiny point of contention that stood between us. A thin, yet sturdy wall. I was happy to watch it fall away, so Cal and I could strengthen our friendship. We might be brothers-in-law eventually.

A hand snaked around my waist, making me feel safe from the wreckage of the rumor.

"Mind if I borrow Cary? The ball's going to drop any minute," said Derek.

Cal gestured that I was free to go.

"Question, do we have to wait until midnight to kiss?" Derek asked.

"Nah. That's for heteros." I wrapped my arms around his neck and kissed him, traditions be damned.

IT WAS A BITTERLY cold January evening when I went over to Derek's new house. It was still empty, but he wanted to get my opinion on furniture. He and Jolene were planning to move in that weekend.

The front door was unlocked.

"Hello?" I called out into the echoey house. Derek had heeded my strong suggestion to hire a cleaning service to do a thorough clean. The place looked brand new and much more spacious without all that junk piled high.

"Derek?" I called out. His car was in the driveway, yet silence greeted me.

This was definitely how horror movies started.

"In here," he called from the main bedroom.

I walked down the hall and found a glow coming from

the room at the end. I pushed open the door to find Derek stark naked on an air mattress surrounded by lit tea lights.

"You stole my trick," I said.

His big, hairy body shimmered in the candlelight. His dick was half-hard and resting against his leg. (Yes, of course that was the first thing my eye went to. I was a gay man, after all.)

"I arranged for a family to come by in a few minutes. The father's a pastor," he said with a smirk.

"Perfect."

"Clothes off, Perkowski."

I didn't need to be asked twice. I practically tore off my shirt. I could ruin one shirt. I had a colorful closet full of them. I kicked off my shoes and almost knocked over a side table with tea lights.

Derek gave me the curled, come hither finger. "You're going to be sore tomorrow."

"Of course I am. I'm a forty-year-old man who's about to fuck on an air mattress."

I straddled Derek's meaty body, feeling his dick pushing against my ass. I ran my hands through his chest hair before bending down to kiss him.

"I take it we're not having a furniture discussion," I said.

He shook his head no. "I love you."

"I love you," I said back. I still got nervous when I said those words to him. They made me feel a different kind of naked.

"You don't have to be scared, Cary. I'm not going anywhere." Derek skimmed a hand down my back to the crack of my ass. I shivered with want, with need, with the security of his body.

I scooted back so I could stroke both our raging hard cocks in my hand. Derek drizzled lube over the action like he was adding chocolate syrup to a sundae, before tossing the bottle aside. The pulsing heat of his erection burned against mine. Derek grunted under me, hissing at my touch.

"Need you inside me," I huffed out. My chest got tight and if I didn't watch myself, I could spill early.

"Need to feel you wrapped around me." Derek thrust into my palm like a caged animal.

With the air mattress straining under us, Derek reached again for the lube. He popped open the cap. This was always the awkward part during sex, the mechanical part. But we just laughed and smiled with each other, no weirdness here.

Derek spread my ass open and slipped a finger into my opening. I unleashed a guttural howl of pleasure. Just the anticipation of feeling his thick cock inside me was enough to get me delirious with lust. It was wild how fast I could go from cautious, normal Cary to a total cockmonster.

"Put it in. Please," I begged. I didn't want foreplay tonight. I wanted to feel myself stretch for him, wanted to feel him completely take over my body.

"Baby. Don't gotta ask me twice." Derek plunged his cock into my hole, pushing past the tightness, lighting me up like the Christmas display in the center of town, which had only just been taken down. I appreciated that he ripped the band-aid off in that sense.

He thrust inside me, filling me up, making me hungry for more. I bounced on his dick as my own leaked onto his furry stomach.

"You feel so fucking good." Derek lay back and interlocked his fingers behind his head. He might as well have been on a beach with a margarita and a good book. There was something oddly hot about his nonchalance. It was laid back domination.

"Don't wear yourself out," I said to him.

"I'm ready to jump in, but I'd say you have it covered."

The fact that we could still banter meant I wasn't fucking him hard enough. I went faster, letting him hit deeper, the sounds of our bodies clapping together in sweaty unison filled the room. He let out moan after moan, testing the limits of the house's walls. The air mattress wheezed under us. It could give out at any moment.

Derek jerked me off, his touch making me levitate. His dick and his hand were pushing and pulling me. I groaned and begged as he gazed into my eyes, his glimmering look telling me to let go.

"Derek." I couldn't believe I got to say his name as he fucked me. This was better than the dirtiest fantasy I'd dreamt of in my letter. I shot my load across his stomach, emptying myself completely.

"That was so hot," he said.

Sweat poured down my face. "Speaking of hot, I just noticed there's no ceiling fan in here. You should call an electrician to get one installed."

"Are you pitching upgrades while I'm still inside you?"

"I never stop working for my clients." I noticed that Derek was still hard and still inside me. "Did you come?"

"Not yet. Um, there was actually something I wanted you to do, if you're cool with it."

"Oooh, what? Tell me!" I couldn't wait to explore all of Derek's interests and kinks.

"I've been curious what it's like to be rimmed. I see that you love it."

Derek putting his tongue anywhere on my body instantly turned it into an erogenous zone.

"It feels amazing," I confessed. I never knew how comfortable he was with that since he'd been living in Straight Land for so long. The thought of getting to be up close and personal with Derek's ass got me hard again. It was another reminder that I was gay because the thought of being up close and personal with a woman in the same way did nada for me.

"Let's do it!" I said.

I got off him. I used my shirt to clean us off. Derek threw his legs back, exposing a pink hole amid a thick dusting of dark blond hairs. His legs were thick and strong, his ass nice and big.

I flicked my tongue over his opening. It was very tight. He grunted above me.

"You doing good?" I asked. "If at any point, you don't like this, tell me and I'll stop."

"Don't stop. It feels weird, but a good weird. I'm not used to being this..."

"Vulnerable?"

"Yeah."

"Join the club," I said.

I swirled my tongue over his ass, pulling his cheeks farther apart so I could get better access. I massaged my finger on his opening, felt it quiver under my touch. With my free hand, I stroked his lubed-up cock. Pre-come seeped onto my fingers, which I then dragged down to coat his hole. Derek's voice cracked with curious pleasure, someone discovering whole new sensations.

Just as he played me at both ends, I returned the favor, stroking him and fingering him, feeling his ass tighten around my finger and tongue as his cock became even more engorged.

"Cary. Fuck. Don't fucking stop."

He clenched around my finger as his cock spurted hot waves of come. It dribbled down his shaft and balls and hit my tongue. Derek was a mess. He was my mess.

I stretched out next to Derek, pushing the mattress to its limit. I rested my head on his shoulder. We stared up at the ceiling together, the quiet of the neighborhood bringing down our heart rates.

"I was going to bring you a bottle of champagne to celebrate the new house. This was much better," I said.

"I hope you're ready to help me christen every room in this place."

31

DEREK

I loved sleeping in my own bed in my own room. I loved not hearing the loud noises of Josh and Quentin playing at seven in the morning. After a year of upheaval, Jolene and I were finally home.

The house was perfect for us. Small enough to feel cozy but not suffocating. Except when we had to share the bathroom.

"Are you almost done in there?" I knocked on the bathroom door again. Usually, our schedules didn't overlap so this was never a problem. But it was Saturday night, and we were getting ready for a fun night of back-to-back parties.

"Give me a minute!" she yelled back.

"You said that ten minutes ago." I tightened my tie, not used to this article of clothing around my neck. I had to check that it was on correctly.

Jolene yanked the door open. "It's all yours."

She scooted past me, her hair flowing down her back in cascading waves, pretty as ever in a black dress...a black dress that seemed a bit shorter than the ones she usually wore. *Uh oh. It's starting.*

"How's the tie?" I asked.

"Perfect. You look handsome, Dad. Cary is going to love it."

I smiled at the prospect of him seeing me in a suit. I couldn't wait to celebrate his victory as top salesman tonight. He was going to be getting a plaque and everything. Jolene gave me a crash course in using the swanky features on my iPhone so that I took the best pictures.

I snapped out of my excitement to study my daughter's face. She was always so happy, so easygoing. How had I been blessed with such a wonderful daughter? This had been a tumultuous year.

"Jo, let's go to the living room."

Jolene sunk into a plush armchair that Cal lobbied for me to get while I sat uncomfortably on the arm of the couch.

"We've been through a lot this year. But you, especially. I want you to know that you are my priority. How are you feeling about Cary? Specifically me dating Cary?"

I was still getting used to my daughter knowing I was dating a man. I regularly checked in with her over lots of father-daughter stargazing to see how she was handling dear old dad having a boyfriend. She was remarkably unfazed. She said that I might not be bisexual at all. I might be demisexual or pansexual. Maybe I was old-fashioned, but it was a little weird hearing my thirteen-year-old daughter say sex so many times.

"Cary's cool, Dad."

She really liked Cary and was excited about the prospect of him being around more. The two of them got along great, though I wondered how their relationship would handle the conflict that came between kids and their caregivers. It would be a bridge we would eventually cross, and we would get through it. Cary knew that he wasn't a replacement for Paula, and he didn't try to be.

"You mean it? You're not just saying that? I want us to have an open dialogue."

"That sounds like something Uncle Russ would say." She cocked an amused eyebrow.

I hung my head. "Guilty."

THE CEREMONY WAS HELD at a fancy banquet hall I'd always driven past but never had the chance to visit. I took tons of phenomenal pictures when Cary and Hannah went up to receive their plaques for salespeople of the year. Portrait mode for the win. Their boss also bestowed them with leis, pre-welcoming them to the Bali trip for top sellers. I found out later Cary got a plus one. I was going to Bali!

I looked around for the Morris brothers, but they were the only agents who had decided not to show up.

Jolene and I schmoozed with Cary and his co-workers. Hannah took her to the bathroom and helped her with a makeup emergency, leaving me and Hannah's husband John to have a conversation about semiconductors where I smiled and nodded.

We left the banquet early to hightail it to Stone's Throw Tavern. *A Mountain Man Christmas* had proven to be so popular that the network was rerunning it into January. They finally realized that audiences were so desperate for queer romances onscreen that they were willing to rewatch a Christmas movie a month after the holiday ended.

"For the record, I don't give a crap about this movie. But others do, so I might as well capitalize on it." Mitch told me at the event. All of the tables and chairs were organized to face the wall of TVs above the bar. He had stubbornly held out on doing a premiere during the Christmas season, but Charlie finally convinced him to acknowledge the movie once it became a hit.

Lucien and Skip made an appearance, too, taking selfie after selfie with fans. They looked wildly different when not dressing up as Mitch and Charlie. Jolene ran over to get a selfie. She had watched the movie three times already.

"Cary, where's your plaque?" Charlie asked, more excited than a dog whose owner had a plate of food.

"I left it in the car. Why would I bring—I'm just kidding." Cary whipped open his winter coat and pulled the plaque from the inner pocket.

"It's so shiny!" Charlie's eyes glowed. Cary let him hold it. "When do you leave for Bali?"

"Not until June." Cary beamed with excitement. I was excited, too. Mostly at the thought of having sex in a hotel bed overlooking the ocean.

"Nice work, Cary." Mitch clapped me on the shoulder. He let out a groan as yet another fan squealed over meeting Lucien. "I can't wait for this movie to die down."

Judging by the initial reception, that wasn't going to happen for a while.

"You should air it here every Christmas," I said.

Mitch groaned again.

"Oh cheer up! It's okay to be in the post-holiday spirit," said Charlie, who was wearing a tight muscle T-shirt with the movie's title stretched across his chest. "Mitch has been talking nonstop about the movie."

"Only that they drove me crazy for a month."

"'Drove me crazy,'" Charlie repeated with large air quotes. "You loved all of it, you gorgeous Grinch."

"Why don't you go refill the ice, Tiny Tim?" Mitch cocked an eyebrow at his husband.

"Hey, I'm not tiny where it counts. Porterfield out!" Charlie backed away, blending into the crowd. Mitch rolled his eyes at his perpetual fratboy, but a loving smile on his lips let the whole world know he was crazy about him.

Cary and I moseyed through the crowd to order drinks at the bar. He hugged the plaque to his chest as if shielding a baby from commotion.

"Are you ever going to put that thing down?" I asked.

"No. I hope you're up for threesomes." Cary held up the plaque and gave it a kiss. It was the culmination of twenty years of hard work, so I couldn't blame him.

"Proud of you." I winked at him.

I ordered two Mountain Man Martinis, tonight's drink special. Typically, I wasn't a martini guy, but I'd make an exception. Someone tapped me on the shoulder as I took out my wallet. I turned and stood face-to-face with Bill, Des, and Hank. Next to me, I felt Cary's body tense.

"Hey," Bill said.

I gave him a mere nod of acknowledgement, nothing more. I shifted to shield Cary. "Can I help you?"

"We came to apologize, to both of you," he said, looking over my shoulder. Bill was a man of few words, but he made them count.

I searched out Mitch in the crowd, certain he told the guys we'd be here tonight.

"We were assholes," said Des.

"Fucking assholes," Hank added. "We're sorry for bringing up that dumb story. We're sorry, Cary." Hank waved over me. "I think we had earth science together, right?"

"I think you guys should go," I said. They weren't going to ruin this wonderful night for him.

"We mean it," said Des. "We feel bad about how we left things. We were joking around at the bar, and we should've stopped when you asked. That's no way to treat a teammate or his boyfriend. And we're not just saying that because we want you to join the Comebacks. Though our defense is fucked if you're not on the team."

Cary pushed past me to face them. "I'm putting gearhead behind me, but it wasn't fun living through that. It's not fun being a gossip item. You guys were on top of the world in high school. You have no idea what it was like."

"My son is bullied." Hank's jaw tightened, his permasmile vanishing. "He's the kind of kid we would've teased back in the day. But he's more intelligent and more interesting than all of us. He's going to be a professional math genius and leave all us idiot jocks in the dust. I guess this is karma." He shrugged his shoulders. "You were right, Derek. If it was my kid being talked about, I'd feel awful."

"I'm sorry he's going through that," said Cary.

Bill clapped my shoulder. "Having you back here, being on the ice together, it's something special. I know you felt it."

I had a flash of playing hockey again, the thrill of being on the ice. I'd never heard these guys apologize, so for them to come here meant that they were sincere. I looked to Cary. I wasn't going to do anything that made him feel uncomfortable, and if that meant giving up on the Comebacks, then so be it.

"You heard 'em," Cary said, a smile cracking his lips. "Their defense is fucked without you."

The guys' eyebrows perked up in unison.

"I guess I'll see you at practice," I said. "But if I hear any jokes about having sex with cars, then I will rip your balls off."

"Ball." Des held up a finger.

We broke out laughing. The guys hugged Cary and congratulated him on his plaque. As soon as Des mentioned he was in the market for a new place, Cary switched into real estate agent mode.

While the PRG event was at a fancy banquet hall with delicious catering, I much preferred this party.

Cal and Russ arrived a little bit later. Cal and I had made a plan that he'd come to the firehouse once a week for lunch. It would be a brotherly bonding session.

"What do you think, Russ? Should we let them in?" Cal asked, crossing his arms.

"I think it goes without saying," his husband replied.

"Into what?" Cary asked.

"The Single Dads Club!" Cal said, throwing an imaginary handful of confetti in the air.

"I'm thinking that we should probably change our name," Russ said.

"Can't. I already trademarked it and am getting merch made." Cal giddily sipped his drink.

THE NIGHT WORE on until finally Charlie stood on a bar stool and announced that the movie was about to begin.

It was standing room only. Mitch had to be pleased with the turnout at least. The Single Dads Club shoved to the back of the room. It was no different than when we used to sit in the last row of the auditorium during assemblies.

"Did I miss the movie?" Leo swept in, unbuttoning his

swanky peacoat. His twins went up front to sit with Jolene. His boyfriend Dusty brushed flurries out of his blond locks.

"No. Hasn't started yet," Mitch said.

"Shoot. I'll keep driving around the block then."

"Oh come on. It's a good movie," said Dusty. "I've already watched it twice."

I gave Dusty a tight hug. It was great getting to know him, and I was floored by the gorgeous shelving unit he'd made for my living room. The man was likely a better carpenter than Jesus.

There we were. My friends and I reunited, along with our spouses. (Technically, there were two more dads I had yet to meet in the Single Dads Club, Buzz and Shane. They were living in Seattle but were planning a trip back this spring.) For the first time in forever, I had a friend group again. I never realized how much loneliness had seeped into my entire being in Alaska. Sure, I had Jolene, but she couldn't prop up my social life for me. I had good friends here, real friends. I had teammates. Why had I been so stupid to leave this town so quickly, so desperate to grow up and break free? We couldn't go back in time, but I would treasure every moment I had with these guys.

We hung in the back of the bar as the movie played, restraining ourselves from yelling out comments. We weren't really into romances, but the movie grew on us. Cary had been turning me into a softie, while also making me hard all the time. Make it make sense.

Lucien stumbled into our peanut gallery halfway through the film.

"Good work, Lucien," said Mitch. "It's kinda weird seeing myself up there, but you make it work."

"It's not you, Mitch. You merely provided a smidgeon of inspiration."

"Is that why I caught you raiding my closet?"

"*Inspiration*," Lucien enunciated.

"You guys did a great job with me. But am I always that perky?" Charlie asked.

"Yes," replied everyone except me and Cary, though if we got to know Charlie better, we'd probably say yes, too.

"I have to say, you and Skip seem very believable as a gay couple. I'm impressed," said Cary.

"Well, funny you should say that." Lucien scratched his head.

"What do you mean?" asked Leo. "Funny how?"

"We really wanted to be true to our characters. I'm a firm believer in doing my research as an actor, really going the extra mile as it were."

"Oh my God." Cal threw his hand over his mouth. "Did you have sex with your co-star?"

"No comment." Lucien strolled off, leaving us wondering just how good of an actor he was.

EPILOGUE
FOUR MONTHS LATER

Derek

When I bought my house, I thought one bathroom would be enough for Jolene and me. And it was... until Cary happened.

Three people sharing a bathroom was rough, especially when one of those people owned enough creams, soaps, and hair product to fill a CVS. I once asked Cary why he had four different types of hand cream, and he looked at me as if I were the crazy one.

I knocked on the bathroom door again. I had to take a wizz so badly I was two seconds from going in the backyard.

"Cary, are you almost done in there?"

"Almost. Just working on my hair."

"What do you mean working on it?"

"It's a process!" he yelled back.

"It looks great!" I said, making an assumption. His hair always looked great, never a strand out of place. I once made a suggestion that he buzz it off for summer, and again, he looked at me as if I were the crazy one.

Fortunately, I found those quizzical looks nothing but endearing. Watching Cary's face change with each new expression was quickly becoming a favorite pastime.

"Can I sneak in and use the can quickly?" I whispered through the door.

Cary opened the door a crack, his big eyes a ray of sunshine on this spring day. "I don't think we're there yet in our relationship." He slipped me a peck on the lips. "By the way, you're really cute in the morning."

Cary hadn't moved in, but he spent multiple nights here per week. It started back in February by accident. A bad snowstorm meant he had to stay the night. We were both nervous about how Jolene would react. I had wanted more preparation before I asked Cary to spend the night. As a dad, I was supposed to be having lots of talks with my child, right? But she just laughed and said I worried too much. That night, the three of us had stayed up late watching movies and eating popcorn before retiring to our bedrooms. Having Cary sleep in bed with me felt wonderfully natural, as if we were following the expected order of things.

Our relationship continued to flourish and strengthen. He spent more time over here, and each time, he further entrenched himself in our lives. We ate more meals together. He drove Jolene to her internship when I couldn't. He and his dad repainted our bedroom. He helped me put down mulch in the spring. Frankly, I was surprised at how handy Cary was. The fancy clothes threw me off. But needing to fix up clients' homes for showings had forced him to become a de facto handyman over the years.

I hated the term partner. Partner sounded too clinical. Cary was my boyfriend, but he truly was a partner, too. We worked together as one unit.

Except when it came to the bathroom.

"Cary, I just need thirty seconds."

He opened the door, his face covered in a white mask, yet another magical lotion that made his skin creamy and smooth.

"Are you auditioning for *Mrs. Doubtfire*?" I asked.

"You know, Derek, some moisturizer would do you good."

I went into the bathroom without commenting. Little did he know that sometimes, after he went to bed, I'd smear on some face cream.

After I did my business, I found Cary and Jolene at the kitchen table. Cary was helping her apply something to her face. It seemed that each week, Jolene's face became slightly more dolled up.

"What is that?" I asked.

"It's concealer," Cary said. "Someone's breaking out."

"Ugh. When will it stop?" Jolene grabbed the mirror from the table and checked her face while Cary continued dabbing it on.

"That's the thing about puberty. It gives you acne, but it also gives you boobs," he said, rubbing in concealer onto her cheek.

I cleared my throat, not wanting to think about my daughter having breasts.

"Derek, chill. Your daughter is becoming a woman. It's a good thing."

"Have we covered them all?" Jolene asked.

"Actually, I see Centaurus forming on your forehead." Cary held up the mirror to show her.

"Please stop naming my breakouts after constellations. I'll never want to look in a telescope again."

"Fair. But the accuracy is uncanny. I wonder if you're manifesting astronomical acne." Cary thought on that for a moment before remembering he had a job to do.

I loved watching the two of them interact. There'd been some friction here and there when Cary had to be the parent and put his foot down. But it was mostly little things like Jolene watching too much TV or checking if she did her homework. We both steeled ourselves for a potential rebellious streak in her.

"This is so not the day for my face to wage an all-out war against me," Jolene said, a new kind of desperation in her voice.

"Why? What's going on?" I asked. I grabbed the nonfat Greek yogurt container she'd requested and scooped her some.

"Well, um, I forgot to mention it before, but I'm having a friend pick me up for school this morning."

Cary and I looked at each other, then at her.

"You have friends that drive?" he asked.

"His mom is the one driving and picking me up."

"His?" I asked, the pronoun hanging heavy in my mouth. "As in a boy?"

"Yeah. He's kind of...we're kind of like...going out." She swooped out of her chair and raced to the kitchen counter for the yogurt, her back turned to us.

Cary put a calming hand on my forearm, helping to quell what he called my patriarchal urges. I wasn't trying to be sexist, but I was also a teenage boy once. He made me meet his eyes and signaled for me to chill.

"His name is Arjun. We've been dating for three weeks," Jolene said confidently. For a middle schooler, three weeks was substantial.

"That's great. Can your dad and I say hi to him and his

mom when they stop by?" Cary asked, and I tried to follow his lead.

"Correction: we *will* be saying hi." I *tried* to follow his lead. Was it wrong of me to want to know who my daughter was getting in a car with?

"Dad, please don't embarrass me."

"I'm not going to embarrass you. I'd like to meet this boy's mom and jot down her license plate."

"Dad!"

Cary stood up, keeping a hand on my chest. "Your dad is just going to say a quick hello, and that's it. He won't embarrass you. I will keep him on a tight leash."

I held up my hand as if swearing on a bible. Although now that Cary had mentioned leashes, my mind was wandering to some interesting places.

A little bit later, after Cary and I had gotten dressed and Cary had washed off his face, a sky blue SUV pulled up the driveway. Cary and I followed Jolene outside.

"How does my face look?" she asked Cary.

"Clean, clear, and under control." Cary winked back at her. "Now go get your man."

She heaved out a sigh of relief. Under her confident demeanor was a trace of nerves. Being a teenager meant she was always nervous about something. She beelined to the car and got into the backseat.

"Why is she getting into the backseat with him?" I grumbled.

"Where else would she sit? Did you want the mom to strap her to the roof of the car like a christmas tree?" Cary said out of the corner of his mouth before putting on his big, agent smile and waving at the mom. "Hello! I'm Cary, and this is Jolene's dad Derek."

The mom and her son got out of the car, leaving Jolene

no choice but to follow them. She couldn't escape that easily. The mom was dressed sharply like Cary, a Burberry trench coat over a powersuit. Her son was like most boys his age: skinny, awkward, his proportions a bit off. He wore thick glasses and a mischievous glint danced behind them.

"Hi! I'm Sarita. Nice to meet you." She shook our hands with a firm grip.

"Thanks for driving Jolene," I said.

"My pleasure. She's on the way, so it's no trouble. Here's my card in case you need to get in touch with me." She handed over a creamy, thick business card. Cary peered at it over my shoulder. Something told me he was already wondering if she could be a client.

"You ready?" Sarita turned back to the kids.

Her son gave her a thumbs up.

"It's nice to meet you, Arjun." I shook the kid's hand and was ready to give him a slightly firm shake, but he beat me to it, his hand squeezing around mine.

"You too, sir."

Cary gave an exaggerated nod of approval at the sir line.

"You kids have a good day at school," I said. Jolene gave me a silent nod of gratitude for not going full dad on him.

Sarita walked back to her car, typing a message on her phone. Arjun held Jolene's hand.

"Arjun, a word," Cary said just before they made their way to the SUV.

"Yes, sir?" he asked.

"You treat her well, and with respect. Because if you don't, if you hurt her in any way, I will find out, and I will rain down vengeance upon you. Are we clear?"

Arjun turned a sheet of white, his eyes jumping behind his glasses. Jolene's jaw hit the ground, in part shock and part embarrassment. As the only other adult, I tried my best to keep my composure.

"Y-y-y-yes," Arjun responded.

"I think what Cary means to say is, have a good day."

Sarita honked the horn, making both kids jump again. Arjun raced to the car, Jolene right behind him.

Cary and I waved them goodbye as the car drove away.

"What the hell was that?" I asked once they were gone.

"I have no idea."

"I thought I was bad cop."

Cary bit his lip, seemingly as rattled as everyone else. "I had some gearhead flashbacks." He took a sip of his iced coffee. "Don't mind me. Just a boy with lingering trauma."

"Hey, what do you know? I've got lingering trauma, too."

"OMG. We're twinning."

I wrapped an arm around him and pulled him flush against me. We were forever works in progress, but perfection was overrated. I'd say we were doing pretty well.

I planted a soft kiss on his lips, getting a taste of his beverage. "I got you."

We stood there a moment, enjoying this embrace, one of millions of tiny moments together.

"We need to work on our bathroom schedule. This morning was a mess," I said.

"Everyone sharing one bathroom brings people together. There was only one bathroom on *The Brady Bunch*, and they were a super tight-knit fam."

"I will not accept a Caryism at this time. Maybe we need to add another bathroom when you move in."

"I'm moving in?"

"Eventually," I said with a smirk of inevitability. We were going to be husbands one day. I felt it in my gut. No two ways around it.

"You know..." Cary threaded his fingers through mine, his sweet brown eyes peering up at me. "Rather than go through all the trouble of building another bathroom, we could buy a bigger house. I happen to know a great real estate agent."

Cary: One Month Later

You knew you were in a relationship built to last when you and your significant other could survive a twenty-two-hour flight together. Fortunately, Derek's shoulder made for a perfect headrest.

We stepped off the plane and were whisked off to our resort in a private car. I kept looking at Derek, then looking out the window at the ocean, not believing my luck at either. The past five months had been nothing short of incredible. I loved waking up with Derek and falling asleep in his arms. I loved spending time with Jolene. I loved knowing that I had a person, a permanent plus one, a special someone with whom I could share my wild spigot of emotions. The fear that Derek was going to turn on me eventually subsided, trickling back into my ocean of anxiety like low tide. He was a good one.

We drove down a windy road clustered with palm trees until we reached a clearing, and there it was. The resort was a massive property right on the water, the crystal blue ocean framing its majesty. I wanted to cry when I thought about little, scared Cary Perkowski feeling like his life was over post-gearhead. *Look what we accomplished, buddy.*

"Damn," Derek uttered over my shoulder. "Maybe I should get into real estate."

"I have some magenta shirts you can borrow."

He kissed my neck. His fingers slunk down my arm and squeezed my hand. "I'm proud of you, Cary."

"Me, too." This year was off to an even better start. With the year almost half over, Hannah and I were on track to exceed our sales from the previous year. The Morris brothers could barely keep up. More stories had come out about shady activity they'd pulled with clients and with other agents. I heard a rumor that they were thinking of leaving the real estate biz and going into cryptocurrency. And honestly...that tracked.

The concierge handed Derek and I drinks inside coconut shells with an umbrella sticking out. It was my first-ever drink with a little umbrella in it. I instantly became more relaxed. During check-in, we received our itinerary of different activities that would be going on. Mixers, cocktail hours, team-building exercises. Real estate agents from across the country would be here, and agents loved to schmooze.

After receiving our keys, a member of the hotel staff brought us to a golf cart and drove us to our bungalow. Derek tried to carry in his own suitcase, but the staffer politely but insistently stopped him. We were a long way from a Best Western.

"Holy shit." My eyes bugged out of my head when I saw the room. It was an open-air unit right on the sand. We could go from our king-sized bed right onto the beach, no doors or windows stopping us. The rhythmic slapping of the waves on the sand lulled me into relaxation.

Needless to say, I had never stayed at a resort anywhere as nice as this one.

The hotel staffer set up our luggage on racks and pointed out all the important parts of our room. There was a wall that could slide to separate us from the beach if we wanted.

Once he left, I collapsed on the bed. I stared up at the large ceiling fan slowly turning. This was truly paradise, and I got to share it with Derek. I made a silent resolution that we would take a vacation like this with Jolene once a year. Life was meant to be enjoyed.

"There's a shower and a soaking tub," Derek said, when he returned from the bathroom.

"Did you use the bathroom, or did you just scope it out?"

"The latter. Smell this." He stuck his hand in my face, and I inhaled a coconut butter-scented hand lotion that made me want a pina colada in my hand pronto. "This is quality stuff."

"I mean, do you expect anything less?" I gestured around the luxury room of our luxury suite. I pulled the itinerary from the side table. The schedule and all the formal lettering brought me away from my paradise mindset for a moment. "There's a welcome mixer at three-thirty. Then dinner is at six. There's also a company picture we need to show up for. Smart that they're doing it now because we get all sunburned. There's also a golf tournament we can sign up for."

"Do you play golf?" Derek asked, joining me on the bed and instantly pulling me into a cuddle.

"No. It's too slow, and the clothes aren't tight enough."

Derek stroked a soft hand through my hair, drawing circles on the back of my neck. "We should probably get ready for the mixer. It's coming up. Maybe we can meet up with Hannah and John."

"We should," I said. "But first...we need to have sex."

I took Derek's hand and put it on my crotch to alert him that I wasn't bullshitting.

"You're horny after a twenty-two-hour flight?" he asked.

It was twenty-two hours of legs touching and hands touching, of glimpsing Derek in a T-shirt that stretched across his chest and shorts that stretched across his beefy thighs, of smelling him and listening to him grunt his delight at the airplane meal, of smiling at him and watching his ass walk through the airport, of watching him lift up our heavy suitcase, arms flexing. Not to mention the excitement coursing through my veins about being at a luxury resort in freaking Bali.

I rubbed Derek's hand on my crotch, getting him to stroke me over my jeans. Yes, I always wore long pants when I flew. I couldn't explain why.

"Derek, I'm going to be brutally honest with you. I am ridiculously horny, and you have the nerve to be hot. If you don't fuck me hard, I think I will either spontaneously combust or drown myself in the ocean."

"You should drown yourself in the soaking tub. It'd be more comfortable, and there's this camomile body scrub—"

"*Derek!*"

"Come here," he growled in my ear. He picked me up, threw me over his shoulder, and plunked me onto the dresser, where he proceeded to kiss the life out of me, his beard scratching against my skin, his rough hands grabbing at my chest. I wrapped my legs around his waist and unconsciously humped against him.

He chuckled against my lips. "Damn."

"Shut up. Don't laugh at me in my time of need." I yanked his shirt over his head and buried my face in his chest, dug my fingernails into his back. I wasted no time undoing his shorts and shoving them below his knees, while Derek got to work unbuttoning my shirt.

"Why did you wear a button-down shirt on our flight?" he said as his fingers struggled.

"Because I like to dress up," I said before dragging my teeth down his neck. I would never be one of those people who wore sweatpants or pajama pants on their flight. When did our society decide it was acceptable to go out in public looking like you just rolled out of bed?

"You brought more of these shirts with you, right?" Derek asked. Yet before I could answer, he ripped it open, buttons going asunder. I should've been upset about losing a perfectly good shirt, but I was too turned on.

I hopped off the dresser and immediately went to work sucking Derek's thick cock. I was well past foreplay. I needed the whole thing in my mouth. I ignored Derek's chuckle above me.

I loved how comfortable we were with each other. There was no putting on a certain appearance for Derek. We could laugh during sex. We could spend time together in silence. Every moment was special in its own way. And watching Derek bond with my parents whenever we went over there warmed my heart.

Jesus, why was I thinking about my parents? I made a mental note to send them a postcard, then returned to my regularly scheduled lusting over my boyfriend.

"Fuck, I'm close, baby."

"You'd better not be that close." While I gave myself a mental high-five for my excellent fellatio skills, if Derek came before he had a chance to rail me, I would drown him in that soaking tub.

Derek pulled me up as if I were a feather found on the floor. He unbuckled my belt and shoved my pants to my ankles. He then threw me over his shoulder again and walked us into the bathroom. I got what he was talking about. It was like a mini spa with low, calm lighting.

"On your knees," he commanded.

I caught my reflection in the mirror as I went down. I checked out Derek's hairy, strong body, a body I'd dreamed about for decades that was all mine.

Derek turned around, sticking his fat, juicy ass in my face. I spread him open, finding the spot of pink. I licked a stripe down his crack.

"God, yes. Eat that hole." His moans echoed off the walls, becoming more vulnerable as I went on.

My tongue turned him to putty. I gave his cheeks a hard slap, his delightful squirm under my touch making my dick harder. Derek watched me through the mirror as I went to town on his ass. He pushed my head deeper inside. I slipped my tongue inside his clenched hole, eliciting more lusty groans.

I stood up and grabbed the lube from the toiletries bag on the counter that Derek had smartly brought in. Without thinking, blinded by my own need, I slicked up my cock, then his hole, and pressed inside.

"Shit." Derek let out a gasp as I entered him. Over the past few weeks, we'd experimented with me being on top, and Derek was a fan. Hell, a guy who enjoyed getting rimmed that much was sure to enjoy bottoming. I'd always thought of myself as a perma-bottom, but I found that I relished the control that being on top gave me. I was grateful to Derek for trusting me this much. And watching a big jock writhe and moan thanks to my cock was a delicious sight. Revenge of the gay nerds.

"You feel so good." I kissed his back, the light, sweat tinged hairs fluttering my nose. "I love watching your big ass get filled with my cock."

"Fuck me, Cary."

"You mean 'wreck me daddy.'" I snorted a laugh, but I was also a tad turned on by the statement. I was forty. I could technically pull off daddy vibes.

I grabbed his hips and thrust into him hard, with a desperate need to connect with this man. Derek nudged his ass up, giving me a better angle.

"Feels so fucking good having you inside me." Derek grunted. "Wreck me."

Yeah, that was totally hot.

I pumped into his thick cake, watched my cock disappear inside him. Then I pulled out suddenly.

"On the bed," I demanded. I wanted to stare into his eyes as I came. When did I become such a romantic?

Back in the room, Derek flopped onto the bed and drew his legs up. A warm ocean breeze drifted in. Sure, I had a gorgeous beach view, but I'd rather look at this burly fireman heating me up. I watched the orgasm build behind his eyes, as desperation gave way to climax and Derek shot all over his stomach.

I slid my fingers through his mess and used it to coat my dick. I cupped his bearded cheek as I fucked him. We locked eyes, saying everything that words couldn't. I buried my face into his chest hair, inhaling its sweaty scent as I came.

We took a moment to catch our breaths. I gazed into Derek's crystal eyes, his squinty smile setting my heart afire. He wasn't my friend's cool older brother. He wasn't a popular jock. He wasn't a mystery waiting to be solved. He was Derek, a scared, lonely guy looking for the same things I was in life.

After wiping ourselves off with the uber-soft, luxury towels, we sat on the floor, our backs against the bed, watching the waves crash on the shore.

Could things get any better than this?

I had no idea, but I couldn't wait to find out.

"Do you want to take a shower together?" I asked.

"It doesn't look big enough for both of us, unfortunately." He'd gotten a good look at the bathroom, so I took his word for it.

"Well, that's homophobic."

He turned to me, his eyebrow raising. "Nothing says we can't try."

———

Thank you for reading!

Want to stay in the know about what I'm working on next? Join the Outsiders today to stay in the loop and instantly receive free short stories at www.ajtruman.com/outsiders.

Please consider leaving a review on the book's Amazon page or on Goodreads. Reviews are crucial in helping other readers find new books.

Join the party in my Facebook Group and Instagram. Follow me at Bookbub to be alerted to new releases.

And then there's email. I love hearing from readers! Send me a note anytime at info@ajtruman.com. I always respond.

ALSO BY A.J. TRUMAN

South Rock High

Ancient History

Drama!

Romance Languages

Advanced Chemistry

Single Dads Club

The Falcon and the Foe

The Mayor and the Mystery Man

The Barkeep and the Bro

The Fireman and the Flirt

Browerton University Series

Out in the Open

Out on a Limb

Out of My Mind

Out for the Night

Out of This World

Outside Looking In

Out of Bounds

Seasonal Novellas

Fall for You

You Got Scrooged

Hot Mall Santa

Only One Coffin

ABOUT THE AUTHOR

A.J. Truman is a gay man living in Indiana with his husband, son, and fur-babies. He writes books with **humor, heart, and hot guys.** What else does a story need? He loves spending time with his family and occasionally sneaking off for an afternoon movie.

www.ajtruman.com
info@ajtruman.com
The Outsiders - Facebook Group

Made in the USA
Middletown, DE
29 July 2024